AT THE COUNTRY HOUSE

A gripping cozy crime mystery full of twists

JANE ADAMS

A Rina Martin Mystery Book 5

Originally published as
The Dead of Winter

JOFFE BOOKS

Revised edition 2021
Joffe Books, London
www.joffebooks.com

First world edition published by Severn House Publishers Ltd in Great Britain in 2011

Cover art by Dee Dee Book Covers

ISBN: 978-1-80405-071-2

PROLOGUE

'Oh,' he said. 'They've sent you, have they? Well, I'm not about to change my mind, so you may as well go and tell them that.'

'I already have. I said you'd be leaving. That there was nothing more anyone could do about it.'

'Right then.' He sounded a little deflated, as though he had expected a little more fuss and his leaving to cause more consternation. 'Well, I'm packed and I'm going.'

'Of course you are.'

The blow to the head was sudden, sharp, utterly unexpected and instantly fatal. There was very little blood, and a towel wrapped tightly around the head, a plastic shopping bag over that, took care of any post-mortem seepage.

The bedroom door locked to keep out any casual nosiness, it remained only to remove the car.

The killer left by the back door, wearing the dead man's coat and scarf and carrying his suitcase and battered leather shoulder bag. Out the back way and across the lawn, through the small door that led into the carriage house and then into the gravelled area where the cars had been parked.

The only danger point was the gated road, the only drivable way from the house to the narrow country lane that everyone referred to as the Main Road. Had there been another car coming along the gated track then one of them would have to give way, drivers would scrutinize one another, and it would be obvious that the current driver of the car and its owner were not one and the same. This was unlikely though, as only the local farmer regularly came up that way; everyone else was inside the house and not likely to want to go out that afternoon in the pouring rain.

Luck held; car and suitcase temporarily disposed of in a gully at the edge of the wood, a walk back across the fields, keeping close to the high boundary hedges and out of sight, was all it took. Wellingtons washed and back in the boot room. All done and dusted, and then only the little apology for not returning sooner to the waiting company.

'Sorry. I needed a bit of fresh air before I felt like talking to anyone.'

Nods of agreement, and a few disgruntled mumblings, though these were soon set aside.

'Oh well, he's gone. We'll have to carry on without him.'

'Yes, he has definitely gone.'

There was much left to do, and the company got back to doing it.

Only one other of them understood the implication: that 'gone' had a more permanent meaning than the simple departure of a discontented guest.

ONE

Aikensthorpe House, 3 January 1872

'You will wear the diamonds?' It wasn't really a question, even though he had phrased it as such. He held the black leather box in both hands, presenting it to her.

'I will wear the diamonds,' she confirmed. He liked to see her well decorated, this husband of hers. He needed to see his prized possessions properly presented, and she was never left in any doubt that she, too, was one of his treasures.

He laid the black box down on her dressing table and shooed her maid aside as he opened the latch and withdrew the exquisite necklace. She bowed her head forward, exposing the nape of her neck so that he could fasten the clasp.

'There.' He smiled at her in the mirror as she looked up, and Elizabeth managed a small twitch of her lips in return. 'Beautiful,' he said, his hands—fat, clumsy hands, she thought—hovering over her bare shoulders.

He straightened then and drew back, as though suddenly recalling the presence of her maid. 'I will let you finish dressing.' His fingers brushed her curls as he stepped back, and she could feel how much he wanted to touch her and also how much this awkward but, she had to admit, generous and caring man was in awe of her.

She just wished that she could love him in return. She just wished, oh so very hard, that he could somehow, miraculously, be younger, more attractive, less prosaic.

She relaxed as the bedroom door closed and her maid resumed her task, arranging *Madame's* hair and tweaking the bright stones in their floral settings into better position. More diamonds were then fixed into her hair, a task her husband would, fortunately, never dream of attempting. She could imagine the fat and clumsy fingers tugging at her ringlets as he tried to fix the fragile little clips in place.

'Madame will go down now?' Her maid stepped back and handed Elizabeth her handkerchief, well perfumed with rose water.

'Thank you, Abigail, that will be all.'

She waited until the maid had left and then paused to survey her reflection in the cheval glass, tugging at her skirts and arranging her neckline impatiently. The pale rose silk looked well against her skin and made her dark hair look even more richly brown. She nodded to her reflection. She would do. She practised her social smile before leaving her bedroom, checking in the glass that it looked appropriately cheerful but still just that little bit aloof. Then frowned impatiently, recalling her mother's instructions and schooling. 'You must always be a *lady*, Elizabeth dear.'

After all, she supposed, that was why Albert had married her, adding her name and lineage to his money and business acumen. Everyone had been happy. No—everyone who *mattered* had been happy, and Elizabeth was under no illusion that she was anything other than at the bottom, the very end, of that particular list.

But—and it was quite a considerable but—Albert was kind to her in an awkward sort of way, he denied her nothing and indulged her interests, and he supported what he called her quest, her talent.

Her small smile was more genuine as she left the room, anticipating the events that would follow this evening. This was to be her triumph, the first of many that would, she believed and hoped, set her free once more to go out into the world, acclaimed for what she truly was.

TWO

Now

'We're lost,' Joy said.

'We can't be lost. We've got a satnav.'

'Which has brought us into the middle of a muddy field in the middle of nowhere in the middle of a rainstorm.'

'Well, yes,' Tim agreed, 'but I'm sure it knows what it's doing, and it's not *exactly* the middle of a field, there's a road.'

'There's a track. A cart track if I'm being generous. Oh, God, look, there's yet another gate that needs opening.'

'Well, it did say on the sign that it was a gated road. There's bound to be gates on a gated road, I'd have thought.'

Joy glared at him. 'And who's the silly sod getting soaked opening them every time?'

Rina leaned forward in the rear seat and peered out through the windscreen. The rain was coming down in curtains, but she could just make out the five-barred gate blocking their way. 'Do you want me to do this one, Joy?'

The girl turned with a quick smile. 'Don't be daft, Rina. No sense more than one of us getting soaked, is there?' She waited until Tim had pulled up close to the gate, then dashed out, held it open as he drove through, and threw herself back into the passenger seat, water streaming from her hair.

'Sure you shut it properly?' Tim asked, risking life and limb in the process, Rina thought.

'I'm sure,' Joy said tightly. 'I'm quite sure. How many more of those bloody things do we have to deal with?'

'Hopefully that should be the last. We're almost there, according to the satnav. You're steaming the windows up,' he added, and Rina cringed. Tim could be so downright stupid sometimes.

'Look,' she said, hoping to distract a now furious Joy. 'I think I saw something, just ahead.'

They all looked, straining to see anything through rain so thick and treacly that the wipers could barely cope on their fastest setting. A few hundred yards ahead, something more solidly grey emerged and coalesced from the overall gloom. Geometrically imposing, crenellated . . . Rina thought that Aikensthorpe House positively *glowered*.

The track transformed into a gravel drive for the last few hundred yards, and the drive then curved about a circular lawn and deposited them in front of a flight of wide steps.

'Are you sure this is the place?' Joy was suddenly doubtful.

'Of course it is. There can't be two Aikensthorpe Houses, can there?'

'So, do we just park up here, or what?'

'Maybe,' Rina said, 'we should all go inside and find out, then Tim can take the car to the car park or wherever. No sense us all going with him and then getting wet walking back, is there?'

'No,' Joy agreed firmly, 'there is not.' She glared in Tim's direction, an action completely lost on him.

Rina hid her smile. Joy wouldn't stay mad for long, and a quick word with Tim would remind him that he needed to pay more attention to his fiancée, even when his mind was otherwise occupied—and right now it was full of the potential of this weekend at Aikensthorpe. Neither Rina nor Joy was particularly enthused by the idea of a weekend conference well stocked with both stage magicians and experts in the esoteric, not to mention the thought of attending lectures on the links between circa nineteenth-century stage magic and the rise of spiritualism, but they both knew Tim would be in his element and really hadn't felt they could refuse to come.

Joy had accompanied him, of course, simply because she wanted to be with Tim; Rina because she needed him to give her a lift back to Frantham on the Monday morning. True, she could have taken the train to Exeter and then Honiton and then got herself a taxi home, or she could have taken up Bridie Duggan's offer of one of her employees driving her back, but Rina really didn't want to put anyone out now that the nightclub staff were finally getting to take their holidays after the frenetic Christmas and New Year. As for the train, the dual threat of industrial action and ongoing repairs, which she knew had caused chaos for the past weeks, had really put her off that option.

'Stay here a bit longer,' Bridie Duggan, Joy's mother, had urged. Rina had been tempted. She and Tim had enjoyed a wonderful few days with Bridie in Manchester, the first real break from responsibility Rina had experienced in a very long time. She had shopped and lunched and gone to the theatre, and the thought of extending her freedom was a tempting one. She had finally declined, knowing that those she had left behind at home would be missing her; that she, in fact, was missing them. If she came with Tim, they could drive home as promised on the Monday.

'Ring this Aikensthorpe place,' Bridie had instructed. 'Chances are there won't be another room available and the decision will be made for you.'

It had seemed like a sensible plan.

It turned out, however, that there'd been a cancellation. Yes, there was room for 'another delegate'. She would be very welcome.

And so here they all were, Rina thought. In the middle of nowhere in the middle of a rainstorm, as Joy had said.

'Ready?' Joy asked. 'Right, let's make a run for it.'

Three car doors opened, three people ran up the granite steps and through the double doors at the top. Rina glanced back towards the car, which was barely visible now as the rain began to fall even more heavily.

They stood dripping collectively on the wooden floor, surprised by the sudden quiet as the heavy doors swung closed and shut out the noise of violent weather.

'Oh,' Joy gasped, and Rina silently agreed. This was positively baronial. Set before them was a wide entrance-way with a centre-piece of sweeping staircase. Off to the left was a massive fireplace of carved blue-grey stone; on the right, what appeared to be an improvised reception desk, currently unmanned. They were in the correct place then, Rina thought.

The trestle-table reception desk was strewn with leaflets and programmes and various books and magazines pertaining to the magical and spiritual arts. A handbell, which reminded Rina of her school days, had been set on the corner of the table with a sign next to it that exhorted them to 'please ring for attention'.

Squelching her way across the polished wooden boards, Joy rang the bell loudly. They waited, wondering how anyone could ignore that insistent clang, which must have echoed through the entire house.

About a minute later, though it had felt longer to those dripping in the hallway, a young woman scurried through a door to the right of the reception area.

'Sorry, sorry, oh my goodness you're soaked! I'm Melissa, let's find out who you are and get you to your rooms there's tea and coffee making facilities and I can get you sandwiches if you're hungry.' She paused for breath and looked them up and down. 'Oh,' she said. 'You must be Mr Timothy Brandon and his guest, and you must be Mrs Martin. Our last-minute replacement.' She looked very pleased with herself, and Rina was possessed by a sudden desire to tell her she was wrong.

'I left the car at the bottom of the steps,' Tim said. 'Should I move it?'

'Oh, no, leave it until the rain stops, there's plenty of space for anyone else arriving. There's a car-parking bit round the back if you want to get it out of the way. There'll be the buses arriving tomorrow from the other convention, and we're not exactly easy to get to.' She beamed. 'Luggage?'

'Oh, yes.' Tim looked expectantly at the two women.

'You don't mind, do you, Tim?' Rina said. 'I think Joy and I will go up and find our rooms.' She returned Melissa's beaming, but now faintly puzzled, smile.

'Oh, er, yes. OK.' Tim looked a little put out.

Rina and Joy watched him go.

'*I* had to open all the gates,' Joy said. 'It's his turn to get soaked. Tell me, does it do anything else round here but rain?'

'Oh, yes,' Melissa assured them. 'Apparently, they're forecasting snow for the weekend.'

* * *

Rina sat beside the window in her allocated room, drinking a very welcome cup of tea and trying to understand the lie of the land beyond. The rain had slowed, just a little, but the wind had increased in strength and alternately slammed great waves of water against the window or blew it swirling away. In the brief gaps between these alternatives, Rina had been able to make out a sweep of what she assumed was lawn and a line of trees beyond. Her room was at the rear of the house and on the second floor. It had been, she was told, part of the nursery wing, as they used to call it. Her room had been the nanny's bedroom, and the bathroom now occupied what had been the adjoining bedroom where her small charges would have slept. It was almost stubbornly quiet, here at the top and rear of the house, and Rina decided that the previous owners of Aikensthorpe must have been of the 'children should be neither seen *nor* heard' school of thought.

A gentle knock on the door announced Joy's arrival. She had changed out of her sodden jeans and was now dressed in what she called her 'softies'. Tracksuit bottoms, T-shirt and a zippered, hooded top. Thick, stripy socks with separate toes completed the ensemble, and her long red hair had been towel dried and then left loose. Rina, used to the younger woman's mature attitude, sometimes forgot that Joy was ten years younger than Rina's beloved Tim, but dressed like this, and with her cheeks slightly flushed from the hot shower, she looked like a teenager, not a young woman of twenty-one.

Joy held a plastic carrier bag in her hands. 'Jeans,' she said. 'Caked in mud. Melissa said I could stick them in the washing machine. I just wanted to see if you had anything that needed to go in.'

'No, I think I survived relatively unscathed,' Rina told her. 'Has Tim dried himself off?'

'Oh, yes, and found the guidebook and gone exploring. Some place, isn't it?'

'It certainly is.'

Joy flopped down on the edge of Rina's bed and tucked her feet under her. 'Am I the only one wishing I'd told Tim to come on his own?'

'No, there are at least two of us. This really isn't my thing, but now we're here, I think we should view the whole weekend as life experience and remember that it's only a couple of days.' Rina smiled. 'Think what leverage you'll have next time you want him to go shopping with you.'

Joy giggled. 'Trouble with that, Rina, is I'd much rather take you or Mum or even the Peters sisters. But I'm sure I'll find some other way of spending my brownie points.' She leaned over and touched Rina's short grey hair. 'You're going wavy. Must be the rain.'

'It always has that effect. I didn't mind when I was younger, but I think I'm getting on a bit for the frizzy look to be a good one. I've got a hair appointment booked for when I get back to Frantham.'

'Ah, at Miss Prince's salon?' Joy giggled.

Rina smiled back. 'Miss Prince knows how to deal with us ladies of a certain age.'

'Rina, darling, you will never be a "lady of a certain age". You are far too special for that. Have you phoned home, by the way?'

'Yes, and spoken to everyone. Bethany and Eliza send their best love as always and want to know when they'll see you again, and the Montmorencys said to tell you they've found a new chocolate cake recipe you just have to try.'

'Oh my God, not more chocolate cake.' Joy's eyes softened with affection as she thought of the Peters sisters and the Montmorency twins, who comprised Rina's eccentric household. Ex-performers all, as was Rina, Joy had come to know and love them well since she had entered their lives so precipitously the year before. Her brother had been killed, and Rina and her cohort had helped track down his killers. Joy had come to regard them all as part of her extended family. Tim, the youngest member of the household by a good thirty years, had rapidly become something more than that.

'Mac was there, with Miriam,' Rina added, referring to DI Sebastian McGregor and his partner. They had promised to keep an eye on everyone in Rina's absence.

'Oh, how are they?'

'A little tense. Mac's hearing is on Monday; they'll be driving up to Pinsent this weekend. By Tuesday I expect he'll know if he still has a job.' She smiled. 'He offered to make a detour and pick us both up on Sunday morning if we find we can't last the weekend. Tim could collect us from Pinsent on Monday, and you could come down for a few days.'

'Rina, that sounds like a plan. Let's see how desperate we get. I've been looking at my schedule for the weekend. I'm attending a talk on the Universalist Church, whatever that may be, followed by a lecture and practical demonstration of various circa nineteenth-century mediumistic practices, and in the afternoon something to do with the design and construction of a Davenport cabinet, which I'm assuming is some sort of magic box. I'll tell you now, anyone asks for a volunteer and I am out of here.'

'It's a long walk home.'

'True. You're right, though. Tim loves this stuff, and we love Tim—and it should be interesting, at least. His Christmas show was a massive hit. I think he's hoping to get more inspiration.'

Rina nodded. She'd been to the Palisades twice to see Tim perform over the Christmas period. The owners of the art-deco hotel had recently renovated the little theatre and removed a partition wall that had been erected sometime in the seventies, so the main dining room and theatre space again became one. It was now wonderful for cabaret, live music and table-to-table close-up magic, which Tim loved to perform. For Christmas, though, they had really set out to produce something spectacular, and Tim had reconstructed a version of Pepper's Ghost, a Victorian illusion that set mystical beings dancing across the stage; and, in his version of an old set-piece called The Artist's Dream, he'd co-opted one of the cabaret dancers to play the part of the ghostlike artist's muse, visiting him while he slept. It had been a beautiful, charmingly old-fashioned interlude, and Rina had seen several of the audience dabbing their eyes.

It had all been rather wonderful, Rina thought, and a fantastic contrast to the intimate close-up magic and mentalism that formed the remainder of his act. It was partly because of those performances that Tim had been invited here, to Aikensthorpe, for this event. Whatever this event actually was. Rina found she was still a little hazy about the details.

'OK, I'd better get these into the washing machine,' Joy said.

'I'll come down with you. We should talk to that Melissa woman, find out what exactly we've let ourselves in for this weekend. Is it my imagination, or has Tim been just a bit evasive about it all?'

'You know, I was thinking the exact same thing,' Joy agreed. 'It's not like Tim. Usually, he's blinding us with science or explaining everything in minutest detail.'

'Maybe he's been sworn to secrecy,' Rina joked. 'Not giving away the magic secrets or something.'

'Hmm, more likely there's something going on he thinks we won't approve of,' Joy said. 'Or that would have made us both say no to him.'

Rina looked at the younger woman in mild surprise. 'You think it was really important to him that we both came, then?'

'You know, I think it was. I got the distinct impression he'd have cried off if we'd said no. Tim is one of the bravest people I have ever met, but for some reason he had reservations about coming here alone.'

* * *

They found Melissa in the hallway arranging pamphlets and ticking things off on a very long list. She was only too pleased to break off and explain how the weekend would proceed.

'Right, well, first there are the full weekend guests—that's you and Mr Brandon and about a dozen of the others—and then there are the people just coming over for the talks and lectures tomorrow, and then you full weekend guests will all be involved in the main event tomorrow evening. Then, of course, there'll be the debriefing and film show on the Sunday. We're likely to have a full house again for that, I'd have thought.'

She had emphasized the words 'main event' and waved her hands, jazz style, just in case they might have missed the point, but had moved on to Sunday's itinerary before Rina had the chance to ask her what the 'main event' actually was.

'What main event?' Rina asked when Melissa paused for breath.

Melissa didn't seem to have heard. 'We're expecting two coaches tomorrow: about one hundred and thirty people, I believe. They'll be arriving for breakfast and staying for all the talks and so on and then leaving just after dinner when, of course, we hand over to the re-enactors and you, few, *special* people.' She giggled.

Rina and Joy exchanged baffled glances.

'Special people?' Joy asked.

'Who are staying for the seance, of course. That starts at ten and ends, well, whenever. Then there'll be the debrief on Sunday and—'

'*Seance*?' Rina interrupted.

Melissa was now the puzzled one. 'But of course. Isn't that what you've come for?' She glanced from one to the other.

'Where's Tim?' Rina demanded.

Melissa pointed towards a door at the opposite end of the reception area.

'Thanks, Melissa,' Joy managed as she fled after Rina, still clutching the plastic bag containing her muddy jeans. She was giggling by the time she caught the older woman. 'Your face, Rina. You looked . . .'

'I *am*,' Rina confirmed, and Joy stopped laughing. 'Look, sweetheart, you know I adore Tim, I'd help him out with anything, but he should have told us what he was getting us into.'

'Well, we don't really know as yet,' Joy said. 'I mean, do you actually trust a woman who does jazz hands every five minutes, not to exaggerate? Wow, will you look at this place?'

There was no evidence of Tim in the large room, but, Rina had to agree, it was worth a 'wow'. The panelled walls were carved in a linenfold pattern reminiscent of much earlier centuries and yet looking 'right' for the opulent space. Above that, a fresco of Adam-style plasterwork—which, beautiful and intricate as it was, didn't quite work with the panelling. Three massive windows—covered by heavy russet velvet curtains that, to Rina's eye, looked contemporary with the house . . . and were showing every one of their hundred-and-fifty-odd years—would have provided guests with a view of spectacular gardens. At least, Rina guessed they were spectacular, but today it was impossible to see anything through the damned rain.

A fireplace that evidently shared a chimney with the one in the reception area dominated the wall opposite the windows, though unlike its blue stone counterpart, some neo-Jacobean woodcarver had been let loose to create a whole forest of trees and swags and unlikely beasts, flanked by mermaid-like creatures, naked from the waist up and wearing the most elaborate headdresses decked out in flowers and fruit.

Nothing about it was right, Rina thought, and yet she found it strangely appealing. Whoever had the job of making the fire surround and overmantel had been having a wonderful time.

Joy bent closer to look at the mermaids. 'She's wearing one of my Great Aunt Madge's wedding hats,' she said.

'Ah, I have yet to meet the redoubtable Aunt Madge, haven't I?'

'Yes, Mum is saving that treat. Too early a meeting with Aunt Madge would be a test of even the strongest friendship. I bet Tim is through there.'

French doors opened on to what looked like woodland, and Rina was puzzled until she realized that they in fact gave entrance into a very elaborate conservatory. No, she corrected, more of an orangery, far too grand to be labelled a mere conservatory. Large expanses of window let what light there was enter through the rear of the garden room, and the roof was more glass, supported by the most beautiful and over-engineered cast-iron arches. There was nothing in the least bit temporary about this structure: nothing that, in Rina's mind, equated with the flimsy UPVC structures people tagged on to the rear of their semis.

The floor was tiled in what looked like marble; elaborate cast-iron grates ran the full length for drainage. Heavy planters, big enough to hold substantial trees, stood against the piers between the windows and, though the trees themselves were now overgrown and untidy, Rina could see where they had once been espaliered and fanned against the walls.

'There's a pond.' Joy was astonished. 'Oh my God, don't let Mum see this. There'll be no peace till we get one.'

Rina laughed. Bridie's house comprised a collection of themed rooms—Rina usually stayed in the art-deco suite—and Bridie was a devil for going to auctions and buying impossibly large furniture just because she liked it. She'd given refuge to the biggest sideboard Rina had ever seen and a draw leaf table designed to seat about thirty, the spare leaves of which were carefully stored and regularly inspected against the time when she had to host a meeting of Commonwealth leaders.

'So, where is Tim?' Joy asked.

'Got to be through there.' More doors, this time leading to a library and then into a smaller study. These rooms must form a wing at the back of the house, Rina thought, matching the nursery wing where her bedroom was, on the opposite side of the house.

Tim appeared to be inspecting a large round table. With him were three other people, two men and a woman, setting up cameras in the corners of the otherwise empty room.

Tim himself was beneath the table.

'Timothy Brandon, come out and explain yourself,' Joy demanded.

Four pairs of eyes focused in her direction, only Tim failing to notice her tone.

'Ah, you've found us, good. Great location isn't it?' He scrambled out from beneath the table, face lit by excitement.

'Seance?' Joy demanded.

The young woman with the camera laughed. 'Oops, someone's in trouble.'

Joy glared at her, then back at Tim. 'Explain.'

The older of the cameramen extended a hand. Rina shook it automatically. 'I think Melissa is bringing us some tea and coffee,' he said. 'Back in the hall. How about we all go and sit down and I'll give Tim a hand on the excuses front?'

'Do I need a hand?' Tim asked, then took a closer look at Joy and Rina. 'Ah, looks like I do.'

Joy, in turn, shook the older cameraman's hand. 'Toby Thwaite,' he said.

Rina had heard the name before. Her eyes narrowed as she dredged up a vague memory. 'You and Tim were at university together.'

'We were, yes. I took the route into electronic magic, and Tim took the more direct approach. I filmed his Pepper's Ghost show at Christmas; that's when I asked him to be the fourth man for this job.' He gestured towards the unmanned camera set up in the far corner. 'This is the rest of my team: Robin Hill and Viv Grieves. They're both students of mine.'

Hellos all round. Rina studied the younger pair: Robin, with dark floppy hair falling over his eyes and the demeanour of an excited ten year old. Viv, with richly brown skin but unusually light hazel eyes. She was very pretty, Rina thought, noting that Robin seemed to think so too. She guessed they were just a little older than Joy.

'Robin, I think, is hoping he'll see a bona fide ghost,' Toby went on, 'and Viv here is determined she's going to spot who's pulling the strings.'

'So . . . ?' Joy let the question hang.

'Tea,' Toby said. 'Hopefully, some sandwiches too. I'm starved.'

They all trooped back into the main hall. A table had been set up near to the fire, and Melissa was busy dragging seats over. Tim and Viv moved to help. Toby spotted the tea and coffee and hot-water jugs set out on the console table.

'So,' he said. 'I'll be mother, shall I? Mrs Martin, what would you like?'

'Rina, call me Rina, and I'd like some tea, please. No sugar.'

Sandwiches and cakes had been laid out on the table. Melissa smiled at her. 'Glad you've met people. Dinner will be at seven, but I hope this will hold you all until then.' Another bright smile and she was gone. Rina was relieved they had been spared the jazz hands this time.

'What does she actually do?' Joy asked.

'Ah, Melissa, well, she actually runs this place. She's got caterers coming in for this weekend, but mostly it's just Mel and some part-timers. She does a fantastic job.'

'Runs this place? As a conference centre?'

'Well—' Toby continued to hand around the refreshments—'believe it or not, in summer they use this as a wedding venue. October to March it will, hopefully, also be conferences, but the company that owns Aikensthorpe has been properly up and running less than a year, and they need to get the secondary accommodation finished before they can really get that off the ground. They're converting what used to be estate cottages and the stable block. Melissa took over last April, and she's trebled the bookings since then, prices too. Lucky we booked early on.'

He sat down and helped himself to a sandwich. 'Eat,' he said. 'Before Viv and Robin get stuck in. Typical students,' he added, 'always up for free food.'

'And you're not?' Viv objected.

'Oh, I don't deny it.' He laughed.

Viv flopped down in the low chair beside him, and Robin pulled his own seat closer. Joy tucked in beside Rina on the little sofa, and Tim wedged his chair between that and Toby's seat.

'How much trouble am I in?' he asked.

'Depends,' Joy told him. 'Have a sandwich. You don't think straight when you're hungry, and I want this explanation to be a good one.'

Rina sipped her tea, surveying the little group. The film people obviously knew each other well, and Toby appeared to have some knowledge of Melissa and this house. He and Tim also seemed to have fallen back easily into their old friendship, which was interesting for Rina who knew very little about Tim's youth. She and Joy were very much the newcomers here.

'So,' she said. 'I suggest we start at the beginning and get the context right. What is this place, why are we all here, and why, Tim dear, did you not tell us what was going on?'

Toby smiled at her. 'You'll need more tea,' he said. 'This is at least a three-cup story.'

He waited until everyone had settled with sufficient food and drink before beginning. Outside, the night was drawing in early; looking at her watch, Rina saw it was only four o'clock, but the darkness was profound. She wondered if they could close the curtains. As if reading her thoughts, Viv and Robin got up and pulled the heavy drapes across. 'Shut the night out,' Viv said. 'It's a bit grim, isn't it? Makes you wonder why on earth they built a house in such an abandoned place.'

'Ah, there speaks a true urbanite.' Toby laughed. 'So, on this dark and stormy night, let us begin.

'Aikensthorpe Hall was built in 1854 by a rich mill owner by the name of Albert Southam. Like many rich men of his age, he was also interested in experimentation, in science and in religion. You've got to think of the historical context here. Spiritualism was just getting started, the Universalist Church was suggesting that anyone could be saved, not just the select few, and Darwin was suggesting that we might not be the result of one single, once and for all, act of creation. Science was moving into the seance room and photographing the phenomena, and both the stage magicians and some of the more unscrupulous mediums were making use of early special effects. God and his angels and the possibility of life after death had become legitimate areas for experimentation and investigation. Literally, nothing was sacred any more—or at least not so sacred that it couldn't be profaned by the scientific nosy parker poking it with a stick. It was a truly fascinating time, and we've got some real experts lined up for the weekend.'

'Melissa mentioned coaches arriving tomorrow?'

'Yes, that's right. There's been a big conference up in Leeds this last week; some of the delegates are decamping here tomorrow for the lectures. I think Melissa would have loved to stage a full-scale convention, with all the delegates on-site, but the accommodation really isn't ready. So, we're bussing people in for tomorrow . . .'

'We?' Rina enquired.

Toby grinned at her. 'Guilty,' he said. 'No, actually, I got dragged into this by David, that's Professor Franklin. He'll be master of ceremonies tomorrow. I got to know him about eighteen months ago. He's written quite widely on the use of early photography and also what you could term magic tricks in a religious context. He's supervising Gail Perry, who'll be our medium at the seance. Gail is a PhD student writing about the various quasi-scientific movements that sprang up in the North of England particularly, and it was her research that uncovered the strange events here in the winter of 1872. That's what tomorrow's reconstruction is all about. Hopefully without the subsequent insanity and violent death.'

He took a bite of his sandwich, and Rina glared at him, so obvious was his enjoyment in making them wait.

'Oh, for goodness' sake,' Viv said. 'They had this seance one night—in fact, the anniversary is tomorrow, which is pretty good timing, don't you think? They'd had loads before, everyone seems to have been at it back then, but this was different. Everyone involved had spent Christmas and New Year together, and during that time they'd invented a ghost.'

'Invented one?' Joy was amused. 'Why?'

'Well,' Toby butted in, taking his story back again. 'It actually prefigured a thing called the Philip experiment in Toronto about a hundred years later. A group of Canadian researchers under the direction of a Dr Owen and his wife got together and created a persona called Philip. Over several months they discussed who he might have been, decided he was a seventeenth-century English aristocrat with a string of mistresses.'

'No, just one mistress. She was burned as a witch, they decided, which of course is terribly inaccurate,' Viv interrupted again.

'Inaccurate?' Joy asked.

'We hanged our witches,' Rina told her. 'Burning was for heretics.'

'That's right.' Viv nodded enthusiastically. 'They did it different in Scotland, but in England it was the hangman who dealt with convicted witches.'

'Anyway,' Toby laughingly reasserted, 'in essence, the modern group *created* Philip, but the Philip they invented and then tried to contact in the seance room behaved pretty much the same way as any other ghostly presence reported in the literature. The table they used was rapped on and moved and even performed on the television in front of the cameras. Of course, it could all be a bit of clever camera trickery and a lot of manipulation—'

'Or it could be that they accidentally stumbled on something real.' It was the first time Robin had contributed to the conversation. He blushed, Rina noticed, noting too that Viv reached out and grabbed his hand and glared at Toby as his laughter exploded.

'We're all entitled to our opinions,' Viv told their professor sternly.

'I'm not saying I *believe* that.' Robin was defensive. 'Just that we should keep our minds open as well as our eyes.'

'Which saying is, I believe, a direct quote from our dear David Franklin.'

Rina looked sharply at Toby, noting the hardening of his tone and the increased pressure of Viv's hand on Robin's. Ah, not so happy families, then, she thought.

'So, you're saying this Philip behaved as though he was real and not something they'd made up?' Joy was intrigued.

'Appeared to, yes. There's a lecture on it tomorrow. I think there's been quite a bit of follow-up work done.'

'But the interesting thing for us is that they did something just like that here, a whole century before.' Viv was evidently excited. 'And we get to reconstruct it and to film the whole thing.'

Rina wasn't so sure she shared Viv's enthusiasm.

'Sounds creepy,' Joy said.

'Well,' Toby agreed, 'we all hope so.'

'But you said that all the people involved had been together over the Christmas,' Rina objected. 'Surely, that isn't the case this time. We only arrived this afternoon.'

'Ah, well, that's what makes it so perfect,' Toby reassured her. 'In the original experiment they brought in observers who stood in the corners of the room. A further two observers actually participated in the seance, knowing nothing about the character they hoped to summon. They were meant to be like controls for the experiment.'

'The analogue for which you've scuppered by telling us about it,' was Rina's somewhat tart observation.

'Well, yes, but we agreed we had to tell you both something. Tim's felt guilty as hell bringing you both here and not spilling the beans.'

'I hope he has,' Rina said, looking closely at her protégé, who smiled sheepishly at her.

'I'm sorry,' he said, and she could see in his eyes that he was.

'I should think so too. We don't do secrets, Tim.'

'No, you're right, we don't.'

She could feel the attention of the group upon them as they made this very personal exchange. Felt their relationship being reassessed, but was satisfied that her Tim really was contrite. She wondered, though, what Toby had said to him to make him even contemplate the keeping of such a secret. Tim was terrible at hiding anything—except, of course, when he was performing. The thought that Tim could have called upon his performance persona and made use of it in the real world disturbed her profoundly. He would not have done this lightly, so what had Toby said or done to make him think, even for a moment, that it might be a proper thing to do?

Deciding that a full interrogation was in order for later, she turned back to Viv, knowing how much that would annoy Toby—and the need to annoy Toby was oddly insistent. 'You mentioned death and madness?'

Viv grinned. 'Bit of an exaggeration, really. One woman had a fit of the vapours and had to be revived with smelling salts, and another left the room screaming—a man, actually, not a woman. Then there was the mysterious death of Dr Pym, one of the guests that night, one of the neutral observers.'

'He fell off his horse on the way home.' Toby was dismissive. 'Too much port after dinner.'

'Ah, but he was supposed to stay overnight, and after the seance he refused to stop and wanted to go home. The servants brought his horse round for him, and there's eyewitness reports that he and Mr Southam were having a right barney. He called Southam an irresponsible idiot, and Southam called him an arrogant sceptic who would do anything to deny the truth. It's all in the inquest notes,' she added.

'Viv has read everything she can lay her hands on.' Toby got up and refilled his cup. He was drinking coffee, Rina noted, in quantities that would have had her flying without the aid of any special effects or ghostly presences.

'So, what happened to him?' Joy asked. 'The doctor, I mean.'

'Weeell, so far as we can make out from the inquest, he fell off his horse and hit his head on a rock.' Viv shrugged. 'Apparently, he took off in a right temper, and you've seen what it's like round here. Really rural—'

'Rural?' Toby laughed. 'You make it sound like we're camping up the Amazon.'

'Far as I'm concerned, it might as well be.' Viv grinned. 'Give me shops and pavements any time. Anyway, as I was saying, the village is about five miles away, and he took a route across country through Aikensthorpe wood. That's over that way.' She pointed at the window at the front of the house. 'If it ever stops raining, you'll be able to see it.'

'It's still on manor land,' Robin said quietly. 'The house was named after the wood. Aiken is Old English for "oak". The local guidebooks say it's a real, authentic patch of wildwood.'

'Sounds lovely,' Joy said. 'Is it walking distance?'

'Only if it stops raining long enough for you to see where you're going and you have a pair of wellies,' Viv said.

'Melissa has a stock of wellingtons,' Toby told them, looking at Joy with what seemed, to Rina's eyes, slightly predatory interest. Her somewhat irrational dislike of the man increased.

'Well, if it clears up, Tim and I might borrow a couple of pairs and go and see,' Joy said. She reached out and took Tim's hand, then leaned over the arm of the sofa and planted a very deliberate kiss on his cheek.

Tim looked surprised, then smiled at her and returned the kiss. He inched his chair closer.

Rina was pleased at the look of disappointment that flickered across Toby's face.

'So, accidental death then,' Joy said cheerfully. 'He probably rode into a branch.'

'Ah, but what about the look of sheer terror that eyewitnesses report, frozen on his face? His lips drawn back in a rictus or . . . oh, something or other.' Viv laughed, then seemed to reconsider. 'Sad though, don't you think, that a man should die just because he had an argument with a friend? My mum always says you should never let the sun go down on your anger—you never know what will happen, so you should never part with harsh words.'

'Oh, God,' Toby groaned. 'Homilies from Viv's mum.'

'My mum says that too,' Joy said. 'Something like it, anyway.' She smiled at Viv.

Bridie would certainly express it differently, Rina thought, but she could well believe Bridie would have her version. Rina considered it to be good and sensible advice.

'It was the last seance they held here,' Robin told them.

'Which is kind of a surprise,' Viv said, considering it. 'You'd almost have expected them to try and get in touch with him, wouldn't you? That's what they did when the gamekeeper died.'

'Gamekeeper?' This bit was evidently new to Toby.

'You should have read the background notes,' Viv chided. 'The gamekeeper was the first seance, about two years before. He got shot in what was reported as a hunting accident, but there was some doubt. Southam and his little gang decided to do some psychic investigating. Actually, he did some real investigating too. He called in a detective all the way from London to look into things. They had regular seances every few weeks after that, until the one where everything went wrong and the room was sealed up.'

'They called in a private detective?' Toby seemed to pounce on the fact 'I must take a look at that. Anyway, that's the end of the story, really. After that last seance, as Viv said, the anteroom it took place in was sealed up, and no seance ever conducted here again. It was something of a cause célèbre locally though, and it made a splash in the national papers. Various mediums and the like claimed to have been in touch with Dr Pym, and the general shenanigans took a good year or so to die down.' He got up, and the others saw that as a cue to move too. 'Viv and Melissa have put notes together for you about the house and such, and there are mini biographies of speakers and such in the conference packs. The other re-enactors will be here for dinner soon. See you all then.'

Rina felt she could hardly wait. Mac's offer to collect them early was looking more attractive all the time.

THREE

Taken from an article in the Times and Herald, *1870:*

> *Commiserations must be extended to local philanthropist Albert Southam, Esq. and Mrs Southam, who have returned only a scant month after their marriage to the news of the death. It is understood that Mr Creedy died in a freak accident. Mr Creedy, undoubtedly an experienced shot, and a man well practised in the use of firearms, seems to have tripped and fallen on his own gun. The shotgun discharged and hit Mr Creedy in the chest and abdomen. Those who came to the scene only shortly after discovered the man not yet dead, but mortally wounded. He is reported to have managed to speak a few words thereafter, before succumbing to his wounds [. . .]*
>
> *An enquiry being held, a verdict of accidental death has been returned. Mr Creedy leaves a widow and two young sons. It is in keeping with the generosity we have come to expect from Mr Southam, Creedy's employer, that he has assured the family that a small pension will be paid to the widow and that they will be found accommodation on the estate.*

Tim and Joy went to their room. No doubt, Rina thought, to reconcile properly, so Rina's planned interrogation would have to wait. She wandered back to the nursery wing, taking time to look over the old house. It had evidently been a very rich establishment, and Rina admired the elaborate carving that ornamented the banisters and balustrades and the rather good portraits that lined the first-floor corridor, some of which, judging by the costumes, pre-dated the house by a good couple of centuries. She had read that the newly rich in Victorian England often bought the family history of others and put it into their freshly built extravagances. She'd also heard they bought their books by the yard to fill their impressive but unread libraries and wondered how true either assertion was. The library here at Aikensthorpe looked impressive; she must go and take a proper look later.

She wondered too when the little anteroom the seance had taken place in had been unsealed and had a dreadful suspicion it had been very recent.

Viv had handed her the prepared information pack as they had parted, and it was now tucked beneath Rina's arm. It was a substantial piece of work, if the chunkiness of the folder was anything to go by, and Rina guessed that if Viv had prepared it then it would be very thorough. She had engendered a sneaking liking for the mercurial Viv and the quiet Robin, but she was very hard pressed to find anything to like in the outwardly affable Toby; the sensation that he had put pressure on Tim to . . . well, not exactly to *lie*, but certainly to be guilty of the sin of omission, was very insistent, and she wondered again what influence Toby possessed that had enabled him to do so. Tim was an honourable and, in all the best ways, a rather simple character, honest and direct. Rina was very annoyed, but no longer so much with Tim.

Walking slowly along the landing, she continued her perusal of the portraits, finally discovering one of the same Albert Southam who must have built this place. A portly, red-faced man, with rather sad blue eyes, he peered out at Rina, looking as though the artist had caught him in the act of searching for his glasses. She wondered if the painter had been trying to create some sense of the intensity of Albert's character; in truth, he had made him look ever so slightly constipated.

Southam's wife hung next to him on the wall, and she was something of a surprise. Looking at the dates, Rina was surprised to find that both portraits had been executed in the same year. Eighteen seventy, just two years before the fateful seance. And, coincidentally, Rina recalled, the same year the unfortunate gamekeeper had died. Elizabeth Southam was very much younger than her husband and very much prettier too. Her dark hair had been dressed in the fashionable ringlets of the period, and her dark eyes examined the viewer with lively intelligence. The artist had clearly enjoyed painting her far more than her husband. There was, Rina fancied, an intimacy about the painting that belied the formality of the pose.

The light on the landing wasn't very good, and Rina squinted, leaning close to try and read the engraved words on the little plaque attached to the frame. The date and Elizabeth's name and status were in large enough letters to read fairly easily, but the rest was small and difficult to define.

Rina licked her finger and drew it across the surface of the brass, removing some of the dirt. 'Painted on the occasion of their wedding,' she read out loud. 'So, a rich old man and a pretty young bride.' Looking at her again, Rina couldn't believe that Elizabeth had been much more than Joy's age in this picture. Had she loved Albert? Rina wondered. Was there something about this man apart from his wealth that had attracted this young and very pretty girl? Or had it been a marriage of convenience, a business arrangement between families? Maybe the contents of Viv's extensive information pack would tell her.

Rina chuckled to herself. Always interested in the human stories, Rina's curiosity was often her undoing and, if she was now truly honest with herself, she knew she'd have to go through this weekend just to satisfy it.

She had reached the stairs to the next floor, and she climbed them slowly, listening to the sounds of the old house as it settled: the clang of pipes not quite up to the job any more, and the creak of wood drying out after years of neglect and damp. She was glad that someone was restoring this formidable old pile. It deserved the care.

Two flights of stairs to her floor, and then the corridor to the nursery wing. Had it ever been occupied? Had that young bride gone on to become a mother? Had it been her wish or Albert's that their progeny should be so hidden away from the rest of the household, or had they merely been following the custom of the times? Or had Elizabeth perhaps been a second wife and any children from an earlier marriage?

Reaching that upper corridor, only the servants' quarters now above her, Rina paused to listen. The landing was broad, and a window looked out on to the gardens at the rear of the house. Another flight of stairs rose up to the attic space where the servants would have slept. *Her* corridor then led back into the right-hand wing, the library and anteroom being on the ground floor of the left. Windows on one side of the hall, rooms on the other—though, so far as she could tell, hers was the only one currently in occupation.

It was so very quiet. Rain still pattered against the window, the house still creaked and groaned, but other than that there was only silence.

Impulsively, Rina turned and began to climb that final flight of stairs up to the attic space. The stairs were steeper here, and narrower, and that strange muffling of sound was even more profound than it had been on the lower floors. Rina's own house was also more than a century old, and also had an attic space that had been the housemaid's room and was now co-opted for extra visitors, but there the similarity ended. Rina's house, Peverill Lodge, was never silent. It could be quiet, when everyone was asleep, but sounds of people and music and radio, and sometimes, in the evening, television, permeated even through closed doors. The clatter of cooking pots in the kitchen, of laughter and conversation and the Peters sisters playing songs on the piano that they had performed in their younger days, all conspired to create a friendly background chatter. Rina hadn't really thought about it until now, but the smothering silence of Aikensthorpe and of this wing in particular brought to mind just how much she missed home and how intensely she loved her noisy, eccentric little household.

At the top of the servants' stairs was a tiny landing and two doors. Rina guessed that the layout must be echoed in the other wing and probably elsewhere in such a big house. Many servants would have been required in Southam's day, both inside and out, caring for the household and the extensive gardens. She lifted the latch on the right-hand door and, finding to her surprise that it was open, she went inside.

The light switch was just inside the door. It was modern and plastic, and the wires were carried up the wall inside equally plasticky white trunking. Downstairs, although it was obvious that rewiring had taken place, the new fittings were brass and the wiring hidden inside the walls. It was interesting though, Rina thought, that the plastic switch and trunking were the only modern interruptions in a room that had barely been touched in a century. Wooden floorboards, a little cast-iron bedstead, a washstand laid with green tiles on which a bowl would have stood, a small fireplace with the grate still in place, and even a candlestick on the plain wooden overmantel.

A small window, dirty and with a cracked pane, was set high up in the wall, and the occupant of the room would have had to stand on the bed to see out. She figured that views were not something servants were expected to look at. A second door led through into another bedroom, this with two beds set at right angles to one another. No new light switch in this room, just signs that it had been used for storage by the electrician. Reels of wire and cardboard boxes still containing some of the new fittings had been set on one of the beds. Another fireplace in this room, another wash stand, and also a small bedside cupboard. Rina could not resist a look inside. Newspaper had been used to line the shelves; Rina recalled her mother and aunt doing the same, though the Peters sisters made certain that in Rina's house pretty, scented drawer liners replaced the utilitarian newsprint. She took the paper out, loving it when she found such unexpected links to the past and, turning the paper into the light, was happy to see the adverts for Goddard's powders and Beechams salts. She blew the dust off, fished a second liner from the bottom shelf and slipped them both inside the folder that Viv had given her. She'd enjoy looking through those later. Who could tell what snippet of old news might be hidden there?

A final glance around the room told her there was nothing more to see, unless . . . Rina crouched down by the fire. Paper had been burned in the grate. She sniffed. Recent burning, she thought, and then poked at the pages, which crumbled away almost to nothing. Almost. One corner of a page remained, a white triangle with a single page number. Rina fished it out, but beyond the number six, it told her nothing. Probably, she thought, something the electrician had burned. She hoped he'd checked the chimney was working first.

Curiosity largely satisfied, she returned to the landing and closed the bedroom door. The second room was also unlocked, but she got no further than the entrance. This room really had been used for storage—generations of it, from the look of tangled chair legs and boxes and a stack of what might be old curtains just inside. She felt for a light switch, found none. Evidently not even the most desultory renovations had been carried out here. She'd have to find a torch and come and have another look later on. Tim always kept a flashlight in the car; she could borrow that.

She made her way slowly back down the dimly lit stairs. She could make out the pattern of old wallpaper, torn here and there to reveal the strata of earlier generations. The stair carpet was worn sisal, from the time when sisal was cheap and functional and not just a statement of environmental concern. Rina was a fan of good wool twist. You couldn't beat it for hard-wearing.

Back in her room she put the kettle on for tea, not so much because she wanted it but because the sound of boiling water was a human, familiar sound and the silence in the room was now crowding in on her; even the rain seemed to have stopped, though she'd been unaware of it until now. It was too dark to see much from the window, even when she turned out the light, though she could just make out the heavy cloud and the line of trees. Was that the infamous Aikensthorpe wood? The little clock on her bedside table told her that it was only a quarter to six: still more than an hour to go before dinner. Rina realized with shock that she was actually bored. She could not recall the last time that had been the case.

'Pull yourself together, woman,' she chided. 'Have a bath, get changed, drink some more tea and have a look at that folder Vivian gave you. There, that's your next hour sorted.'

Feeling better now that she'd made a plan, she went through to the bathroom to see what fancy complimentary bath stuff Aikensthorpe had to offer and turned on the bath taps, glad of the additional noise. Melissa had left three little bottles of bath gel and a basket of pink soaps that looked far too pretty to use. There were still bars on the windows in the bathroom, a remnant from when the room had been the nursery and implying that at some time there had actually been children here. Original feature or not, Rina thought, she'd have had them removed. It made an otherwise spacious room feel oddly claustrophobic. She pulled the blind fully down, hiding them from sight.

In addition to the connecting door from her bedroom was a second exit leading back out into the corridor. It was locked from the inside; the new lock, like the faux traditional electrical fittings, had been selected so it did not look completely out of place in the setting, but it didn't look quite right either: too modern and just too brassy. Rina turned the key and peered out on to the empty corridor, not sure what impulse had led her to do so. Glancing to her left, she could see the completely new door at the end of the hall that had been knocked through to the outside world. Solid and white, and bearing the legend 'Fire Escape', it looked horribly intrusive. Just down the corridor from Rina's room was another door, slightly ajar.

Rina frowned at it. She'd passed the door before entering her room and could not recall seeing it open then. On reflection, she realized, this was what had made her unlock the bathroom door and glance out: the faint, subconsciously recognized sound of another door being opened.

Another guest, presumably, though they were awfully quiet and why leave the door open like that?

She closed her own and locked it again. 'Rina, stop making mysteries where there are none,' she told herself sternly. 'The sooner you get yourself home and normal again, the better for everyone.'

The bath had run now, and the selected gel filled the room with the fragrance of rose and honeysuckle. Making up her mind that she would knock on the other door on her way down and introduce herself to the new guest, Rina made her tea and fetched her dressing gown.

'Tea and a good soak, that's what you need, you silly old woman,' she chided herself. 'All this talk of ghosts and death and other nonsense is getting to you.' But even so, she could not resist the urge to check the locks on both the doors before succumbing to the invitation of perfumed water and hot tea.

Something just wasn't right here, Rina thought. She'd met 'not right' far too often for her to mistake it—and whatever it was, it was certainly present in this beautiful old house.

FOUR

'I'm still not happy about this, David.' Gail swallowed more of her drink and refilled her glass from a bottle on the sideboard that dominated this little parlour next to the main dining room.

'Don't you think you've had enough?' He kept his voice low, glancing uneasily at the assembled company.

'None of your business.' She knew he hated being shown up; sometimes she just enjoyed provoking him. He was such a stuffed shirt.

'What is my business is that I need you in good shape for tomorrow, so pull yourself together. The Martin woman and Tim's girlfriend are incidental. We need them to be neutral witnesses, that's all; everything else is as it was before Simeon left.'

'No—' she shook her head—'it isn't. They're strangers, David. They'll completely ruin the vibrations.'

'Oh, now you *are* getting too precious. Gail, you do what you do well enough, but don't start believing your own press. This is an experiment, not a performance.' She swallowed more wine and glared at him over the rim of her glass. Professor Franklin moved closer. 'Gail, I want this to be a success, just as much as you do. More, probably, let's face it; I've got rather more to lose here.'

She opened her mouth to retort, then shut it again, turned away from him, pretending to study one of the many pictures on the panelled walls.

'Gail, tomorrow will be a great success. The first of many. But you have to take hold of your emotions. You are here to *play* a part, not to *live* that part.'

'You just don't believe I can really do it, do you?'

'My mind is open. There are, as they say, many things in heaven and earth that—'

'Go fuck yourself.'

'Gail,' he chided. 'Please. You're letting your emotional responses overrule your analytic. Deep breath, put the glass down and remember the exercise I taught you. Take control of your emotions, keep focused on what is really important here. Do you really want to be lumped together with the stage magicians and the illusionists and the charlatans? Or do you want to build a reputation as a meticulous researcher? Someone not afraid to delve into the psyche of those who delude themselves, but who can remain separate from all of that, untainted by it—'

'Have you actually listened to yourself? Talk about believing your own press. David, I—' She broke off. Tim and Joy had just entered the room, and she fell back into a moody silence.

'I thought you liked Tim Brandon.'

'I do,' she said flatly. 'That isn't the point though, is it?'

* * *

Edwin Holmes glanced in the direction of the argument raging beside the window and accepted a glass from Rav Pinner. 'Not a happy bunny,' he said.

'Is she ever? But I don't think David helps. He is a tad sanctimonious.'

Edwin laughed, his blue eyes twinkling. 'Ah, but he's a famous man, don't forget. He has to be aware of how the world sees him.'

'So he likes being seen as a sanctimonious bastard then? That's his public persona?'

'Now, Rav, don't be cruel. What do you think of our new guests?'

'I've not met them yet. The girl is pretty,' he said thoughtfully, looking approvingly in Joy's direction. 'Toby tells me Tim Brandon is very good, and I've seen some film of his work; it seems to me that he understands the Victorian mindset.' He shrugged. 'You know Mrs Martin has something of a reputation, don't you?'

'Reputation? Of what kind?'

'I looked her up. She's made quite a splash as an amateur investigator. It seems she never quite let go of her television role.'

Edwin laughed. 'I believe she played a Miss Marple type of character, didn't she? I watch so little television. Have you seen the show?'

'Yes, a few episodes.'

Jay Stratham had been listening to the conversation. 'We get them on one of the cable channels back home,' he said. 'Very British. Do you think dinner will be long? I'm starved.'

'We're still a few minutes early,' Edwin told him.

'I suppose we are. Well, Edwin, Rav, if you'll excuse me, I'm going to have a talk with Mr Brandon.'

'You're going to talk shop,' Edwin predicted.

'What other kind of conversation is there when magicians get together?'

'Quite,' Edwin said, watching with amusement as Jay strolled over to where Tim and Joy were standing. 'She *is* very pretty,' he added wistfully. 'Oh, to be a great number of years younger.'

'Age has its own virtues,' Rav told him softly.

'Does it?' Edwin asked sadly. 'I'm really not sure I can think of any.'

* * *

The dining room was through another door in the main reception area, and drinks were being served in a little anteroom off that. When Rina arrived, Tim and Joy were already there. Joy had changed into a simple, blue shift dress, and she had left her long red hair loose. She looked stunning, Rina thought and noted that the male attention in the room seemed more or less evenly split between her young friend and Viv. Robin stood next to his girlfriend looking very proud with Viv's hand clasped in his own. On the face of it, Rina thought, they made an odd pair: Viv so utterly confident and self-possessed, and Robin shy and uncertain, good-looking in a somewhat understated way with his very dark hair and very bright blue eyes and rather pale skin. He'd make a good goth, she decided.

Viv spotted her and grinned broadly. 'Red or white? Or I think there's some sherry.'

Rina went over to them. 'Sherry would be nice, actually.' Sherry before dinner was a commonplace at Peverill Lodge. 'I had a quick look through the information you prepared for us. You've done a very efficient job.'

'Thank you.' Viv looked both pleased and surprised. 'Robin gave me a hand. It's really interesting stuff, don't you think, and isn't this just an amazing house?'

'It is,' Rina agreed. 'Tell me though, what do you actually think happened that night? Hype aside, do you think they really experienced anything?'

Viv and Robin exchanged a glance. Rina was slightly taken aback; she'd expected an immediate affirmative from Robin.

'Weeell.' Viv stretched the word to breaking point. 'We've talked about it a lot, Robin and me. I mean, I'm a major sceptic, but Robin really believes there is something else out there, you know.'

'I don't think it's all ghosts and ghouls,' Robin put in quickly. 'I mean, I'm sure most things that seem strange have a perfectly ordinary explanation, and I'm not sure that calling things ghostly or psychic or supernatural really helps anyone.

I mean, they're happening here, in this world, aren't they, you know? Which kind of implies that they belong here and not somewhere else.' He trailed off, and Viv took over.

'What we mean is that yes, there is something we haven't explained yet, but it becomes difficult to talk about because of the semantics involved. It separates people into two separate camps, you know, believers and non-believers, when what we should really be saying is we don't know what's going on, but something *is*, so we should just observe, explain what we can and then accept that there are elements we don't have a handle on yet. It's like . . . I've got a friend who's doing an archaeology MA. She says that in really important sites they deliberately leave areas un-dug because each generation has better ways of examining the evidence and understanding what went on there.'

'We shouldn't be afraid of saying we don't know, is what we think, I suppose.' Robin blushed, the pale cheeks flushing a very bright red. 'And that we need new words, a new vocabulary, so we don't get tied up in the way all the words we use have extra value and meaning added to them. If I say I want to see a ghost then everyone thinks I must be some kind of religious loony. What I really mean is that I'd like to see something interesting, something I can't explain and can't figure out or reproduce using special effects or stage magic.'

'And that night, back in eighteen seventy-two, I think those two groups clashed,' Viv said. 'The people who wanted to see, but who also believed, clashed with the people who couldn't accept any of it. I think they quarrelled because Doctor Pym thought his friends had dragged him into a situation that was pointless or maybe even evil. I don't know what you've managed to read yet, but Pym was dead against all the experimentation that was going on. I couldn't find out why, but he seems convinced it was dangerous and he thought Mr Southam was becoming obsessed.'

'It wasn't the first seance he'd attended though,' Rina objected. 'They seem to have been a regular occurrence, according to your very thorough notes.'

Viv looked pleased. She didn't get much praise for what she'd done, Rina thought.

Robin was thoughtful. 'I don't think he was against trying to speak to the dead. He'd claimed to have received messages from his dead wife, hadn't he?'

Viv nodded.

'So, what was so different about this time?' Rina asked.

Again, that swiftly exchanged glance between Robin and Viv. 'Maybe because they told him they'd *invented* the ghost,' Viv said. 'I think that upset him. I think he felt cheated and used and began to doubt that the earlier messages had been real.'

'That's what we think, anyway.' Robin shrugged. 'It's all a bit speculative, but then, all of this stuff is a bit speculative. I mean, we're not even dead certain their ghost was fully invented.'

'Oh?' Rina was intrigued.

'Well,' Viv said. 'One letter I read suggested it was another attempt to contact the gamekeeper. Elizabeth seemed to agree with some of the local gossips that the shooting hadn't been an accident, but—' she shrugged—'I don't know. Edwin is convinced it wasn't about the gamekeeper, so . . .'

'And what do you think?' Rina asked them both.

'I think everyone looks at the evidence and sees just what they want to see,' Robin said. 'No change in that. I can't imagine Mr Southam would have been too pleased to have all of that dragged up again though. I mean, he'd been seen to have done his bit, called in the detective, looked after the family.'

'Whatever actually happened,' Viv added, 'it ended in disaster.'

'And how do you both feel about this group having invented their ghost?' Rina asked.

'I'm just intrigued,' Viv said. 'I mean, if nothing happens, then nothing happens, but if it does, it's going to be very interesting.'

'Have they tried to raise the same character? The same one as the original seance? That's assuming it wasn't the gamekeeper, of course.'

'Well, that's a bit of a problem too. No one could really agree on what or who that was—assuming it *definitely* wasn't Mr Creedy the gamekeeper, that is. It's not like the Philip phenomena we told you about. That's well documented: a lot of it was filmed or recorded at the time, and there are tons of notes. What happened here is fragmentary, and a lot of it is from the coroner's report and eyewitness statements, and Mrs Southam had left here by the time the rest of the statements were taken so we don't know what she thought about it and that was kind of central to the event.'

'Her portrait is on the first-floor landing,' Rina commented. 'She looks very young.'

'She was twenty when she married Albert Southam. He was fifty-three.'

'And she left?'

'The morning after the seance, very early. Pym's body was found after she'd gone. She never came back here.'

'Where did she go?'

'Italy,' Robin said. 'The family had a villa in Rome or somewhere close. She went there and never came back home again. Albert Southam died five years after, and this place was rented out. She didn't even come back for the funeral. The room was walled up, and it was a condition of the tenancy that it was never opened up again—and it wasn't. Not until a month ago when Melissa got the builders in to take the false wall down. The room was just as they'd left it. Table, chairs, even what was left of a bowl of roses on the table. Melissa took pictures as the work was being done.'

'I'd like to see those,' Rina said thoughtfully.

'Pity she didn't get someone to film it.' Robin was regretful. 'Surely there was someone here with a video camera, or even a mobile phone.'

Viv laughed. 'Well, anyway, the room was opened and the re-enactors started to prepare.' She pulled a face. 'We got here two days ago to set up, but no one's told us anything much yet.'

Joy left Tim's side and came over to join them. 'He's talking shop,' she said. 'I'll not get a word in.' She didn't sound as though she minded too much. 'I read through your stuff,' she told Viv. 'I didn't realize that Mrs Southam was the medium.'

Rina had missed that. Joy had evidently been more assiduous in her research.

Viv nodded. 'She was at it before they married. Only private parties and stuff, not in public, though there were impresarios who tried to persuade her father and offered big money. She came from what they called an "old" family, lots of tradition and no cash, but then she married Albert Southam and I suppose that sorted that.'

'They met at a seance,' Robin said. 'I'm not sure if that's my idea of an ideal first date.' He glanced at his watch. 'Dinner in a couple of minutes,' he added. 'I'll give you the quick biographical tour before we go in, so at least you'll know who's sitting next to you.'

'Thank you,' Rina said. 'I think that might be a good idea. Start with the man Tim is talking to.'

'Ah, well, I'm not surprised they're so engrossed. That's Jay Statham. He's American—'

'*African* American,' Viv corrected him with a little giggle. 'You know how Toby likes us to be politically correct. He's a nice guy,' she added. 'Jay, I mean.'

'And Toby is not?' Joy evidently couldn't resist. She'd spent far too much time with *her*, Rina thought.

'Oh, he's OK, he's just a bit . . . Anyway, Jay Stratham. Magician and technical adviser. He writes books about the history of magic and also advises film companies and stuff. We're lucky to have him here. He's going to be the fourth camera on the night. I was just standing in for him today.'

'What will you be doing?' Joy asked.

'I think, if I remember the seating plan right, sitting between Rina and that man over there who's talking to Toby.'

Blond, close cropped hair, his expensive suit cut to emphasize the musculature beneath, Rina felt an immediate sense of familiarity. 'Oh,' she said. 'That's Terry Beal, isn't it? The one who does all those action films.'

'Didn't know you watched that sort of thing, Rina.' Joy was amused.

'The twins like them.'

'Stephen and Matthew?'

'No, dear, Bethany and Eliza. They like all that over-blown muscularity. Some things don't change even when you reach the age to know better. What's he here for?'

'His agent got wind of what we were doing and arranged it,' Viv said. 'I think he's playing an exorcist in his next film or something. Over there, the Asian man is Rav Pinner. His dad is English or Welsh, I forget. Anyway, he's a physicist, he's a member of one of those debunking groups, but the old man he's talking to is Edwin Holmes—'

'Grand old man of psychic research,' Robin said. 'I'm quoting Toby there. He's lovely, and he and Rav seem to be really good friends even if they do sit up all night arguing.'

'And playing poker,' Viv added. 'Rina, just in case you're tempted, don't. They are scary good, they really are.'

'And the girl standing next to the middle-aged man?' The pair of them were standing in the corner of the room, observing. Occasionally, the man had spoken to the girl, but she seemed almost to be ignoring him.

'Oh, yes, them.' Viv frowned. 'Sorry, he gives me the creeps. If you had to describe a stereotyped shrink then he would be it. You get the feeling he's judging you all the time. Anyway, that's the famous professor, David Franklin. Gail is the medium; she's one of his research students. I think Toby mentioned that?'

Rina nodded, recalling that he had said something about her. She didn't look comfortable with her mentor, Rina thought. In fact, she looked as though she'd rather be just about anywhere else.

Still full of misgiving for the weekend, Rina could not help but be intrigued by the company and speculate as to how events might unfold. It would, as she had said to Joy, be interesting if nothing else.

Out in the hall the handbell rang and then Melissa appeared. 'Dinner is ready,' she said. 'Sorry it's a few minutes late, but the rest of the temporary staff don't get here until morning, so I'm pretty much it.'

They followed her through from the anteroom in which they had been chatting to the formal dining room.

'Do you happen to know who else is on my corridor?' Rina asked Viv. She had knocked on the door of the room opposite hers before coming down, but had received no reply.

'You're on the nursery floor, aren't you? I don't think there's anyone else up there. Melissa said the renovations are only part complete on that floor.' She glanced curiously at Rina. 'Any particular reason?'

'No, not really. I just noticed that the door along from mine was open.'

'Probably Melissa,' Robin speculated. 'She's still using a lot of the un-renovated rooms for storage.'

'Probably was, then,' Rina agreed, but something, she felt, was wrong with that analysis. Melissa was a bustler: she scurried and hurried and made noise wherever she went. Some people moved quietly and calmly, some did not—and Melissa was definitely a did not. If Melissa had been in that room, Rina would have heard her.

FIVE

Aikensthorpe, 1870

It had been only a few weeks after their return from honeymoon that Elizabeth had been told about the Reverend Spinelli. Ellen Creedy had been so desperate and so distressed when she had come to see her new young mistress that Elizabeth had felt bound to do something.

'Those that were with him said he told them,' Ellen whispered. 'Mr Creedy swore that he'd been shot at, that it wasn't his weapon that went off.'

'Who on earth would shoot your husband?' Elizabeth had, at first been reluctant to listen. Albert was doing all he could to help the family: he had kept a roof over their heads at no rent and given them the promised pension—more than most employers would have done, Elizabeth well knew.

'He said it, ma'am, he told them. Oh Mrs Southam, forgive me, but I can't get out of my head that he was killed and that the man who killed him is still out there.'

'Did he name someone?'

Mrs Creedy nodded emphatically. She leaned forward and whispered a name that at the time meant nothing to Elizabeth. Spinelli.

'I will look into this, Mrs Creedy,' Elizabeth had promised. If nothing else it would add a little excitement, she thought, to a life which had proved dull since their return from Europe.

Later, she had summoned those employees who had been there on the day of Creedy's death and asked them to confirm what his widow had said.

'And what do you think?' she had asked both the estate manager and the head gardener who had been first on the scene and watched the gamekeeper die.

The gardener shuffled his feet, twisting his cap between his hands. He shook his head. 'I saw nothing, Mrs Southam, nor heard nothing either.'

'You can go, Michael,' George Weston, the manager of her husband's estate, told the man.

Elizabeth opened her mouth to protest, but a slight shake of Weston's head caused her to hesitate and keep silent until the man had scurried away.

'Mr Weston?'

'Please understand, Mrs Southam, that you cannot expect those who are vulnerable to the wrath of their superiors to speak freely. I will confirm Creedy's words, but I do ask that you leave the servants out of the matter. For their sake.'

Elizabeth frowned. 'Very well, Mr Weston, and what will you tell me?'

Weston hesitated for a moment, and then he said, 'Creedy's weapon was unloaded when I took it from his hand. It had not been fired.'

'You lied to the police?'

'I lied to the police. I perjured myself at the inquest. Creedy asked me to do so. I did not see fit to deny the wishes of a dying man, especially as I fully understood his reasoning.'

Elizabeth rang the bell and ordered the maid to bring them both tea.

'Sit down, Mr Weston,' Elizabeth commanded. 'And you will explain your reasoning to me.'

* * *

It was after nine by the time Rina headed back to her room. She had decided she would call Mac and ask him to look some things up for her on his computer. She had become used to having Internet access this past year and really missed it now. She supposed she could have asked Melissa if there was a terminal she could use, but really didn't want to draw attention to the fact that she was checking up on her fellow guests and doing a bit of her own research to supplement Viv's very able appraisal. It didn't seem very polite, apart from anything else. She'd been relieved to have been seated at dinner with Joy and Tim, and their other table companions, Rav and Terry, had proved to be amiable and easy. Much to her surprise, Terry Beal, internationally acclaimed action hero, more famous for his muscles than his brain, was a bright, intelligent soul who had been far more interested in finding out about his fellow diners than talking about his acting career. Best of all, he knew of Rina. Her lead role in the TV series *Lydia Marchant Investigates* was familiar to him and affectionately recalled.

'I used to watch it with my mother, and now I catch it on reruns when I'm travelling. You'd be amazed at how many languages it's been dubbed into or subtitled for.'

Actually, Rina thought, she knew precisely how many—and picked up a nice little royalty cheque on a regular basis. Lydia Marchant had paid for Peverill Lodge in the first place; now she did her bit to help with the running of it, and Rina was profoundly grateful to her alter ego.

'It must have been hard to give it up. What did it run for? Ten years, twelve?'

'Eleven series,' Rina told him. 'And three films, but it had run its course by the time it was finally axed. You know, there was a twelfth series commissioned?'

'No, I didn't realize that. What happened?'

'Oh, change of mind at the top. Some new executives drafted in wanted to modernize, and apparently Lydia Marchant was too old-fashioned for them. Every so often someone will talk about a revival—I've even had a couple of meetings about it—but I doubt anything will ever happen.'

Terry Beal had looked keenly at her. 'Would you want to?'

'I wouldn't say no. It could be fun.'

'It could indeed.' He flashed a smile and leaned across the table. 'Leave it with me,' he said, and Rina had smiled back, trying to ignore the frisson of excitement at the thought that he might in fact be able to do something. It *would* be fun, she thought, after all this time.

Rina arrived at the final landing and, on impulse, turned off the light so that she could see out of the large window. The rain had ceased, the sky cleared and she could now see the two wings leading back from the main body of the house and the outbuildings Melissa had told her had been the stables and accommodation for live-in outdoor staff. There was a yard beyond, but Rina's view of this was blocked by the tall, pitched roof of the carriage house. All of this, Melissa had told her, was to be converted into guest accommodation for the conferences she hoped to host. The space between the wings was grassed, skirted by paths, and beyond that was a larger expanse of lawn, which stopped at a line of trees. Aikensthorpe wood was out of sight on the other side of the house, but Rina assumed that this line of tall trees must be an outcropping from it; they looked too densely packed to be merely a field boundary. She released the catches on the sash window and eased it up, glad to find that it had not been painted closed as so often happened with these old windows. Cold, damp air flooded on to the landing, taking her breath. There's snow on that wind, she thought. It might not be there in the morning, but it wouldn't be long after. Checking the latch was secured and she was not about to be decapitated by a falling sash, she leaned out and looked towards the unlit windows of the seance room. Melissa had shown her the pictures she had taken when it had been unsealed. When she had entered the room that afternoon, Rina had assumed it was windowless, but now she knew that close fitting shutters, matching the wall panelling, had been fastened tight over them.

'They drew the shutters that night and they were never opened again,' Melissa had said. 'The room was closed and locked and that was that.'

Robin had been accurate in his description of the room's contents, but in addition to the remains of roses still in a silver bowl, Rina had noticed a single glove left on a chair, a lady's paisley shawl draped across the back. It was these small items that spoke so eloquently to Rina. Something had frightened the participants so much that they had departed in haste and sealed the memory inside, not even venturing back to retrieve their possessions.

She started to close the window, glancing first at the still lighted windows of the dining room and the little anteroom where they had gathered before dinner. The curtains had not been fully drawn, and a shaft of light that fell on to the paving stones and the sodden grass was momentarily broken as someone passed between light and window. She had left Tim and Jay Statham deep in conversation with Rav, and Joy playing poker with Edwin and Gail. Rina, having seen Joy play before, felt sorry for the other two.

A slight movement attracted her attention, and she looked towards the rear of the stable block. Now her eyes had become accustomed to the light, she could see a small door fitted into the grey stone wall. A figure moved beside the door and then opened it. Rina could see a light come on, and then the door closed again. She frowned, annoyed with herself that she had seen no one leave the house and could only guess who the figure might have been. Tall and slim built, she would surmise Melissa. Not that it mattered, she told herself. It was just that she liked to know these things.

She was about to move away from the window and go to her room when a second figure detached itself from the shadows by the library wall and walked swiftly across towards the stable door. Intrigued, Rina noted that whoever it was walked the length of the lawn rather than down the path, as though to avoid the sound of gravel crunching beneath their feet. Rina leaned out a little further. This second person was male, and something in the way he pushed back his hair caused her to believe it might be Toby. He paused, glanced around, then opened the small door and went inside.

'Well,' Rina breathed. 'Now, isn't that interesting?'

Or was it, really? So Melissa and Toby were meeting in the stable; there could be so many and varied reasons for that. Romantic, perhaps, or something merely practical to do with the events of the weekend.

Telling herself not to be such a busybody, but knowing that the habit was far too ingrained for her head to take the blindest bit of notice, Rina withdrew and began to close the window, only to pause as a third person stepped into view. He—she was pretty sure it was a he—moved out into the patch of light slanting through the dining room curtains and stood looking towards the door in the stable wall. For perhaps a couple of minutes, he didn't move, and neither did Rina. She couldn't place him. Carefully, she compared her mental images of the males in their party to the figure standing there, dressed, unlike Melissa and Toby, in a heavy coat and what she assumed was a thick scarf or hat muffling the shape of his head.

Too heavily built for Rav, and not Robin either—far too tall, and definitely without Robin's slightly apologetic little stoop. Tim she would know anywhere, and Jay Stratham had a distinctive way of moving that was quite unlike this man. Jay thrust his head forwards when he walked, as though listening for something, or stalking some mysterious prey. The old man, Edwin Holmes? No, definitely not him. Terry, maybe, or possibly the professor?

The figure moved, and Rina retreated, suddenly uneasy about being seen. She watched as the figure marched confidently across the lawn, heading towards the line of trees. He didn't seem worried about being seen, but then, she thought, why should he be? Melissa and Toby, the seeming objects of his interest, were in the stables, and no windows looked back out on to the lawn. The rest were in the dining room or anteroom, and both of these had their curtains closed. He, whoever he was, had no reason to give any thought to a potential spy in an upstairs window.

'There's trouble in this,' Rina said to herself as she eased the window closed. 'Just mark my words.'

* * *

Reaching her room, she put the kettle on, the routine of tea making and drinking always guaranteed to help get her thoughts in order. Then, mug in hand, and notebook with a list of questions on her lap, she phoned Mac, knowing he wouldn't mind being called so late. Mac, like most police officers, and his partner, Miriam, a CSI, often kept peculiar hours.

'No, there's nothing wrong,' she reassured him. 'I just felt the need to chat with someone back in the civilized world.'

'Frantham? The civilized world? I'm not sure it's made it into the twentieth century yet.'

'Quite,' Rina said. 'How is everything back at home?' she asked rather wistfully.

'Missing you and planning celebrations. Anyone would think you'd been on a year-long expedition to unknown climes, not ten days in Manchester. So, what can I do for you?'

'You can Google a question for me, if you would. Mac, this is a strange place, and my fellow guests are no less odd. Nice enough, I suppose, but . . .'

'But?

'Oh, just but. Do you have a pen and paper? Right. Can you just do me a quick background check on the following? Who they are and what they do and that sort of thing. I've been told the basics, but I do like to be properly briefed.'

'Are you investigating, Rina?' Mac was laughing at her.

'No, not exactly. Mac, you know that feeling you get when everything looks all right, but there's something that doesn't add up. Something that's just off?'

'All too well. Rina, is everything all right up there?'

'So far as I can tell, I suppose it is.'

'But?'

'So far it is just a "but". Humour me, Mac?'

'Always, you know that. I'll give you a call if I come up with anything I think you need to know, otherwise I'll drop the notes in on Sunday morning.'

'Thank you,' Rina said. 'You're definitely coming up early then?'

'We may as well. Neither of us can settle, so Miriam's looked out some places of interest up that way. We've decided to drive north tomorrow, take in some sights, and we've booked a bed and breakfast in a village about five miles from where you are. You know snow is forecast?'

'I guessed as much.' Rina smiled as she said her good-byes, suddenly feeling much better at the thought of Mac and Miriam being close by. She got up and wandered over to her window. The light from the room blocked the scene outside and merely showed Rina's reflection.

'You're looking old,' she told herself. 'Old and tired and bored. You need a challenge, Rina Martin. Something more than retirement by the seaside.'

She dropped the curtain back into place and sat down on the side of the bed, a sudden unexpected wave of loneliness sweeping over her. True, she had some wonderful friends and a busy life, but it had been dawning on her for the past few months, ever since it became obvious that Joy and Tim were really serious about one another, that something was missing. True, that particular something had been missing for many years, since her beloved Fred had been taken from her after only five years of happiness. She slowly took the watch from its place on her wrist and studied it, stroking the little gilt face and the rather worn leather strap. Fred had given this to her, and though she had another, everyday watch, this was still her treasured possession, worn on those occasions when a little extra nerve was required. She wasn't sure why she'd felt that need tonight, but she had, and the talisman had worked its usual magic, calming and reassuring her.

There was something no one in her little household knew about, not even Tim: something that accounted for the sudden surge of anger when she had discovered what he had landed them in the middle of.

'Seance indeed,' Rina snorted, and then closed her eyes and blinked back a stray tear.

When Fred had died, she had fallen apart. The man she loved had gone, taken not by some great drama but by a simple bout of flu which had turned to pneumonia and not responded to anything the doctors had to offer. A few weeks after the funeral she had been walking aimlessly through town and seen an A-frame advertising a visiting medium. It had seemed so obvious that she should go in and see if her Fred could talk to her. Rina had never bothered with such a palaver before, but, sometimes . . .

So she'd gone along to the temperance hall that evening, and she had watched the woman on the little stage as she searched the audience for someone who could 'take the initial M' or who 'had an auntie recently passed who liked violets' and she had hoped that something would come to her. And as she had watched, she had grown angry and then enraged. It wasn't that Rina was against religion or against those who claimed to be able to speak to those who had 'passed over'.

Died, Rina thought. They had died.

It was the randomness of it all; the blandness or meaninglessness of so many of the pronouncements. Surely, she thought, if you wanted to transmit a message to a loved one via some talented stranger, then you'd make bloody sure the message was particular enough to be unequivocal and not just something that would have been quite at home in the most platitudinous of greetings cards?

She had listened to the fifth or sixth assertion that Uncle So-And-So was happy and at peace and seen the looks of gratitude, the undoubted comfort the grieving had received, and had felt nothing but anger. Had heard the exhortation that a bereaved parent should 'finish the bottle of pop' their dead son had neglected to drink and, unlike the rest of the audience, not been overwhelmed by the fact the medium had known about the remaining soft drink so much as consumed by outrage that anyone, dead or alive, should waste time on such banality.

Rina had left before the rage broke free and became words; it wasn't in her nature to be cruel or derisive of those who so clearly needed and wanted such contact. After all, hadn't she thought she was one of them; hadn't she gone looking for such comforts?

Leaving as quietly as she could, she stood outside the hall and sucked deep breaths of cool air. It had rained, and she drew into her lungs damp wind that carried the tang of sea salt, despite the fact that she was at the time a good fifty miles inland, and, bemused and wondering, tears had begun to flow as she recalled how Fred had always loved the sea.

And then the voice in her ear, close and clear as though he stood beside her: 'What do you want to bother with all that for, lovely? You and I, we can chat anytime you like.'

Rina had spoken to no one about that moment, but she knew it had been her Fred talking to her. It had not been some desperate self-delusion; neither had it been imagination. Fred had been there, and Rina had felt both comforted and newly bereaved.

SIX

Aikensthorpe, 1872

Elizabeth breathed slowly and deeply, preparing herself before the others in the party joined her in this little panelled room. They had met here, for the same purpose, many times, but tonight was different, the preparation was different and her performance would be faultless.

She patted the diamonds back into place and smoothed her hair, then took her seat at the round table, facing the door. Elizabeth knew that she looked spectacular. 'Ethereal', Albert had said, 'perfect', and she felt a sudden surge of affection for her fond, foolish husband and reflected on the strangeness of the fact that a man so ruthless and efficient in his business dealings should be so easily manipulated in his emotional ones. Had he not been so obviously happy to have won her, then she might even have felt a little guilt.

The door opened and the company trooped in, quiet now, anticipation palpable. They took their seats. Albert to her right; Dr Pym and Mrs Francis directly opposite her with Mr Francis, her lawyer husband; then Mr Weston, Aikensthorpe's estate manager, and, of course, the Reverend Overton. The Reverend seated himself directly next to

Elizabeth and smiled conspiratorially. She looked away rapidly. Stupid man, Elizabeth thought. He could give the entire scheme away, just because he couldn't keep control of his emotions.

Her old friend, Miss Esther Grimes, had taken her place at Dr Pym's left, and between her and Albert was the object of this exercise, the Reverend Spinelli.

Odious man, Elizabeth thought, but tonight she would finally see him brought down, and how she would enjoy his disgrace.

Spinelli caught her eye and smiled, inclining his head in a little bow. 'An atmospheric setting, Mrs Southam. I am sure the evening will be invigorating.'

Elizabeth returned the bow and then closed her eyes, focusing. She heard the two servants they had selected as neutral observers come in and stand in the corners closest to the door, and the heavy door was closed and the room darkened, lit now only by a single candle nestled in the heart of the rose bowl placed at the centre of the table. A slight shuffling of feet betrayed the nervousness of the maidservant, and Elizabeth could imagine the sharp look that Banks, the butler, would cast in her direction. The shuffling ceased, and a close silence descended.

The servants had been a last-minute addition. 'We should employ some observers,' Spinelli had stated. 'Eyes of those that are not involved in the proceedings.'

Albert had reluctantly agreed. Elizabeth had some qualms about involving Pym in this; he was an honourable man and was not going to take kindly to being involved in such trickery. Spinelli though—now, he was the object of it all, a man truly deserving of being cut down to size, and Elizabeth was the mechanism by which this odious little creature would be destroyed, his reputation tattered and crushed. Justice would be done.

She allowed herself a little smile at the thought. 'If everyone would please join hands,' she said quietly. 'I feel the spirits are with us and ready to begin.'

SEVEN

They knew they had to move the body before the weather really got too bad for it to be possible. Simeon Meehan had been shifted twice already: once into an outbuilding, and then into the boot of the car belonging to the Aikensthorpe Estate.

It was late, rain still fell intermittently, and the journey down the gated road was a nightmare of slipping and sliding and spinning wheels and anxiety that the noise of wheels and revving engine would carry.

The journey back was yet another trauma, and it was after four in the morning when they returned to the house, entering via the rear door and disposing of wellingtons in the boot room.

'It's done now,' he said, and his companion nodded uneasily. 'We'll move the car later. If we get the chance. If we don't, it doesn't matter, we'll be long gone.'

'I suppose so.'

He cast a suspicious look at his companion. 'Don't let me down,' he said. 'You know what I do to people who let me down.'

EIGHT

Morning brought the promised coachloads of attendees—mostly male, Rina noted with amusement—and it also brought the first flurries of snow.

'Bet the buses had fun coming through the gated road,' Joy said. 'Look at the mud.' The pair of them had taken up residence on the stairs, sitting halfway up the first flight so they could people-watch. They could see the new arrivals through the wide-open doors. Melissa had laid down big rubber mats, but even so the polished wooden floor was now mired in black clay and wet with melting snow.

Rina nodded. The trackway wasn't much more than rutted earth for the most part. Closer to the house, a few tons of gravel had been spread about to give the impression that the cart track was in fact a drive, but the section from the road crossing the fields left a great deal to be desired.

'I wondered about that,' Rina said. 'Don't you think it odd? A big house like this usually has an impressive entranceway. There's a coach house, which presumably housed coaches, and yet—'

'No convenient way in or out,' Joy said, nodding. 'I find a lot of things odd about this house. It has a sort of not quite finished feel to it. Almost as though after Albert Southam died everything stopped. Did he finish the drive, do you think? Or was that just another job he didn't get around to?'

'Another job?' Rina was intrigued.

'I read some more of Viv's notes. Apparently, formal gardens were laid out just after he and Elizabeth got married, but all work stopped after she left. He had plans to install more bathrooms and better plumbing, but that stopped too—and the improvements Elizabeth urged him to make to the workers' cottages? He never finished them either. It's like life was just frozen off after she had gone, and I still can't figure out why she left when she did. As *suddenly* as she did.'

'She was gone before they discovered poor Dr Pym's body,' Rina said, nodding. 'It's an odd event all round. The man who rented this place after Albert died sounds very strange too.'

'Oh, the mad scientist.' Joy laughed. 'Some of his books are in the library; I found them this morning. There wasn't much he wasn't into: he wrote volumes on electricity and microscopy and he had a telescope on the roof. Maybe he liked to be well away from the rest of the world so it didn't matter that guests had to trek across three counties if they wanted to visit. Who *are* all these people?'

'Apparently, a mixture of stage magicians, psychical researchers and special-effects people. Melissa says it's quite unusual to have them in the same place, and I think she would love to stage a regular event here.' Rina paused to study the new arrivals; the demographic was largely male, white, thirty to fifty, she would guess. Most were deep in conversation, some looking around with interest, a few pausing on the threshold as though to assess the atmosphere before deciding to commit.

'Good morning, did you sleep well? When do we get breakfast?' Terry Beal loped up the stairs and plonked himself down beside Joy.

'Surprisingly well, thank you,' Rina told him. 'You?'

'Oh yes, and I've been for a run already. I'm starving now.'

Joy laughed. 'Where did you run to? You must have looked like a mud wrestler by the time you got back.'

'Too right, I did. I ran back down what they laughingly call the gated road and then cut across towards the wood. To be honest, I didn't do the miles I usually do this morning. I was sliding about all over the bloody place, fell twice. I could just imagine my agent's face if I had to ring and tell her I'd broken my leg after slipping on a cow pat. If Melissa really wants to make a go of this place, she needs to install a gym at the very least. Maybe even a sauna.'

'I've never really fancied saunas,' Rina said.

'Me neither,' Terry Beal agreed. 'The one time I tried one I came out looking like a beetroot and feeling sick as a dog, but my wife loves them so we installed that and a hot tub last year.'

'What does your wife do?' Joy asked.

'She's an artist,' Terry said, and they could hear the pride in his voice. 'We met at school, lost touch for a while, and then ran into one another fifteen years ago. I was doing voice-overs and adverts and anything I could blag my way into; she had just had her first solo show. We'd neither of us got any money—not much in the way of prospects either—and we started off sharing a flat with another girl we'd been at school with. Anyway, one thing led to another, and we got married six months after that and I made the first Matt Bianco film the following year. The rest, as they say . . . I meant to ask last night, how do you both feel about this spiritualist stuff? Only, I've got to admit, I'm not really looking forward to it.'

'No?' Joy was intrigued. 'What bothers you?'

'Oh, I don't know. It's all a bit . . .'

'Contrived, artificial, nonsensical?' Joy suggested.

'Not a believer then?' Terry was evidently amused.

'Well, from what we've been told, we don't need to be. The ghost is invented, the company are a bit weird, to say the least, and I'm really only agreeing to do this to be supportive of Tim.' She paused, head on one side as she thought about it all. 'I went to one of those psychic evenings they do at the local pub. Mum wanted to go.'

Rina was surprised. And then not surprised. Bridie Duggan was not a woman to leave any stone unturned when she went looking for answers, and she had, after all, lost both a husband and a son in the past twelve months.

'And? What was it like?' Terry seemed genuinely interested. 'I've thought about it, you know, but it seems . . . Anyway, I'm a bit too recognizable to go down to my local pub to hear a medium. Can you imagine the tabloids?'

'Do they know you're here?'

'Oh, I'm sure the agency publicity machine will make sure of that—*after* the event, at least. Of course, it all depends what happens tonight. If we all go stark staring mad then I guess it'll be a quiet trip to some exclusive health farm and a distinct lack of comment from the studio. Though if something interesting happens, well, I'll be talking about my preparation for the new role on every chat show between here and LA.'

'That would be good publicity for Aikensthorpe, I imagine?' Rina said.

'I expect so.'

'Are you scared?' Joy asked bluntly, and for a moment Rina thought she might have offended the action star—then he nodded.

'Actually, yes. It's like a mix of stage fright and that feeling . . . You know, when you're a kid and there's some old house or bit of the wood or park or something that no one wants to go near and then someone dares you and . . . Well, you get the picture. I feel like I'm about nine again and scared stiff of Mr Howard's dog.'

'Yeah, I know what you mean,' Joy said. 'I'm not happy about the idea of being filmed, either, though I suppose that won't bother you?'

'Less than it might, but it's still different. When I'm making a film, I know what I'm doing. It's scripted, and if I get to the point where I really don't want to do that stunt—or my insurance won't cover me for it—there's always a stuntman. This is me tonight, and it feels just a bit weird, if I'm honest.'

'But isn't it *you* when you give the interviews?' Joy asked him.

Rina laughed.

'Ah, Rina knows it's not, don't you, Lydia Marchant? No, it's still not fully you—there's a persona you adopt, even without realizing it, that's sort of in-between the character you're playing on stage or in the film and the real you. It's like a compromise person: one that only talks about certain things and keeps others very private and still has that little bit of glamour about them from the role. At least, that's the way it is for me. How was the psychic evening you were telling us about?'

'Weird,' Joy said. 'There were two mediums or whatever: one gave like messages and stuff, and the other did tarot readings and used a crystal ball. Mum had a reading done, and it was just a bit disturbing how close the woman was to what had happened. She saw two tragedies and a lot of pain and a strong man supporting Mum in the background who would become even more important to her in the future. It all made sense. Then the psychic woman who gave the messages, she kept trying to tell Mum about a cat. I mean, Mum has nothing against cats, but we don't have one and I don't think we ever have, but this woman was insistent, like it was really important.'

'But the tarot reading, you said that was accurate?'

'Yeah, my dad and brother both . . . Well, we lost them both last year. The strong man in the background made sense, and I hope the rest is true, too, that Mum and our friend Fitch will get together. I know dad would want them both to be happy; he wouldn't want Mum to be on her own.'

Rina nodded; she hoped for the same thing. Bridie was deserving of happiness. 'Looks like we're going to get breakfast now,' she said.

'Oh good, I'm fading away to nothing here.' Terry stood and stretched, exhibiting bulging biceps and frighteningly flat abdominal muscles. 'You said you lost your father and your brother? I'm really sorry to hear that.'

Rina could hear the curiosity and wondered how Joy would respond.

'Thanks,' Joy said. 'There was a car crash. It was all a major shock.' She got up from the stairs and led the way down to breakfast, leaving Rina to walk with Terry Beal.

Yes, there was a car crash, Rina thought, but it was all a bit more complicated than that. She didn't blame Joy for not wanting to explain.

'I hope I've not upset her.' Terry Beal seemed genuinely concerned.

'No,' Rina assured him. 'You did nothing wrong. Oh, and I meant to ask—I was told that there was only a room for me because someone had dropped out. Do you know who?'

Terry shook his head. 'I think it might have been a Professor Meehan,' he said. 'He was on the original list my agent got for me. He was some kind of historian, I think. Melissa said he had family problems and had to leave early.'

'But he was meant to be the other neutral witness?'

'Sorry, Rina, I really don't know. Come to think of it, though, he can't have been, because he was here over the Christmas. Originally, they asked if I'd be a neutral observer, then when I got here they said there'd been a change of plans and that I'd need briefing and you would be standing in for me, if you see what I mean.' He shrugged again, 'Sorry, Rina, I didn't really ask. This is just a job on the road to preparing for a job, you know?'

They descended, joining the crush in the main hall where Rina and the others had drunk coffee the day before. Small tables had been set out here and in the dining room, and buffet tables set up in both rooms. Even so, it was crowded. Joy had already commandeered a table and waved at them. 'You get me something to eat and I'll keep our seats.'

'Right you are. What about Tim?'

'Oh, we've lost him. He was in a huddle with Rav and Jay last time I spotted him.'

Terry had grabbed two trays. 'It's like being back at school.'

'I hope not. The food at my school was dire. So,' she asked as she filled two plates with bacon and scrambled egg, adding mushrooms and toast for Joy, 'what is this mysterious part you're researching? Someone said you were playing an exorcist.'

'Someone was right,' Terry confirmed. 'I've got to admit I had mixed feelings about it, but we thought we should try and expand my range a bit. You can't spend your entire life throwing yourself off buildings and escaping from burning cars. Not unless you happen to be Bruce Willis, that is. I started out on stage, playing some quite serious roles, and last year did Shakespeare in the Park in New York—only a small role, but I got the taste for the serious stuff again. I'm making an art house film this spring: low budget, and all rather gritty and grimy, where I get to play a writer who spends more time boozing than he does putting down the words. Shall we take these to the table? Then I'll go back and get us some drinks. Tea?'

'Lovely,' Rina told him. He left Rina to unload the trays and returned a few minutes later with cups and teapot. 'So, this other role? The exorcist?'

'Well, I got offered it a year ago and said no, it wasn't me. Then they came back with a rewrite. It's set in the Midwest of America in the nineteen twenties, and this preacher in a travelling show has a sideline doing exorcisms. It all gets very dark, and he's very corrupt and isn't above creating the phenomena just so he can then get rid of them. For pay, of course. It's brooding and menacing, and I still get to throw myself off things, but the action stuff is more integrated into the story rather than: OK, we blew up a helicopter and thirteen cars in the last film, how can we top that this time?'

'And how is this preparation for that?'

Terry shrugged and loaded his fork with mushrooms and egg. 'Beats me,' he said. 'Like I said, it's a job on the way to another job. So long as someone pays me for it, I just go where I'm told.'

* * *

The morning had been surprisingly enjoyable, Rina thought as she met Joy again after lunch. Joy was buzzing with excitement. 'Gail and Tim are doing a thing,' she said. 'Now, in the carriage house.'

The carriage house, dining room and library had been the locations for the three lecture strands that morning, leaving the large hall free for serving meals. It worked well enough, Rina thought, though it did mean that Melissa and the temporary staff had to carry everything through from the kitchen on the other side of the entrance lobby. Not exactly convenient.

'What is Tim doing?'

'He and Gail are doing some kind of demonstration. I'm not sure.' Joy grinned at her. 'It'll be good, anyway. Tim's doing it.'

Following her out of the orangery and running across to the little door Rina had seen Melissa use the night before, Rina reflected that Joy was probably right. Tim's performance techniques had expanded exponentially in the past year, especially since he'd abandoned his hated alter ego, the Great Stupendo, the clown act he had developed for the children's parties that had once been his bread and butter work.

Stupendo, orange wig and clown costume, had been ceremoniously cremated in Rina's back yard just a few weeks before he'd met Joy and following a particularly acrimonious children's party—and a particularly unsettling choking incident. Tim didn't like to talk about him these days.

They crept into the carriage house and took up position at the back of the already packed room. Rina gathered that this was something of an impromptu performance. She recognized some of her fellow delegates from that morning. Professor something who lectured in parapsychology and comparative religion, and Ray who designed special effects, and Margaret who said she was some kind of researcher, though Rina was pretty certain she was actually a journalist. She took far too many notes and seemed to specialize in asking what she presumably felt were searching questions.

Tim stood on a raised dais at the end of the carriage house. Gail—their medium for that evening and Professor Franklyn's PhD student—stood at his side. She looked no happier, Rina thought, than she had the previous evening when she'd been talking to the professor and given the impression she'd like to run away.

'Ladies and gentlemen.' Tim had switched into performance mode, and Rina could see he was enjoying himself. Made even taller by the dark suit he wore and more angular and ascetic looking by the oddly angled lights, Tim Brandon was the archetypal magician in Rina's eyes. She could tell that he had slipped into his mentalist persona: the one he made use of in his cabaret performances at the Palisades. He studied his audience, making momentary but deliberate eye contact with seemingly random people, holding their gaze for just a fraction too long for comfort before shifting to someone else. Even among these experienced diehards, Rina thought, you could still feel that thrill of anticipation.

Gail, on the other hand, stood with eyes cast down and made no attempt to interact. Tall—though not as tall as Tim, who was over six feet—Gail was blonde and almost fragile looking. Rina had gained the impression that Gail was doing all she could to keep apart from the rest of the company, and she was slightly surprised that the younger woman would agree to this display—whatever it turned out to be. Professor Franklin stood at the side of the room, watching Gail intently, and Rina found herself watching him in turn.

He thinks he's a Svengali, she thought, and I suspect Gail is about to teach him otherwise.

'My friend, here—' Tim was indicating Gail—'was born with a gift. She is what some people choose to call psychic, a channel for that which few of us would claim to understand.'

Gail looked up for the first time and stared out across the assembled audience. Still she made no attempt to engage them, leaving all of that to Tim.

'Clever,' Rina murmured, realizing for the first time that Tim and Gail were playing their own game. She glanced at

Professor Franklin and, judging by his expression, understood that he, too, had experienced that revelation.

'I make no such claims,' Tim went on, 'but what I do claim is that anything Miss Perry might be able to do by her means, I can replicate using mine.'

Gail glanced briefly in his direction and then closed her eyes.

Tim seemed to take that as his cue. 'Let us begin,' he said.

Gail took a deep breath and released it slowly; Tim continued to scan the audience in that slow, deliberate way. Rina, who had seen him do this countless times, could not help but smile. She felt a little nervous though; his performances were usually for the entertainment of the paying public, well oiled with drink and relaxed by the good food and convivial atmosphere of the Palisades. Here, the audience was not on his side—or Gail's. They were predators, Rina thought, who would be only too happy to trip him up.

'I'm sensing something,' Gail said. 'A woman. Her name is Jane or Janet.' She opened her eyes and scanned the audience. 'She passed over not long ago, a year, maybe two, and it was very sudden.'

Nothing. Rina held her breath. To her surprise, Tim took the baton.

'She was quite young,' he said. 'Thirty, thirty-five, and had been in good, though not perfect, health.'

He's found his mark, Rina thought. His broad focus had shifted, and now he looked at someone on the right side of the room. Rina could not see who.

A man coughed. 'Um, that might be my daughter-in-law,' he said. 'Her name was Janet—'

'But you called her Jan,' Gail interrupted.

'Yes, we called her Jan.' Rina could hear from the change in the man's tone that he was hooked now. Reluctantly so . . .

'She had children,' Tim said. 'A boy and a girl.'

'No, a girl and a boy,' Gail corrected him. 'The girl was born first. She was—'

'Seven when her mother died, or, no, eight, and the boy was six?'

'Almost six,' the man said.

'She sends her blessings,' Gail said. 'She sends her love.'

'And she forgives you for the argument you had with her. Don't feel guilty,' Tim added. He held the man's gaze a moment longer and then shifted his attention, moving on before anyone could react. 'I'm getting something, a series of numbers, not a phone number, not a lottery number, or is it? Is it someone who plays the lottery every week? You, madam. You play the lottery each week.' He paused, got a giggling acknowledgement.

Oh, she'll be easy, Rina thought. She's already engaging with him.

'Birthdays,' Gail said. 'You play birthdays . . . and one anniversary date.'

'Don't we all,' someone said, and Tim laughed with them.

Gail smiled, but there had been a fractional pause. She takes herself far too seriously, Rina thought.

'No, not just birthdays—you play ages,' Tim said. 'Now, let me focus on this. Think it, please, madam. See the numbers in your mind. See them as clearly as you can—'

'Ten,' Gail said.

'Ah, my lovely assistant has the first one right, doesn't she?'

Gail glared at him and then remembered where she was. 'So would *my* lovely assistant like to guess the rest?'

More laughter. Tim bowed mockingly. So I needn't have worried, Rina thought. They've read the room right. She wondered if Gail's intimations of annoyance were also part of the act they had worked out.

Tim closed his eyes and placed his fingers to his temples, massaging gently as though the receipt of knowledge caused him slight discomfort.

'I'm seeing a four,' he said, opening his eyes again. He wagged a finger at the woman with the lottery numbers. 'Oh, fie on you madam, trying to fool a poor illusionist like that.

She's making me see a four, ladies and gentlemen, when in fact she should be showing me a fourteen, isn't that right, madam?' He reached behind him and picked up a notepad and pencil from a small table Rina had not noticed before. 'As you can see,' he said, flicking the pages open for the audience to look at, 'nothing is written on this pad. I will now attempt to ascertain the remaining four lottery numbers and will write them on this pad.'

Rina sensed momentary disappointment. This was a knowledgeable crowd; they would be expecting something like this, for Tim to use a sleight-of-hand gimmick to write the numbers after they had been said.

Tim had finished scribbling now and handed the pad and pencil to Gail. She looked at them and shook her head. 'You've got one wrong,' she said.

'Really?' He leaned over to look. 'I'll bet I haven't.'

'Oh, how much?' Gail challenged.

Rina smiled. The room was happy now; things had once more taken an unexpected turn. She watched, amused, as Tim dug in his pocket.

'I'll bet ten pounds, a packet of mints and some fluff,' he said.

'OK, I'll raise you fifteen pounds, a pack of chewing gum and a lipstick.'

'What colour?' More laughter. Tim waved them into silence and returned to his grave performance tone. 'Madam, would you please tell everyone what your favourite lottery numbers are?'

'Fourteen, ten, twenty-one, seventeen, thirty-six and two.'

'Two? Are you sure?' Tim looked dismayed, Gail triumphant.

'I told you so,' Gail said. She held out the notepad to a man in the front row of the audience. 'Sir, would you mind standing up and reading what is written on the pad?'

A tall man stood, held the notebook up and showed the remainder of the audience, and then read: 'I predict that the remaining numbers are twenty-one, thirty-six and *twenty*-two.'

'And if you would read what is underneath that?'

'It says: and Gail predicts he's got it wrong and the last number is just two.'

Laughter and applause: some of it, Rina could hear, very reluctant. 'Nicely subverted,' she said to Joy. 'Did you know what they were going to do?'

'Not really. They got together for a few minutes before lunch and came up with it. It worked well, didn't it?'

Rina nodded. Tim had joined them now, and the audience, making their way out, offered congratulations.

'I didn't think she'd do it,' Tim said. 'She's very defensive of the psychic stuff, but I think she knew how much it would piss David Franklin off if she stood up there with me and performed.'

'He's an odd man,' Rina mused. 'The sort of man who likes to be in control, no matter what.'

'Doesn't happen,' Joy said. 'Not for anyone. Life has this way of knocking you for six, just when you think you've got it figured out.'

NINE

As they waved the buses off, the snow had begun to fall harder. Rina could not see clearly even across the width of the gravel drive.

'The snow has set in for the night,' Melissa said glumly. 'I can't see the buses making it back in the morning. I'm going to let the temporary staff go home, just in case.'

Rina nodded. 'Is that going to be a major problem for you? Financially, I mean.'

Melissa shrugged. 'The consortium who own this place take out insurance against having to cancel, so I suppose not, but it isn't helpful, not when you're trying to build a business. And you know how it is—even if it's not your fault, you feel responsible.'

Rina patted her arm sympathetically. It seemed odd to see the exuberant Melissa looking so glum. 'It's all gone very well today,' she said. 'No one can predict the English weather, not even a houseful of psychics and mentalists.'

Melissa laughed. 'I guess you're right. You all set for tonight?'

'Ready as I'll ever be,' Rina told her, then noting the younger woman's worried look she added: 'Oh, I'm sure it will all be fine. It's just not really my cup of tea, you know?'

Melissa leant towards her and whispered confidentially, 'Not sure it's mine. In fact, I'm pretty certain it wasn't in the job description—but hey.' She smiled. 'Best get back to the kitchen. Go and eat, in fact, *please* go and eat. We'll have food coming out of our ears if the buses can't make it back. There's only so much I can freeze down.'

The phone in the hall began to ring, and Melissa went to answer it. Rina was making her way back to the big room when she was called back. 'Rina, it's for you. Your friend Mac? Tell him if he fancies a free meal, we've got more than enough to spare.' She smiled, handed Rina the phone and then disappeared back into the kitchen.

'Mac!' Rina was very pleased to hear his voice. 'Where are you?'

'About four or five miles away at the B&B. Is everyone all right? This is mean weather. The landlord says it's going to get a lot worse, so I thought I'd see how bad it was your end.'

'Blizzarding. You know you have to come up a gated road? One thing: if you do make it here and then get stuck, there's enough food to withstand a siege.'

Mac laughed. 'Sounds good,' he said. 'We should be OK on the road. The Volvo is all-wheel drive, and it hasn't let me down yet.'

'Ha, famous last words. When are you coming over?' she asked, a note of wistfulness creeping into her voice.

'First thing in the morning, for breakfast. I spoke to—Melissa, is it? She said that would be fine. I talked to her earlier this afternoon, you were still involved in something, but she said we'd be very welcome. I think she was already worried about the weather; she said she didn't know what would be going on tomorrow.'

'Well, it's got worse since then. We'll be really glad to see you both, Mac. I just hope you don't get stuck. You've got to be in Pinsent on Monday.'

'About that, yes. Well, I'll tell you all when I see you. Miriam's making hungry noises, apparently dinner is about to arrive. Take care of yourself, Rina, and we'll be there bright and early.'

She felt both relieved and slightly lonely when she put the phone back on its cradle and recrossed the hall. That feeling of claustrophobia—strange in so massive a house—that had assailed her on the upper floors now seemed to have spread to the lower. Smothering quiet had descended, strange after the noise and bustle of the day, and Rina felt as though a warm fog had settled upon the place, the doors too thick and heavy to permit the reassuring kitchen sounds to escape, deadening even the conversation in the big room where the others had gathered.

Joy looked up with a smile as she entered. 'I've got a plate for you. Hope you like everything.'

'I'm sure I will.'

'And I've got a pot of tea. Thought it might be a bit too early for the wine.'

Rina sat down beside her at one of the little tables. 'Are you on your own?'

'Only just. Tim's gone off with the camera people to check the set-up—again. Terry went to call his agent from his room. The mobiles don't seem to be working very well. He thinks the bad weather is affecting the signal—not that it was ever great here. I didn't really feel like joining the conversation over there.' She nodded to where Rav, Viv and Professor Franklin were debating something with Edwin Holmes. The old man seemed to be holding his own, his voice quiet and insistent; from time to time objections would be raised before he took control again.

'Gail?' Rina asked.

'Oh, gone off to prepare, I think. She took a tray to her room. Ah, there's Terry. He's surprisingly nice, isn't he? I thought he'd be a real diva. You know, I've quite enjoyed today.'

'So have I,' Rina agreed. She poked at the food on her plate, not sure if she was hungry. 'It's been unexpectedly interesting. It's made me think, though, about life and so on.'

Joy looked puzzled. 'Life?'

'More what I want from it. I think I've just realized how much I miss working, being out doing things. Strange, isn't it, the way ideas suddenly crystallize?'

'I guess it is. I guess Terry Beal has been more of an influence than I thought.' She smiled, seeing the subject of their conversation approaching them.

'Influence? What kind of influence? Bad, I hope.' He sat down, then got up again. His restless energy was palpable. 'You know, I think I'll get more food. Melissa is urging us all to eat, eat, eat, you sort of feel you have to oblige. Can I get you ladies anything?'

'Chocolate cake, please,' Joy said. 'It isn't as good as the Montmorencys', but it isn't bad.'

'I must meet these paragons of the kitchen.' He disappeared for a moment and came back with another tray: food for himself and cake for Joy. 'In fact, I've just been chatting to my agent about a certain lady detective, and we both feel that the time might be right for a relaunch.'

'Really?' Joy was clearly impressed.

'Oh, no,' Rina said. 'I didn't mean you to—'

'Nonsense, this would be a great thing to happen. Now, how would you feel about a guest appearance from, well, a semi-famous action hero type? My agent likes it, says she wants to meet when we finish with this, chase some ideas around and maybe start pitching in the next month or so.'

It wasn't often that Rina was stunned, but Terry had managed it.

'You're serious about this?' Joy was astonished and, Rina could hear, very pleased. 'Rina, you've got to admit it would be great.'

They turned to look at her. 'Slow it down,' Rina ordered. 'Terry. I—'

'Rina Martin, you are a talented woman as well as being a truly nice one.' Terry took her hand. 'We both know we're a very long way from making this happen, but let me give it a shot? Yes?'

Rina found she was gaping at him. She shut her mouth with a snap and then nodded. 'Why not,' she said, 'and if it doesn't happen, then it doesn't.' But she'd be disappointed, she realized with a sudden shock. She truly would.

TEN

Aikensthorpe, 1872

'Mr Creedy, if that is you, will you rap the table twice for me?'

'Creedy? The gamekeeper?' Albert was confounded.

'Hush, my friend.' Dr Pym's voice was soft but excited. 'Let the spirits speak.'

Elizabeth felt a brief pang at involving Pym, a genuine honest soul, and another pang—of fear this time at what her husband would do if this worked against her. She pushed that thought to one side. 'Mr Creedy, if you would be so kind as to confirm your presence here.'

The table rapped. Twice.

'Your wife misses you, Mr Creedy,' Elizabeth continued.

'Ah, the poor widow,' Spinelli whispered. 'So alone still.'

Is she really, Elizabeth thought. Or are you ensuring that she does not feel lonely, Mr Spinelli?

'Mr Creedy,' Elizabeth continued. 'We are told that those in spirit understand the world of the living, can still see and hear those they have left behind, can still feel their grief. Mr Creedy, if that is so, then you will know of the rumours surrounding your untimely death, that persist despite the passing years.'

'Elizabeth!' Albert was clearly not amused. He had indulged her talent, as he saw it, but he preferred Elizabeth's spirit encounters to be unknown, romantic.

'Let her continue, Albert,' Pym said. 'This may help to quiet the rumours.'

'Rumours that have no foundation,' Albert snapped, but he settled reluctantly and allowed Elizabeth to continue.

'Mr Creedy, was your death an accident? There are many people still asking this question, and your widow is deeply troubled by it. Please, if you can answer this question, rap once for no and twice to confirm.'

A pause, and then one distinct and careful rap. They waited, but there was nothing more.

'I say,' Pym said.

'Elizabeth, desist now.' Albert was even more annoyed. He had called an investigator, from London, to look into Creedy's death when the vile rumours had begun, two years ago, and the detective had found nothing to support any of them. Matter dealt with.

Elizabeth knew she had very little time before Albert broke the circle. 'Mr Creedy, do you know who was responsible for your death?'

Two raps this time, unhesitatingly delivered.

'And can you identify this person?'

Two raps again. Looking at her husband, she could see that he was incandescent.

'Elizabeth, enough!'

'Is your killer here?' There should have been more preamble, she thought, but there was no time. Elizabeth gambled everything on one final question.

The table trembled, there was no other word for it.

'Something else is here,' Spinelli almost squeaked. 'Something terrible.'

Bang, and then a second, almost a crash this time, the table lifting beneath their hands and slamming down.

Startled cries, shouts of 'enough' from Albert. But Elizabeth hadn't finished. So certain was she of Spinelli's guilt.

'Did you kill Mr Creedy, Mr Spinelli?'

'Did I what? Dear lady, how can you suggest such a thing?'

'Right, that is it. Elizabeth, go to your room.' Albert stood. The table tipped and fell on to its side.

Pym was fluttering like a debutant. Spinelli stood bewildered, and Elizabeth turned to George Weston for support. Wasn't this what

Weston had told her, what she had believed, what they had plotted for so long to uncover?

He gave no sign, simply looked on with an expression of grave concern on his face. 'Mrs Southam, are you feeling quite well?'

'Am I—' Elizabeth was dumbfounded. 'Mr Weston, you told me that Mr Creedy had spoken Mr Spinelli's name. You said—'

'Mrs Southam,' Weston said gravely. 'If I have put you under any misapprehension then I am deeply sorry.'

'Misapprehension? You said he—'

'I said merely that Mr Creedy asked for the Reverend Spinelli.' He put gentle emphasis on Spinelli's title. 'A reasonable wish, I would have thought. Mr Creedy knew that he was a dying man.'

'But—'

'Elizabeth, you've said and done enough. Go to your room,' Albert interrupted.

'I'm not a child. You can't order me!'

Albert turned to the maidservant now cowering by the door. 'Take your mistress to her room, and Pym, may I trouble you to give her something to settle her nerves.' Albert's tone was restrained, but his face was flushed.

'Settle my nerves? There is nothing wrong with my nerves!'

'Come now, my dear,' Dr Pym said. He reached out and patted her hand, then turned to her husband. 'Don't be too hard on her, old man, you know how women can be when they are in a delicate condition.'

Delicate! Elizabeth blushed. She had told no one but her husband and the doctor that she was pregnant; to have it announced in such a cavalier manner was too much.

'Mr Weston, please.' But even as she begged him to explain what they had done and why, that Weston had heard Creedy's last accusing words, she knew she had been betrayed. Weston would not help her. Weston had his own agenda.

Without another word, she turned and left the room, the servant rushing after her. Dr Pym paused to offer reassuring words to Albert and then followed them. He would listen to her, she was certain of that.

* * *

An oddly celebratory atmosphere prevailed when Rina came back down at ten that evening in preparation for the seance.

Everyone had dressed for the occasion, men in suits and woman in the best dresses they had with them. Gail had gone ahead of them into the seance room—to prepare and meditate, apparently—everyone else seemed to be drinking and eating again, and Rina began to wonder if Melissa had threatened to lock them all in until some specific volume of the food mountain had been consumed.

'So,' she asked, approaching Edwin Holmes as he helped himself to another glass of wine, 'do Joy and I get to know anything about this invented ghost of yours?'

The old man turned and smiled at her, his pale blue, rather watery eyes crinkling at their corners. 'Oh, no, I'm afraid not. You already know far too much. The two, or should I say four, neutral witnesses on that other night knew absolutely nothing. They fully believed in the process, so I can't tell you more than we already have or it would ruin the whole effect.'

Rina frowned. 'But we've already drifted miles from the original proposition,' she argued. 'So far as we know, everyone that night was a believer and, as you say, there was total secrecy when it came to the origin of the phenomena they claimed to be calling up. And,' she emphasized, 'we don't even know who or what they were claiming to be trying to contact, do we? So—'

'You are, of course, absolutely right. We have only a limited knowledge of the spirit they claimed to be trying to summon that night, but I'd still like to keep as close as we possibly can to the original experiment, even allowing for all of those variables.' The pale eyes twinkled. 'Tell me, though, Rina, where do you stand on all of this? Believer, non-believer, or, like our friend Terry, have you not yet made up your mind?'

Rina ignored the question. 'I thought nothing was known about the 1872 invention?'

'Almost nothing. I promise, I will tell you everything I know afterwards, but we really don't want to put any of that into people's minds. Tonight, we must focus on our experiment—the comparison with theirs will be made after the event.'

Rina frowned. She hated to be kept in the dark, but she let it lie and tried another attack. 'You said there were four neutral observers on the night in 1872. I though there were only the two Joy and I are substituting for? Dr Pym and this Reverend Spinelli person.'

'And two servants, drafted in at the last moment. We have Viv to thank for that detail; she found it mentioned in one of the newspaper clippings Melissa discovered a few days ago.'

'Oh?' Rina was now intrigued. 'Where did she find them?'

'In the seance room,' Edwin said. 'In a wooden deed box just inside the door. It was as though someone had put them there right before the door was sealed.'

'I don't recall seeing a deed box in the photographs. And I thought the room had been sealed on the night it all happened.'

'Well, we had assumed that, but to be honest, if any of us had really thought about it that would have been highly unlikely.'

'The police would have wanted to see the room,' Rina said, nodding. 'Even if Pym's death was ruled an accident, any police officer worth their salt would have wanted to check out the background; he'd want to know what made Pym ride off in such an almighty hurry that night. So, where is this box now?'

Edwin laughed. 'I'll get Melissa to sort it out for you later. I think we're about to go in.'

Rina nodded absently and, with Edwin, went over to where Joy waited for her by the door. Her mind was buzzing, and something was starting to feel very wrong. The photographs she had seen that Melissa had taken spoke of a rapid and final departure. The abandoned glove and scarf; the heavy and rather valuable rose bowl, untouched and locked away as though it had been tainted by events; the shuttered windows, never again to be unfastened, no sunlight or fresh air allowed to permeate the stricken room.

And now the box. Where exactly had it been found? Who had put it there, and when and why? She could understand that Albert Southam might have collected accounts of that night; understand, too, that he might then have thought better of the impulse and wanted the records of such disaster hidden away. But if he wanted rid, why not just burn them? Anyway, it would not have been possible to remove everything from sight or consciousness that might bring a reminder of events. Viv had told them that the investigation and the public interest had rumbled on for the following year.

The other question—a question she should have thought of herself: had the police gone into the little room and poked about, or had they merely glanced inside? And the servants: why hadn't they been questioned about their involvement? Rina had read through almost all of Viv's considerable documentation now and could recall no mention of them, unless . . .

'Edwin, the servants—the butler, Banks, and the housemaid, Sally Birch. Is that who the other two were?'

He looked surprised. 'Yes, I believe so. Why?'

'Because, according to the notes Viv gave us, they left the following morning, with Elizabeth Southam. Before Dr Pym was found and before the investigation began. Three people left this house together. My big question is: why?'

Now, it seemed, was not the time Rina would get her answer: they had entered the little room beyond the library. Thick, velvety darkness enclosed them, the only light a single candle in the centre of the rose bowl. Pale pink blooms cast a soft fragrance into the room. Gail was seated opposite the door with her eyes closed. She did not move as they shuffled in and took their seats around the table, Professor Franklin immediately to Gail's left and Edwin Holmes to her right. Rina, Joy and Terry sat opposite the medium, Rina directly facing the young blonde, whose pale hair and skin now looked silvered in the candle light.

Terry is in on the story, Rina thought. So is Tim and Viv and everyone else. Only she and Joy, the so-called neutral observers, had been shut out of what she was now starting to think of as a conspiracy. Her every instinct told her she should leave, now, take Joy and Tim and go and tell the others, even Terry Beal, just what she thought of them and their silly games.

Worse, she now felt angry with Tim all over again. Her much loved mentee had got her into this and had also been part of the group that had planned and constructed this event—albeit not such a central element, as he had spent Christmas and New Year separate from the main conspirators—but she still felt aggrieved.

The four men filming the seance had taken up their positions in the corners of the room: Tim and Toby behind Gail, and Robin and Jay behind Rina.

Beneath the table, Joy grabbed Rina's hand. Her palms were damp.

'Are you all right?' Rina asked her softly.

'No, not really.'

'Quiet, please,' Professor Franklin chided, and Rina glared at him, then squeezed Joy's hand.

'We can leave if you want to,' she said, loudly enough for Franklin to hear.

'No, I'll be all right.'

Melissa was sitting between Terry Beal and Edwin Holmes. Melissa was at the wrong angle for Rina to see her face, but she could see that Terry looked oddly tense and ill at ease. He glanced her way and smiled tightly. Only Viv and Rav Pinner seemed truly at ease, Rav glancing around the room as though looking for trickery and Viv grinning at Rina as though she merely felt excited. Happy, excited, intrigued by life, together these seemed to comprise Viv's default setting, and Rina was oddly glad she was there. Not much would really faze Viv, she thought, and at the moment she felt a real need for calm, unflappable people; Rina found herself feeling anything but calm and unflappable.

Gail opened her eyes, and Rina heard the door behind her snap shut. Too late to back out now, she thought.

'I feel the spirits are present,' Gail said. 'So we will begin.'

It occurred to Rina that this young woman was playing a very odd role. It seemed that she really thought of herself as psychic, as being able to act as a medium between the living and whatever else there might be, and yet here she was tonight, behaving as though all of that was make-believe. Did she feel strange, anxious, somehow traitorous, or had she found a way to reconcile these opposite beliefs? Had Elizabeth Southam, all those years ago, also managed to find a way to ease her conscience?

'We are here tonight,' Gail said, 'to speak to one of our number recently departed. Grace Wright was not a young woman, and her passing was expected, but even so, those of us who loved her had hoped for a few more years before we had to say goodbye.'

Grace Wright, Rina thought. Their ghost was called Grace Wright? Somehow she had expected something far more exotic.

'Grace,' Gail was saying, 'we all hope that you are close by and that you can make contact. If you would all please join hands and ask that our sister, now departed from us, has the strength and will to come through the veil.'

Joy still held Rina's hand. Terry Beal's palm was oddly rough when she took it, the skin dry and warm. Rina watched as everyone linked hands and then, under Gail's direction, closed their eyes. She was used to the low light now and could see Tim clearly, camera focused tightly on Gail. Toby seemed to be making little panning shots, taking in the whole company. Rina glared in his direction as he focused momentarily on her face. She saw him smile.

Everyone else had been obedient and shut their eyes, even Rav Pinner, though his lips twitched as though he found the urge to laugh almost too much. Viv looked solemn, or about as solemn as someone with such a smiley mouth could manage to get. Reluctantly, Rina followed their lead and closed her eyes.

The scent of roses was strong now, and she wondered if the flowers were really giving off such an emphatic perfume or if Melissa had used a scented candle. She could hear the soft sounds of the cameras as someone switched focus, heard the scrape of metal on plastic, perhaps a ring against a camera body, then the shuffle of feet as they changed position. She was acutely aware of those with her round the table. Joy still tense, breaths sharp and shallow; Terry, breathing deeply and rhythmically as though in meditation. Someone, a man, coughed and muttered an apology.

'Now, let go of your neighbour's hands and lay your palms flat on the tabletop, fingers touching those of the people next to you so the link is maintained but you are in full contact with the table.'

Sounds of people rearranging and repositioning themselves. Joy let go of Rina's hand reluctantly, and Rina could sense the relief of the younger woman once their hands touched on the tabletop. She squeezed Joy's fingers reassuringly. On the other side of her, Terry Beal's hands were very large and oddly comforting.

'Now,' Gail continued, 'we all need to focus on Grace. On hearing Grace and welcoming her into our presence. Think about her, ask her to come to us, tell her that we miss her.'

Miss someone who never existed, Rina thought.

'Even those of you who did not know Grace Wright in her life, please, open your minds to her now. Welcome her here.'

It was as though Gail had read Rina's mind and for a second or so she was shaken. No more than that though. Rina remembered the performance Gail and Tim had given that afternoon and knew that Gail was as good as Tim at reading, anticipating, guessing the response of her audience.

Cold reading, as Tim called it.

Her earlier feelings of unease had been replaced now by irritation and, if she was honest, boredom. If *she'd* been creating a ghost it would have a better name than Grace Wright and would have had a far more colourful past than this lot seemed to have invented—an unfair thought, maybe, as she had no idea what life experiences this invented persona was invested with.

'Grace, can you hear me? Rap the table if you can hear me.'

Oh, please, Rina thought. This is just too silly.

The silence seemed to grow more profound as everyone waited.

Nothing.

Rina relaxed. Nothing would happen because there was nothing *to* happen. They'd all sit here for half an hour or so, then someone would call time and they'd all go back to eating the food mountain and discussing what might or might not have happened back in 1872, and Rina was now more impatient to fill in the gaps in her knowledge regarding that event than she was to continue with this faff.

'Perhaps there is someone present who does not want this to happen.' Professor Franklin's voice boomed unexpectedly deep and loud. 'Please, I ask all of you, let your minds be open to the possibility of spirit. Put your doubts and misgivings aside and let us welcome Grace into our presence.'

Inwardly, Rina huffed.

'Grace, please contact us.' Gail's tone was still calm, but Rina heard, or thought she heard, a slight urgency there, as though the girl worried that she could not, after all, make this work. 'Focus, please. Think about Grace. Want her to be here.'

A small draft annoyed the back of Rina's neck, and she wondered if the door had been opened again, though she had heard nothing, then the draft transformed into a chill all the way down her back. She wriggled against the splat of the chair, trying to make sense of where the chill emanated from. A movement from Joy told Rina that she was feeling it too.

'Grace? Is that you?' Gail's voice seemed sharper now and, to Rina's ear, a little doubtful.

Then: *thump*.

A collective cry of *ohs* and *ahs* and a 'what the!' from Terry.

'Rina!' Joy had hold of her hand again.

'Please—' Gail's voice was insistent now—'don't break the circle. Keep your hands flat on the table. If it moves again, please don't be afraid. Grace, is that you? Please, Grace, knock once to confirm.'

As though on command, the heavy oak lifted and jerked and then landed with a distinct thump.

'Yes!' Edwin was triumphant.

'Please,' Gail said, 'don't break the bond.'

Then the table jumped again. Two knocks, Rina thought. Does that mean it is Grace or it isn't? She was intrigued now, but not afraid. She'd seen this sort of thing far too many times in her performing days.

'Rina . . .' Joy gripped her hand more tightly, pressing down on the table at the same time so that Rina's fingers were crushed.

'It's all right, Joy, dear. Just ease up on the grip a little, will you?'

'Sorry.'

'Was that Grace?' Edwin asked.

'I don't know,' Gail said. 'Grace, please confirm that you are here. Just a single rap will do.'

Whatever it is, it isn't rapping, Rina thought irritably. That was a definite tip, not a rap. Though, she moderated, it was probably a little churlish to be splitting such metaphorical—or should that be metaphysical—hairs at this stage in the proceedings. At least something had happened.

'It's cold,' Joy said, and Rina realized she was right. The draft was back, only this time it was intensified—more chill than mere inconvenience—and there was the scent of damp and snow upon it, as though someone had entered the room and brought the outside with them.

'Okaay,' Terry Beal muttered. He sounded a little anxious. 'What now?'

'Wait,' Rina breathed.

'You're enjoying this,' Joy whispered. She sounded very put out.

'I am now,' Rina agreed.

'Quiet, please!' Professor Franklin was annoyed at their perceived frivolity. 'Gail, do you know who is with us now? Is it Grace?'

'Yes.' Gail sounded triumphant, which jarred oddly with Rina's knowledge that Gail and the rest claimed to have created Grace.

'Grace—' Professor Franklin seemed to be taking over now—'are you ready to communicate with us?'

The table jerked again, and it seemed to Rina that it was now in an irritable mood, as though it didn't think much of Professor Franklin either. She wasn't quite sure what it was about the man that she disliked so much, but the instinctive suspicion was there. Maybe Grace felt that too—or Gail did.

'Perhaps we should leave the communication to our medium,' Edwin said quietly. 'We don't want to cause confusion.'

Rina glanced at the professor and was gratified to see his frown. 'Gail,' Edwin said pointedly. 'Perhaps you would like to ask the questions now?'

Rina caught Rav's eye. He looked slightly puzzled, as though only just recognizing the friction between Edwin and Franklin.

'Grace, we have people here who don't know you. May they ask you some questions?' Gail said.

The table tipped again.

'Mrs Martin, Miss Duggan, perhaps you would ask questions now. Things only you might know, but that Grace can respond to with a simple yes or no. Remember those in spirit often know a great deal about our world.'

Like the half-drunk bottle of pop, Rina thought. She glanced at Joy, who looked far from happy. 'All right,' she said. 'Tell me, Grace, do I live far from the sea?'

'Grace,' Gail asked, 'does Mrs Martin live far from the sea?'

A hesitation, it seemed to Rina, and then two thumps of the table.

Rina decided to deviate from the yes/no format. 'How many people live with me?'

Professor Franklin began to object, but Edwin interceded: 'I'm sure Grace can count, Professor.'

'Grace,' Gail asked, 'how many people live with Mrs Martin?'

Five thumps of the table appeared to suggest that Grace could indeed count.

Rina was unimpressed. All of this was the sort of random knowledge that a quick conversation with Tim would have established. She thought hard. What could she ask that no one could know? 'Have I ever visited a medium, Grace?'

Not perfect, Rina thought. There was a fifty-fifty chance of getting it right.

For a moment nothing happened, and then *thump*. Just the one.

Joy cast a curious glance in Rina's direction, as did Tim.

'Is that correct?' Gail asked.

'No,' Rina said. 'I'm afraid she got that one wrong.'

It seemed to Rina that the table trembled beneath her hands, but if she'd hoped for a more emphatic disagreement, none came.

Joy had calmed down now and put a tentative question of her own. 'How many brothers do I have?'

Interesting, Rina thought.

One emphatic thump, and then one more tentative. 'You have one living and one in spirit, so Grace tells me,' Gail said. 'She is telling me that you lost the youngest of the two and that you miss him very much.'

'I do,' Joy confirmed.

For a few minutes more they put questions to Grace, through the medium of Gail, and most of the answers seemed to be accurate. Rina was still unimpressed. She had once worked as a mentalist's stooge and for a season in her youth had dressed in skimpy costume and feathers as a magician's assistant. She was also intimate with Tim's work. Presently, she had seen no evidence that Grace was other than clever trickery. What Rina had yet to work out was how and who.

The cold draft she had felt on the back of her neck seemed to have returned. Joy put another question to Grace, but this time there was no response.

'Gail,' Edwin asked softly, 'has Grace left us?'

'She's still here,' Gail said. 'But there is someone else, a Pat or a Patrick. He passed over only a short time ago—months, perhaps. A very violent death.'

Joy gasped, and she gripped Rina's hand again. 'Rina?'

'Hush, dear, it's all right.' Joy's dead brother had been called Patrick, and yes, he had died a violent death, but even the scantiest of background checks on herself and Joy would have revealed that information. It had been all over the papers. She glanced across at Tim. He had lowered the camera and now stared in their direction, a hint of doubt in his eyes. Doubt, and a flash of anger.

'He says there is someone here he wants to talk to. He says that Grace brought him here. That he was wrongfully killed, a violent, terrible death.'

'I feel him too,' Edwin said. 'Oh, he was very young.'

'*Rina!*'

'That's enough.' Rina was furious now. She let go of Terry's hand and stood up. She could tolerate participating in an experiment, but this was different. This was taking advantage of Joy's grief, and that Rina would not tolerate.

'Please,' Gail said. 'Don't break the circle. We are doing so well.'

'Oh, I'm sure we are.' Rina's anger boiled to the surface. 'Switch on the lights and open that damned door.'

Joy stood beside her now, and Rina could feel her trembling. Tim had put the camera down and took Joy's arm, leading them both towards the doors. He opened them wide and switched on the library light. 'Electric isn't connected in there,' he said. 'Joy, lovely, you have to know I had nothing to do with that.'

She buried her face in his chest and gave in to tears.

The heavy door opened again, and Terry Beal came through. Behind him, Gail and Edwin were asking that everyone stay calm and please remake the circle. Terry said nothing, but went past them into the big hall, and when Tim came through with Joy and Rina he had poured drinks for them all. Rina was oddly satisfied to see that he was as pale as Joy.

'What happened in there? Are you all right?'

Joy accepted the glass and sipped without asking what was in it. She never drank spirits, Rina thought.

'Patrick was the name of Joy's brother,' she said.

'The one that died? I mean, of course the one that died. I mean . . .'

'Yes,' Rina confirmed. She looked closely at Terry, satisfied herself that the man was as shaken as he appeared to be and that he hadn't been the one responsible for such a mean and cruel trick.

'Do you . . . do you think it could have been him?'

Rina glared at him, then softened. 'I doubt it,' she said. 'I think someone just did a good job with their research. Patrick's death made the news all over the country; it wouldn't be difficult to find out about it. Right.' She set her drink down and headed for the reception area.

'What are you going to do?' Tim asked. 'Rina, Joy, I am so sorry about this, I had no idea—'

'I'm going to call Mac and tell him to come and fetch us all. We can spend the night at the B&B; I doubt they'll be booked up this time of year. Tomorrow you can drive us home.'

'Rina, it's too late for Mac to come tonight. It's gone midnight,' Tim objected. 'Anyway, I could drive us.'

'You've been drinking.'

'Not much.'

'Enough to be over the limit. Mac won't mind.'

'No, but Tim's right,' Joy said, seeming to have rallied now. Her glass was empty and her cheeks slightly flushed.

'I really wouldn't want him and Miriam driving across that dirt road at this time of night. It's pitch black out there. And he's probably had a drink too. They *are* staying in the pub.'

Terry crossed to the window and drew the curtain back. 'Actually, it's pitch black and a white-out all at the same time,' he said. 'Look.'

Rina sighed, but looking out through the glass she had to agree. She joined Terry, watching the blizzard, the snow falling so thickly and heavily that it was impossible to see anything beyond the window.

'First thing in the morning then. We are leaving. Agreed?'

'Agreed,' Tim said.

'What if it was Patrick?' Joy asked. 'What if it was and I didn't listen? What if he really did have something to tell me?'

Rina shook her head. 'I don't believe that,' she said stoutly.

'And if it was,' Terry said in a more reasonable tone. 'If he contacted you this time, if such things are possible, then he can do it again. Leave here, do some research, find a medium you feel you can trust and try again. If it was Patrick, then he won't be, well, offended, will he?' He shrugged. 'Look, this is all new to me, I'm just saying—'

'And you're right.' Rina flopped into a chair and recovered her drink, suddenly deflated and tired. The others joined her, a miserable little knot of humanity in a room not designed for the cosiness they all craved. Instinctively, they drew closer to the fire, and Terry poured them all more alcohol from the closest decanter. Brandy, Rina noted, wondering how it would go down on top of the malt whisky she had just knocked back with unusual lack of caution.

'You lied, didn't you?' Tim asked quietly.

'About?'

'About seeing a medium.'

Rina glared at him and then sighed. 'It was a very long time ago. I only thought about it again when we came here.

It was just after Fred died and I felt so terribly alone and I went to one of those public meetings where a medium gives messages. I left only part of the way through. Somehow it all seemed a little odd, not really what I was looking for, though I have to admit other people there did seem to be getting some comfort from it.'

Even if the messages were, to Rina's mind, hopelessly banal.

'And it was as though, as though . . . Well, I felt Fred speaking to me outside, telling me I didn't need any kind of intermediary to chat to him. It was so strange. I've never talked about it.'

'How did you know Rina was lying?' Terry asked Tim.

'Oh, just a feeling.' Tim smiled at her. 'This was a daft idea, wasn't it, Rina darling.'

'Only this part of it; we've enjoyed the rest. But I've had enough now. I want home and my own bed and all my own things around me and my family. Especially my family.'

'Chocolate cake,' Joy said, 'and dessert in blue bowls with loads of cream and the Peters sisters playing the piano.' She laughed a little shakily.

'Can anyone come and eat cake at your house?' Terry asked.

'Oh, only a chosen few,' Tim told him. 'But I think you're in with a shot. Rina, you think someone was manipulating the seance. Rapping the table.'

'Yes, I do. And I think the group didn't just research their imagined ghost, Grace, they researched myself and Joy. It would be easy enough to do, especially these days when everything is on the Internet. Apparently, I even have a *Wikipedia* entry. Terry, were you involved in creating Grace?'

'Oh, not really. Gail, Rav, Edwin and David Franklin and Simeon spent between Christmas and New Year here together, and I think Melissa was involved. I think Toby and Jay Stratham arrived just before New Year, and Viv and Robin just before I did. I got here only a few hours before you all did. Prof Franklin and Edwin briefed me and told me that some friends of Toby's were coming along to be witnesses and that I should be careful not to say too much to you because that would ruin the experiment. I must admit I thought it was all a bit odd, but I was here so I thought I might as well go along with it. When I met you, I did wonder how it was all going to turn out though.'

'Tim, what did Toby say to you to get you to take part?' That question had been nagging at Rina ever since they arrived.

'He said nothing, Rina, I was just returning a favour. He made the film of the Pepper's Ghost illusion I performed at Christmas and The Artist's Dream. He didn't charge, even though it took a good deal of time and the use of equipment I really couldn't hope to get access to any other way. He said he'd do that for me if I acted as fourth camera on something he was working on. Of course, I agreed. Then I asked if Joy could come with me, and then you came into the picture, and he asked if I thought the two of you would mind being witnesses. I thought he just meant it like two members of the audience—you know, "come up and check the chains and locks and that the guy is in the sack" sort of witnesses. By the time I got here and found out exactly what was going on, it was all organized, and I guess I thought—'

'You thought you owed Toby a favour and a deal was a deal.' Rina nodded. Knowing Tim as she did, that made perfect sense. 'I don't like him,' she said bluntly.

'We were very close at university. Being with him now makes me realize just how long ago that was. It felt good to see him again, to have him working with me on filming the illusions, but outside of the work, I don't know, you suddenly realize you've got very little in common with someone you once felt you knew, and that's hard.'

They fell silent, reflecting on the events just passed. 'Bed, I think,' Rina said at last. 'I've had enough, and I need my sleep.'

They all rose, agreeing with the sentiment, when the orangery door opened and the others trooped through. Toby looked oddly serious, and Edwin excited.

'Oh, good. You're all still up,' Edwin said. 'My dear, you have to watch this.'

'Watch what?' Joy backed away. 'I'm sorry, Edwin, but I really have had enough of all this stuff. I want to go to bed now.'

'Oh, but Patrick left a message for you. You have to hear it, my dear. You really do.'

'I don't understand.'

Rina looked from one to the other of the group. Edwin could not contain his excitement. Viv and Robin hung back as though uncertain and puzzled, and Rav poured himself a drink and then leant against the fireplace observing them all. Jay Stratham prowled, looking out of the window as they had done earlier, and whatever had excited Edwin seemed lost on him.

Toby was fiddling with one of the video cameras. 'I've set it up on this camera,' he said to Joy. 'You get the best view.'

'Of?' Rina looked at Rav for explanation. He shrugged, setting the ice in his drink rattling.

'Where did Melissa go?' Tim asked.

'Back to the kitchen to get more food. She's determined to force-feed us, I think,' Viv told him.

'I didn't see her come through.'

'No, there's a little door at the other end of the orangery thing. It's behind a tree.'

Rina raised an eyebrow. It wasn't like Tim to miss something like that. Not like her either. 'So?' She looked at Rav again.

'After you'd gone, Edwin suggested we use the planchette to take a message. I have to say I declined.'

'And?'

'And any of these techniques is open to abuse and self-deceit.' Rav sipped his drink, seeming ready to dismiss it all.

'Why not let Joy decide?' Edwin said. 'Toby, will you show her the film, please?'

'Joy, you don't have to do this.' Rina was annoyed now.

'Sorry, Rina, but I think I do. OK, Toby, show me what you lot got up to.' She sat down on the sofa, Tim beside her, and Toby handed him the video camera. Rina and Terry stood behind.

Toby had started the recording at a point when they were already using the planchette, the wheeled trolley moving rapidly across a board on which letters and numbers had been painted. Rina could not recall having seen it previously. Convenient, she thought, that someone had the foresight to bring it into the room.

'Can you tell us your name?' Gail was saying.

'P, A T, R—Patrick, is it Patrick? That's a yes, a definite yes.'

The planchette moved again and this time spelt out the name Joy. 'I'm sorry,' Gail said. 'Joy had to leave. Was there something you wanted to tell her?'

Everything seemed to stop and then abruptly begin to move again. 'Love her,' the message spelt out. 'Wish her happy.'

'Is there more?' Rina demanded.

'No, nothing very constructive,' Toby said. 'We kept trying, but we just got a lot of gibberish after that.'

Joy said nothing. The colour had left her cheeks again, and she looked unbearably weary. Finally, she got up and took Tim's hand. 'I'm going to bed,' she told them all. 'Goodnight, all of you. We've decided to leave in the morning.'

Protests and pleas to reconsider followed Joy and Tim through the door.

'You can't *really* be going,' Toby said.

'Why not?' It was the first contribution to the conversation that Jay Stratham had made. 'I may well be joining them. I doubt our promised speakers will be back tomorrow, not if this weather continues, so I think I'll be off too. I don't see anything worth remaining for.'

'We could try again with Grace,' Edwin said. 'Jay, there is still so much more to explore.'

'Is there? I'm sorry, Edwin. I understand how important this event has been for you, but frankly I've seen more professional behaviour from carnival fortune-tellers.'

Viv giggled, and Robin looked shocked. Edwin was clearly hurt. 'Jay, I can't believe you would say such a thing.'

'And it saddens me to have to. Edwin, you've been at the vanguard of your field for a lifetime; frankly, this little performance tonight was unworthy of you. That you should lend your name to such a pathetic farce saddens me greatly, it really does. I'm planning on leaving in the morning, if the weather permits, but I won't be participating further. I'm sorry, Edwin, but I can't lend my name or my reputation to any of this, and neither should you.'

'But Jay, please.'

Jay Stratham crossed to where Edwin stood and gently laid his hands on the old man's arms. He spoke softly, friend to friend, ignoring the remainder of the gathered company. 'Edwin, my old friend, only my respect for you bade me say yes to this. I was worried from the start that it seemed off the wall, even for you. No, hear me out. I understand, or I think I understand, what you hoped to do, and it is laudable that you should try and bring such a disparate band together, a credit to your reputation that we should all agree, but frankly, Edwin, I don't believe a word of what's been going on. None of it will stand scrutiny. Believe me. Let it go.'

He released Edwin and walked stiffly towards the door.

He was the third cameraman, Rina thought. What did he film that upset him so much? She glanced at Rav, who had refilled his glass and continued to watch silently from his place beside the fire.

'And what do you think?' she asked him.

'That Jay is correct and we should pack up now, spend the rest of the weekend as each of us sees fit and leave as soon as the weather breaks. Edwin, I too am sorry, but so much is wrong about this set-up. It proves nothing; it demonstrates nothing. You and I disagree on so much, but I've always considered you a consummate professional, a stickler for what you deem to be the truth, even when I've been utterly unable to agree with your conclusions. You need to let go of this, now. At least the weather will spare you the embarrassment of presenting the films to the convention. Bless the weather, Edwin, and leave it alone.'

Melissa chose that moment to arrive, clanking across the hallway with an ageing tea trolley. 'You lot have to eat,' she commanded.

Rina glanced at her watch. It was past one in the morning, and she felt too weary to pursue further discussion. More to please Melissa than because she wanted anything, she chose a couple of sandwiches and announced that she would eat them in her room, then followed Joy and Tim up the stairs. Back in the hall she could hear that the arguments continued, getting heated now as Edwin defended himself and Rav, in quiet tones, tried to persuade him to walk away from what Rav simply saw as a failed experiment. Then the door closed and Rina could hear no more.

Slowly, carrying the unwanted plate of sandwiches, she made her way to her room, got ready for bed and made herself a cup of tea. Rina sat beside the window, staring out at the still falling snow and allowing her mind to collate the events of this weekend. The knowledge that Mac would try and reach them tomorrow soothed her. She needed his clear head and Miriam's observational skills, and just the idea of having as a sounding board people that had not been involved thus far was a happy one.

'What have we all learned from this?' Rina asked herself. 'Apart from not to do it again, of course.'

Nothing really, she had to admit. The one clear but unsurprising revelation was that people clung to the positions they had adopted, even when those positions were under siege. That ideas were precious to those that avowed them and built their reputations upon them: people like Edwin and Rav and Jay, who could still manage to be friends despite their intellectual differences, but who made ready to break such bonds if it looked as though their professional reputations might be compromised.

'People,' Rina said with a sigh. 'You reach the point in life, Fred, when nothing they do shocks you much, it just disappoints.'

She could imagine his response to that. 'Not like you to be cynical, love,' he would have said. 'And there are some who don't let you down, you know that.'

Yes, she knew that, and it was knowing that which always permitted a bit of optimism to remain even when things got bad, to be clung to like a life raft when the world got all too complicated.

Knowing she wouldn't be able to sleep yet, she spread Viv's notes out on the dressing table, moving the old-fashioned dressing table set—moulded glass candlesticks and oblong tray and little bowls—and finding in the process the newspaper pages she had discovered lining the shelves in the servants' quarters.

Happy to be distracted, Rina pored over the adverts for *sunlight soap* and *pink pills for pale people* and the maternity corsets that looked like elaborate birdcages. Turning the pages over, she found a list of sailing times for passenger vessels out of Liverpool and London. Of quayside auctions listing goods brought in from the Indies and China and even Afghanistan. Silk cloth and raw cotton, tea and sugar, spices and tobacco. A report on the visit made by the Duke of York, the election of local counsellors, making special note of the re-election of Mr George Pryor as Mayor. People so long dead and gone, but their stories still resonating down the years. She turned to the second folded sheet of newspaper and opened it out on the dressing table. A familiar face looked back at her—though, in the faded black and white photograph, Albert Southam looked older and more tired than he had in his portrait. She realized with a little shock that she was looking at his obituary and the report on his impressive funeral.

Local industrialist and benefactor of many local charities, promoter of education for both the children of his employees and the employees themselves—apparently, he hired teachers for a number of free night classes—Albert Southam seemed to have left his mark.

The article noted that in the past five years he had been forced to withdraw from an active role in these enterprises due to ill health and that his business and charitable activities had been run by the office of his estate manager, Mr George Weston.

George Weston had been at the original seance, Rina recalled.

The article made no reference to the events of 1872, except to record that Mrs Southam was unable to travel back for her husband's funeral, having been advised by her doctors not to risk the journey from the family's other residence in Rome as her health was too fragile.

'Sad that she didn't even return to give you a proper send-off,' Rina mused. 'What happened between you that night? What upset your world so much that she ran away and you locked yourself up in this place from then until you died? Did you even know that George Weston was running everything in your name? Did you give the orders, or did you even care?'

Tired enough to sleep now, Rina went to bed and managed to doze. She dreamed of planchettes and closed rooms and of her younger self in spangles and feathers and not a lot else, stepping into a magician's cabinet, all ready to disappear. And then she dreamed of Patrick's death, his body washed up on the beach not far from her home, and Joy's precipitate arrival into their lives, cold and dripping wet and defiant and very brave despite being scared half to death.

She woke with a start, thinking that someone had knocked on her door, and then, as she lay in bed, trying to sort out the dream reality from the mundane, she heard the bang again—only, it wasn't on her door, it was coming from above her head. Someone was up there in the attic rooms.

Much against her better judgement. Rina got out of bed and pulled on the fluffy pink dressing gown and rather fancy satin slippers that had been a welcome gift from Joy's mother that festive season, and she slipped out into the hall.

She was very aware that she was the sole resident on this floor in this wing and fervently wished she could summon someone to go with her. She should at least take some kind of weapon. Ducking back into her bedroom, she fetched one of the heavy glass candlesticks from the dressing table and set off alone.

ELEVEN

Aikensthorpe, 1872

The arguments had continued well into the night as Dr Pym tried hard to make Albert see what George Weston had done. That Elizabeth had merely acted with the best intent.

Elizabeth sat at the top of the stairs and listened to the ferment below. Sally Birch, the little housemaid, sat beside her, all wide eyed and frightened, and had left her side only to go and fetch her mistress's shawl.

True, Dr Pym had been put out when he realized that Creedy had not in fact been speaking to Elizabeth, but he was a kind man, she thought, he had forgiven her.

The other guests had left, and finally George Weston left too. He saw Elizabeth seated on the dog leg landing, peering down through the banister rails like a child who has been banned from an adult party. He smiled.

'Are you satisfied, Mr Weston?' she asked bitterly. 'I thought you were my friend.'

'Never, madam,' he said. 'What possible reason could I have to be a friend of yours?'

He climbed halfway up the stairs and leant towards her, a broad grin on his face. 'You should go, madam. Leave here. The scandal will burn for months. It began with the death of Creedy, and now I've added more fuel to the fire. You should leave here before you shame your family name even more.'

'I have done nothing wrong.'

'Of course not, but who is going to believe that? Albert is furious, your friends have seen how you've tried to manipulate him, gone against his wishes. He investigated Mr Creedy's death, he has dealt more than fairly with Creedy's family, and you've gone out of your way to usurp his authority. To shame a good and kindly man.'

'You planned this. From the very start, you planned all this. But why? I don't understand.'

'No, and I doubt you ever will. Just know this, Mrs Southam: you aren't the first young and pretty girl to attract Albert Southam's eye. Just be grateful that you had a family name, an alliance that could be useful to him. Not like my poor mother, who had only what Albert Southam saw. A pretty face and hopes well beyond her station.'

He departed then and left Elizabeth dumbfounded. Angry tears fell, and Sally found her handkerchief and, as Elizabeth seemed incapable of it, wiped her reddened eyes.

'The master will have forgotten all about it by morning,' she said gently, and Elizabeth, mistress of Aikensthorpe, proud wife of Albert Southam, found herself weeping on the shoulder of a fifteen-year-old girl.

* * *

When Rina and the others had left, the arguments had continued. Gail in particular was upset, not only that the circle had been broken and the re-enactment ruined, but also because she insisted there had been someone else in the room ready to communicate.

'Something or someone was blocking him,' she insisted.

'Probably Rina,' Toby joked.

'What did you feel?' Robin was sympathetic and curious.

'I thought . . . It felt familiar, and yet . . . It *couldn't* be him.'

'Oh, for goodness' sake, Gail, stop being so mysterious. It adds nothing to your charm. If you've got something to say, then say it,' Professor Franklin said.

'And you don't need to be so damned rude.'

'She is right about that, David.' Edwin's voice was soft and tired. 'Perhaps Jay and Rav are correct too. I've tried to derive meaning from something that was essentially meaningless.'

Viv got up from where she sat next to Robin and crouched down by the old man's chair. 'Edwin, don't be put off, it really doesn't matter. You did this with all the right intentions. No one thinks anything less of you.'

'You are very kind, my dear, but I've suddenly been reminded that I'm getting old and that maybe I'm also getting desperate.'

'Intimations of mortality, Edwin,' Toby joked.

'Leave him alone.' Viv was on her feet, and she turned angrily on her professor. 'At least Edwin is still open to ideas. His curiosity is still turned full on. You, I don't think you've had an original idea in your entire life. You're boring, Toby. tedious. You try to be so clever, so cynical, you put everyone down just because it makes you feel better.'

'Viv!' Robin was caught between shock and agreement.

'Now who's being rude.' Toby was laughing at her, but everyone could see that she had touched a nerve.

'Please,' Edwin said. 'We should not be fighting like this.'

Robin added his voice. 'No, we shouldn't. Viv and I are going to bed; we've both had enough for one night.'

Viv opened her mouth as though to argue and then changed her mind. Instead, she turned on Toby yet again. 'When we get back to uni, I'll be asking for a new supervisor,' she said. 'And I'll be telling them why.' She marched from the room and Robin chased after her. It seemed to take Toby a moment for her words to sink in.

'What the hell do you mean, telling them why? Little bitch!' He, too, left the hall, and the door swung shut, cutting off the argument that continued up the stairs.

Melissa sighed and started to load dishes and glasses back on to the tea trolley.

'Do you need a hand, my dear?'

'Thanks, Edwin, but I'm fine. I'm going to dump this lot in the kitchen and sort it out in the morning. Later this morning, I mean. I'm guessing it'll be just us lot for breakfast.'

'I suggest we all turn in,' David Franklin said. 'We are all feeling a little fragile, it seems.'

'Good idea,' Edwin agreed. 'Though . . . Gail, you said had a familiar feel to the other presence. Can you tell as any more than that?'

She hesitated, and then she said, 'If I didn't know better, I'd have said it felt like Simeon, Professor Meehan, but he's not dead, is he? He's just gone home.'

TWELVE

Rina paused at the foot of the attic stairs. Instinct and good sense screamed at her that she should forget about this and go back to bed, but curiosity told her that she wasn't going to be able to sleep even if she did. As usual curiosity won. She began to ascend, annoyed at stairs that creaked far more than she remembered and oppressed by the smothering silence she recalled from her previous foray. Anyone up there would be sure to hear her coming. She decided to try a different tack: forget about being quiet and just be the guest disturbed by some odd bumps and thumps in the floor above her room.

'Is there anyone there?' Rina called out. 'Hello, is everything all right?'

No reply, just the gathering silence, like an audible fog blocking her ears.

Reaching the landing, she pushed open the door to the room used for storage. Nothing appeared to have been disturbed. Once she'd got the second door open and the light switched on, it became obvious that no one had been there recently. Rina herself had probably been the last visitor. She went through to the second room, just to be certain. The debris left by the rewiring still sat on the bed, the fragment of paper still in the grate.

Sighing, Rina turned to leave, and then swore under her breath. 'You idiot woman, this room isn't above yours. It turns the wrong way.'

She hurried down the stairs, blaming lack of sleep and the events of the evening for fuddling her brain. So where was the stairway to the other attic rooms?

Back on the landing, she remembered that she had seen that other bedroom door left ajar the first evening they had been here. Could that be her answer? She stood and listened, not sure if she really heard the sound of someone up above or if her overstretched nerves now just imagined it. Back along the corridor, she tried every door. An airing cupboard; a bathroom; an empty bedroom, the mirror image of her own, furnished for guests but still covered down with dust sheets. Then her own room, and next to that the door she had seen left just slightly open.

Taking a deep breath, Rina turned the handle expecting to find yet another bedroom beyond. Instead, she discovered a short and narrow lobby, with an even narrower flight of stairs leading off. Reluctant now, but still determined, and with the candlestick-weapon firmly clasped in her hand, Rina mounted the stairs, senses so stretched that each tiny creak and groan of the wooden treads seemed magnified. Just one door at the top this time. Rina opened it and reached round the frame to find the light switch she hoped would be there. She was relieved on two counts when she found it: first, that electricity had been connected and she was able to see; and second, that it was unlikely anyone would still be there in the dark. Would they? Surely she hadn't made that much noise coming up the stairs.

The room was empty: of people, anyway. A rodent squeaked and skittered into the shadows, and Rina told herself that it wasn't really as big as it looked. She could smell mice up here, musty and musky and damp, and traps, recently set, told her that Melissa was aware of the problem.

So that was what she had heard, perhaps. A trap snapping shut and an unfortunate rodent coming to a sudden end? A fine explanation, except that Rina knew she had heard two bangs and not one. Was it really likely that two traps had been set off in such quick succession? Her experience of mice was that they fled at the slightest sign or sound of danger, and of rats that they were extremely adept at taking the bait from the trap without setting anything off.

She relaxed a little and loosened her grip on the moulded glass candlestick, suddenly aware that she had been gripping it so tightly that the hobnail pattern was now impressed into her palm. This attic had been used as a storeroom too, though someone had started to sort out what was up here. Large boxes, tea chests and the like filled most of the space. It would have been a tight squeeze getting them up here, Rina thought. In the one closest to where she stood she could see newspaper wrappings that had been slightly disturbed, revealing an old teapot. The remainder of the service was stacked beneath, she discovered as she poked about. Next to that was a box of old clothes, some of them from the nineteen twenties and in surprisingly good condition considering the mice population. The slight smell of camphor and lavender that still clung to the fabrics when she examined them suggested why that might be the case. Her mother and aunts had always sworn that camphor and lavender kept both moth and mice at bay.

A wooden crate filled with sheet music had been less fortunate.

Rina glanced around, looking for whatever it was that had made the noises she had heard. Drag marks on the dusty floor looked fresh, and one of the tea chests had only recently been opened: its lid, resting on top, had been splintered and broken by use of something like a nail bar. One piece of the frame now rested on the floor beside the chest; most likely the lid had also fallen and that was what she had heard.

So, who on earth would want to go firkling about in the attic at this hour of the night—or morning, rather. In Rina's experience, late-night firklers were rarely up to any good.

The tea chest in question was half empty. She removed a sheet of newspaper that must have been used to wrap something or other and smoothed it out. It was dated from June 1875, three years after the seance evening and about two year before Albert Southam's death.

Taking the newspaper with her, she left the attic room careful to switch out the light but painfully aware that anyone going there again would be see the extra footprints on the floor and the additional disturbance of dust.

Back in her room, she locked the door and took a clothes brush to her dressing gown and slippers, and then smoothed out and brushed off the newspaper she had found. The bedside clock told her that it was just after five.

Rina decided she'd had enough for one night. She really needed to snatch at least a couple of hours sleep. Her days of being able to work and then party and then sleep through the morning were long past. She switched out the light and crossed to the window, peering out at the snowy landscape. The snow had almost stopped falling, but the sky still hung heavy with the promise of more and it was clearly thick on the ground. She hoped Mac would be able to make it to them in the morning. No, *this* morning, she corrected herself. She was about to let the curtain fall back when something caught her eye. A line of footprints not yet buried by falling snow started from some point close to the house and hidden from her view, but led out across the lawn and towards the line of trees beyond.

THIRTEEN

Aikensthorpe, 1872

Dr Pym had left the house that night with something like despair in his heart. He had never seen Albert so angry, and nothing Pym had been able to say had assuaged that rage.

At the crux of it, Pym realized, was not that Elizabeth had sought to deceive them, or even that she had accused Spinelli—a man Pym had been certain was innocent until this night. It was that Elizabeth had not only acted in opposition to Albert's wishes, but had also done so in such a public manner:

Had she spoken to Albert about her suspicions, or, better still, confided in him earlier, then Pym was certain he could have convinced Albert to look at the matter again. He just had to hope that a new day might bring clarity and calm, and he had promised Elizabeth that he would return the following day to speak to them both once more.

He knew that Albert had other ideas though. That Pym had seemed to take Elizabeth's side had incensed him, and angry words had passed between the old friends that Pym knew would take more than a good night's sleep to forgive and forget.

'She says that George Weston convinced her to do this,' Pym had said. He had realized immediately that this was a big mistake.

'George would do no such thing. This is a female foolishness, hysteria. Jealousy.'

'Your wife is jealous of what, Albert?' Pym tried to sound reasonable. Being one of only a handful of people who knew the truth about George Weston, he knew that Albert was oddly protective of this illegitimate son of his. 'Your wife knows nothing of that unfortunate liaison. You were young. Foolish, perhaps. But you have always done right by the child.'

'And you have always disapproved of my bringing him here.'

'Not exactly disapproved, no. I admit I thought it unwise.'

'Unwise.' Albert's tone was cold.

Pym had sought to justify his view, and the argument had turned nasty. Pym did not want to think of it. Instead of remaining for the night, he had called for his horse and chosen to leave before his host demanded it of him. Pym's only regret now was that he had passed no words of comfort to the poor young woman sitting on the stairs. Her eyes as she watched him leave seemed to follow him still, even as he rode from the house and towards the wood.

He would give Albert a few days to cool his temper and then return. They had been friends since boyhood; surely a little female foolishness could not come between them so irreparably.

'She has brought scandal upon my house,' Albert had said. 'Do you think those who were here tonight will remain silent? My name will become the object of ridicule, and you may be certain that scoundrel Spinelli will use all of this to his advantage. He could sue for slander and claim with justification he had a lawyer witness it.'

Poor Elizabeth, Pym thought. Young and foolish and so eager to do right that she had followed terrible advice and then been betrayed by the very man who had given it. Pym was in no doubt that George Weston had set this whole cascade in motion. Pym made up his mind that he would prove that. Weston would be made to pay.

He had entered the woods at the edge of the estate. Not an easy route, but the most direct to his home and one he had travelled many times. He had instructed the servants to go to bed, telling them he would not be home that night. Tom would have to be woken; the boot boy and general factotum slept on the floor by the kitchen, so Pym could be sure of rousing him; Pym's housekeeper slept far too soundly to be woken by his knocking on the front door.

The horse shied as a shadow moved on the track up ahead.

Pym reined in the horse and soothed it, stroking the animal's neck. 'Who the devil's there? Oh, it's you.' With certainty, the devil, he thought.

George Weston stepped on to the path in front of him.

'Get out of my way,' Pym said.

George Weston struck out at him with the pommel of a silver topped cane. Pym fell to the ground and did not move again.

* * *

Sleep had come briefly, but by seven thirty Rina was up and dressed and back in the small room where the seance had been held.

She tapped the panelling, tipped the table, rapped on the floorboards and opened all of the stiff shutters and let the light flood in, cold and crisp and very white. Soft flakes of snow drifted down, and the footprints she had observed from her window a few hours before had now been obliterated.

Rina sighed, suddenly concerned for Joy and also for Bridie when she learned of all these goings-on. 'Patrick, dear,' Rina said softly, addressing Joy's dead brother, 'sometimes the dead really should keep their distance and let the living get on with what they have to do. Don't you worry, Joy is well loved and she is happy and we all plan to make sure she stays that way.'

'Talking to the dead, Miss Martin?'

She hadn't heard Rav come into the library and was momentarily embarrassed to see him standing in the doorway, a slightly amused expression on his angular face.

'Yes,' she told him firmly. 'I don't happen to believe you need all of this malarkey.'

He smiled at her. 'I tend to agree.'

'I didn't think you held with the spiritual.'

'Oh, I've no argument with the spiritual—or, at least, no argument with people's personal needs and beliefs. I tend to think that's their own business, and besides, I agree with our young friend Robin, it may well be the vocabulary that needs to change. We still need to have the discussion, but perhaps use less emotive language if we can ever hope to reach a proper conclusion.'

'And have you experienced the spiritual for yourself?' Rina asked playfully.

Rav laughed. 'Rina, I grew up with the unlikely parental combination of an Asian Hindu mother and a Welsh Christadelphian father and we lived in a small town ten miles from Cardiff. They made it work by celebrating everything. We spent Diwali with her family in Cardiff and Christmas with his and somehow it all turned out fine. Yes, as a child and a teen I had my "moments", you might say, but for my parents, what might have been divisive turned out to be a bond. They both believed in *something*, and they loved one another, so they accepted the whole of the other person. I have to say, they taught me a very valuable lesson, not in tolerance, but in genuine respect.'

Rina smiled. 'They sound like very exceptional people.'

'Oh, in many ways they are, and what is more, they are still as much in love as ever—and that, I think, is precious.'

Rina nodded. She had to agree with that. 'And when you ceased to believe?'

His smile was a little sad. 'They accepted it because they love and accept me. I know they both pray that I will find a way to reconcile with belief of some kind but . . .' He shrugged. 'My parents and their families learned to accommodate one another, and so they acknowledge my right to find my own particular path as well. I suspect that when the habit of acceptance has been established, it is, thankfully, a hard one to break. But changing the subject wildly, what were you looking for? Didn't Tim and Jay already examine every speck of dust in here?'

'Oh, I'm sure they did, but the trouble with experts is that they tend only to look for evidence of other experts. They sometimes miss what is right under their noses because it doesn't seem clever enough to be relevant.'

Rav was amused. 'A nice observation,' he said. 'And correct, of course. Spiritualists look for the spiritual, scientists for what they see as scientific, psychologists hope to unearth some childhood trauma, and engineers probe for clever devices. Cynics like me, of course, we always just hope to prove someone tried to dupe us.'

'Are you really such a cynic?' Rina asked him.

'Most of the time, yes. Though I am always open to the possibility that life can surprise me. Did you find anything?'

'No,' Rina said. Frowning, she glanced accusingly around the room once more, then looked at her watch. 'Breakfast time, I think, and my friends should be arriving soon, if they can make it through that lot.' She gestured irritably at the snow outside. It had finally ceased to fall, but the sky was filled with more.

'Are you still planning on leaving today?'

'I think so, yes. A lot depends on the condition of the roads. We're a bit cut off from civilization here, so we'll make a decision when Mac has arrived. If it's fairly clear, I think we'll go before the next blizzard. You?'

Rav nodded. 'I think so, but I want to have a long talk with Edwin first. I'd hate to think of us parting on bad terms.'

'He's a nice old man.'

'He is, but of late I've been concerned that he's, well, being less rigorous in his experiments than he once was. There is such a pressure for results in every field these days. Frankly, Rina, I wish he would just finally retire, go and write his memoirs or something and do the occasional lecture. He's always been a man of great integrity.'

Rina looked keenly at the younger man. The dark brown eyes were troubled. 'Sometimes,' she said, 'people get carried away by the desire to demonstrate what they *believe* to be the truth that they can forget truth actually has to be there.'

Rav nodded. 'I don't usually agree with Edwin,' he said. 'In fact, on most scores we are diametrically opposed, but I do like and respect him. In both our fields there are those who, as you say, get carried away by their own desire to prove their points. There are scientists and mathematicians using the same faith based language as religious zealots. Not that they realize it, of course. Our friend Robin is right about use of emotive language; the wrong vocabulary, if you will. I've always tried very hard to avoid extremism in any form, and it bothers me a great deal that, at the end of his life, Edwin should have allowed himself to be drawn into that deep water.'

* * *

In the dining room it was evident that they were diminished in numbers. Gail and Dr Franklin had left very early, Melissa told them. They had left her a note in the kitchen saying that Gail wanted to try and get home.

'They'll be back,' Melissa prophesied. 'The coaches won't be though. The organizers called me to confirm that conditions are too bad—like I didn't know that already! One of the buses skidded off the road last night and had to be rescued.'

'Anyone hurt?' Rav asked anxiously.

'Apparently not. They were crawling along, fortunately. Blasted weather.'

'That's Britain for you,' Rina said cheerfully. 'Is Jay still here? He said he might leave today too.'

'Gone off walking as soon as it was light. He seems to like this weather. I made sure his mobile had a strong signal before I let him out,' she added, and Rina wondered if she'd locked the front door until Jay had demonstrated that fact. She glanced out of the window, gratified that although the snow had started to fall once more, it was only falling lightly. In her younger days she, too, would have been out in it first thing, stamping around in stout wellingtons and taking pleasure in being the first to mark the pristine surface.

Except, she thought, recalling last night and the footprints she had seen, she would not have been the first. She stared hard at the snow that lay thickly, obscuring the lawn and the gravel paths, drifting almost to window height, but could see nothing now. How deep was it? Nine inches, maybe more. Deep enough to be challenging, but not so deep she would not have enjoyed it.

When was the last time she had waded through deep snow? They rarely got a lot in Frantham; it was too close to the sea, and the hills rising behind usually took the brunt of it, leaving her hometown with just a light sprinkle, whichever direction the wind blew in from.

'Morning, Rina.' Tim and Joy arrived, Tim kissing her cheek and Joy giving her a hug.

'Feeling better?' Rina asked Joy.

Joy nodded. 'Much. I slept like a baby,' she said, wondering at that fact. 'You?'

'No, my mind was working overtime, I'm afraid.' They served themselves breakfast and sat down together at the table. Rav, it seemed, had little appetite and was drinking coffee, nibbling toast. Viv and Robin, at the far end of the table, were chatting over plates piled high. They acknowledged Rina and the others, but did not break off from their conversation. Viv giggled at something Robin said, and Rina smiled fondly in their direction.

'They're a nice couple,' Joy said sotto voce. 'Viv is *so* mad at Toby. You should have heard them last night when they came up. I'd just dozed off. She was giving him hell over something.'

'Oh?' Rina, of course, was interested.

'We couldn't hear enough to make it out: it was all fierce whispers, you know, people trying not to be loud and not quite managing it. She told him she thought he was a disgrace and would be asking for a new supervisor when they got back, but that was all we could make sense of.'

'Apart from the fact he sounded like he was threatening her. He said if she made trouble for him, she'd regret it.' Joy shrugged. 'Sorry, Tim, but I think he's a creep.'

Tim nodded. 'He wasn't always like that,' he said quietly.

Terry arrived, looking as though he'd had a full eight hours' rest. He, too, was hungry. He plonked himself and his breakfast down next to Rav and beamed across at Rina. 'How are we all? Bit thin on the ground this morning.'

'You sound happy.'

'Oh, I am. No reason, I just woke up feeling this way.'

'Lucky you.' Rav was sardonic.

'So, what do we do with today? Croquet on the lawn? Big barbecue to use up Melissa's food mountain?' Terry asked.

'I don't think we could even find the lawn,' Rina said.

'Oh, if everyone gets a shovel, we can soon dig it out.'

Tim laughed. 'You're serious, aren't you?'

'Deadly. Every house party should have croquet in the afternoon and tea on the lawn. Really, though, are we going to try and get out of here before it gets worse?'

'Gail and David have already left,' Rav said. 'Jay is thinking about it. He's gone for a walk, of all things. I hope he comes back soon; he's meant to be my lift out of here.'

'Oh, you can always hitch a ride with me,' Terry said.

'We'll be waiting for Mac to arrive, and then we'll see,' Rina said. 'But yes, I think it's likely we will go. I see no reason to stay now.'

'Poor Melissa.' Terry grinned. 'The princess all alone in the deserted palace.'

* * *

Mac and Miriam finally arrived after breakfast was over, though Melissa insisted they sit down to an impromptu second. It had taken them almost three hours to drive five miles, and Mac was not keen to reprise the experience.

'The local radio says the main roads should be cleared later today, but we're nowhere near a main road here so it's anyone's guess. The landlord of the pub told us it's not unusual for them to be cut off for several days when the snow comes in suddenly like this.'

'Great.' Tim grimaced. 'So, Rina, what do you think? We hold on for a while?'

'That would seem to be the sensible option,' Rina agreed. Mac's car was heavy and rugged and all-wheel drive; Tim's car was anything but. If *Mac* had encountered such difficulties, well . . . 'We see what the day brings,' she said. 'If we can make it out to the main road tomorrow, we should be in a better position for getting home. But, Mac, what about your hearing?'

Mac and Miriam exchanged a glance.

'What?' Rina said.

'I've called ahead and told them where I am and what's going on. Seems the weather in Pinsent isn't much better so it will all have to be rescheduled, but I'm not sure I'm going to bother anyway.'

'Mac?'

It was Miriam who answered. She looked so much better than when Rina had last seen her, when Miriam had been recovering from some terrible events. The bright blue eyes shone now, and she tossed back the long dark hair. 'I'm moving into the boathouse,' she said, referring to the little flat Rina had helped Mac to find in Frantham Old Town. 'And I've been offered the chance to go and finish my Master's in September.'

'Well, that's good,' Rina approved. 'It's about time you moved in officially, you practically live there already. But what about work? Will the MA be full time?'

Miriam and Mac exchanged a glance. 'We've been talking,' Miriam said, 'and we think we both need a change of direction.' She looked down for a moment, as though embarrassed. 'The fact is, Rina, I tried to go back into work and I just can't. I've seen the doctor and he's signed me off for another month, and if I'm not feeling better after that I'm going to put in my resignation.'

Rina nodded. 'Miriam, dear, it's bound to take time. You've had a dreadful experience.'

'So I'm going to go back to what I wanted to do in the first place. My MA is in forensic anthropology, that's where I wanted to be. Hopefully, I can pick up some consultancy work, maybe some teaching.' She laughed. 'OK, I'll admit I've not thought it through, but . . . We've agreed. That's the next step, and Mac—'

'Has been offered a job,' Mac said.

'A job? You mean leave the force?'

'Possibly, yes. Probably, even. Abe has offered me work, and I think I might accept.'

'Right.' Their friend Abe Jackson ran a security firm in Dorchester. Rina tipped her head to one side and looked at them both carefully. 'Are you sure you're not both rushing into things? Believe me, I can fully understand why, but—'

'Probably,' Mac agreed. 'Rina, when I accepted the Frantham posting it was clear to everyone I was just being shunted out of the way—and actually I was quite happy to be shunted. I'd had six months on sick leave, and I was still a mess as you well know. But I'm better now. And everything has changed since then. Everything but the job. I'm thinking that now might be the time to change that too.'

Rina nodded. 'Then I will say no more,' she said.

Mac laughed. 'That would be a first. No, Rina, we do hear you, but sometimes you've just got to take that leap.' He fished under the table for his battered old briefcase, and Rina knew he was telling her very gently that he didn't want to talk about their decisions any more. In an odd way she was heartened by that. It meant that these new thoughts were still too fragile to be exposed, too newly formed. Did she hope Mac would change his mind? Rina wasn't sure; she found it hard to think of Mac being anything but a police inspector, but then she also found it hard to reconcile the fact that the close friendship they had formed had actually begun less than a year before.

'What do you have there?' she asked, taking his lead.

'The information you wanted. This house, the other participants in this exercise of yours—'

'Definitely not of mine. I'd have organized it much better than this.'

'I'm sure you would. Right, we have a date with some snow.'

'Snow?'

'Melissa said she has wellingtons we can borrow, and Tim and Joy suggested a walk out to some wood or other,' Miriam said.

'You want to come?' Mac asked Rina.

'No, thank you, Mac. I'll take these up to my room and have a read, maybe a nap too. I didn't get much sleep last night and, well, old bones, you know?'

'Old bones,' Mac scoffed. 'All right, we'll catch up with you at lunch.' He leaned across and kissed her cheek, and as Rina watched them leave the dining room a tear pricked the corner of her eye. Mac had never done that before, and it had been nice. Very nice.

FOURTEEN

Gail had said very little since they left Aikensthorpe. David Franklin drove, concentrating on trying to keep the car in a straight line or simply to keep it moving where the snow had drifted and now packed round the axles. Twice, he had handed over to Gail while he pushed the car out of the drift; more than twice she had suggested they go back.

'You wanted to leave; we're leaving.'

'That's right, blame me for this. Are you even sober enough to be driving?'

'Should have thought of that before, shouldn't you? Damn and blast it.' They had wedged deep again; a snow drift blocking the gated road had grounded the car. He bashed the steering wheel in frustration. 'Bloody hell!'

'Fuck,' Gail said. 'You're allowed at least one. I agree it's an overused expletive, but I think you can have at least one.'

He glowered at her for a moment and then began to laugh uncontrollably. Gail, unable to resist, gave in and joined him. 'Oh, God,' she said. 'What the hell are we doing here?'

'Trying to leave,' David suggested.

'Yeah.' She reached out and took his hand. 'When are you going to tell her, David? I'm sick of all this pretence.'

'Soon, I promise.'

She pulled her hand away. 'That's what you said a month ago and a month before that.'

'She won't agree to a divorce easily, I told you that. She'll make me pay, big time. You've got to see that, Gail.'

'I see it. I see that you're more worried about your money and reputation than you are about me, about us.' She sighed. 'Don't know why I ever thought any different.'

'Gail—'

'Please. Don't bother. Get out and push, and I'll steer.'

'Gail—'

'Don't. Just don't.'

They had to dig the car out this time. Two hours had passed since they left Aikensthorpe, but finally the main road was in sight. David turned the wheel and the car slid sideways out into the road. He swore. 'Frozen,' he said. 'On top of the snow. Must be the run-off from somewhere.'

Gail clung on to the door handle, her face pale. The road curved steeply down the hill, turning out of sight beyond the hedge. It was still not properly light, and the car headlights picked up the dark edifice of hedge and steep bank, the solid white of road. The clock on the dashboard told her it was ten to eight. 'We should have stayed,' she whimpered.

'*Now* you decide. I thought you couldn't stand any more.'

'I didn't realize how bad it would be out here.'

Gail squealed in panic. All semblance of control had been abandoned now. David steered and then oversteered, sent the car into a skid and frantically wrenched the wheel trying to straighten up. Gail screamed this time.

'You are not helping,' David yelled at her. His knuckles white on the steering wheel, he gripped tighter, trying to ease the vehicle on to something approaching a straight line. The road swept down and to the right, and David gave up all pretence of knowing what to do. 'Just hang on,' he snapped. 'Fuck!'

She was right, Gail thought abstractedly as she clung to door handle and the front of her seat and tried hard not to scream. Sometimes only that word would do. The last thing she was aware of, before the car lurched sideways and the headlight picked up the wall of mud and stones that blocked the road ahead, was that she felt that presence again.

'Simeon?' Gail said, and then the car smashed far too fast into the mudslide, tipped and rolled, and the world went black.

FIFTEEN

Taken from an article in the Herald and Echo, *5 January 1872:*

> *It is the sad duty of this writer to report the death of a pillar of our small community. Dr Thaddeus Pym, well known in the country for his acts of charity and his skill as a physician, suffered a fatal accident sometime yesterday night. It is understood that Dr Pym was riding home late from Aikensthorpe House, residence of Albert Southam, Esq. and Mrs Southam. It is understood that Dr Pym had been planning to remain at Aikensthorpe overnight, and therefore his absence was not noted until the following day. The body of Dr Pym, who had been thrown from his horse a scant mile from Aikensthorpe House, was found by a local farmer a little after seven . . .*

No one had been concerned that Edwin had failed to appear at breakfast. He hadn't been the only one; Toby had only come down for long enough to collect a tray and then remove himself back to his room.

For Edwin to also miss lunch, though, seemed strange, and Rav was dispatched to knock on his door and see if he was coming down.

'I can fix him a tray if he'd rather not,' Melissa said. 'But the old boy has to eat.'

'How was the walk?' Rina asked.

'Oh, wonderful.' Miriam's cheeks were reddened by the cold, but she looked so much more relaxed, Rina was satisfied to see.

'The woods are beautiful,' Joy said. 'We counted all the different species in the hedgerow, and according to that the boundary must date back more than a thousand years. Tim found some ruins,' she added.

'Ruins?'

'It looks like the remnants of an old folly,' he said. 'There's a bit of an archway and some wall. It could be anything, but it's just at the point where you get a fantastic view over the valley, so I wondered, you know, if it was a garden feature.'

Rina nodded, was about to tell Tim he was probably right, when Rav reappeared, his brown skin bloodlessly pale. He was obviously distressed.

'It's Edwin,' he said. 'He's dead.'

'Dead?' Viv was horrified. 'How?'

Rav shook his head. 'I don't know. His heart was bad, I know. Maybe the upset of last night, maybe . . .'

Miriam was on her feet. 'Show me,' she said gently.

'You're a doctor?'

'Well, no, actually I'm a forensic scientist, but I'm used to dealing with the dead, so—'

'I'll come with you,' Mac said.

'Had I better call an ambulance?' Melissa's hand fluttered nervously. 'This is horrible. Just horrible.'

'Bit late for an ambulance if he's dead.' Toby was sardonic.

He looked hung-over, Rina thought. She followed Mac from the room, leaving Tim and Joy to sort out the various stages of upset in the dining room.

Edwin's room was on the first floor and in the wing above the library.

'In here.' Rav held the door. He was calmer now, but his lips were still slightly blue. Rina wondered if he, too, had heart problems. They stood beside the door while Miriam and Mac went to inspect the old man's body. It was obvious from first glance that Edwin was indeed dead, and to Rina's eye he had been dead for quite some time. The cheeks already looked hollow; the lids of Edwin's eyes were slightly retracted. Rina found herself thinking of the old custom of putting pennies on the eyes to keep them closed.

'Poor Edwin,' she said softly. 'You say he had heart problems?'

Rav nodded. 'I know he'd had angina for years. I don't know how bad it was, but—' He broke off, watching intently as Miriam touched Edwin's hand where it lay on the light blue quilt. He lay on his back, head propped awkwardly on too many pillows, one hand extended on the covers, the other tucked under the blankets.

Gently, Miriam checked for a pulse at wrist and throat that they all knew would not be there. Flexed the fingers, checking for the first signs of rigor. Opened the lids and looked into the dead man's eyes. Then she turned his head and peered at his neck as though puzzled by something.

'Miriam?' Mac questioned.

'Do you have your torch?'

Mac rummaged in his jacket pocket, produced a key ring that had a small flashlight attached.

'There's blood here on his neck. Not much, as though he scratched himself on something. Rav, do you know if Edwin took tablets to thin his blood?'

'Warfarin? I believe so, yes. He used to complain it took an age to stop bleeding if he cut himself. Miriam, what's wrong?'

She didn't respond immediately; instead, she looked again into the old man's eyes and then stepped back from the bed as though to take in the scene from a better perspective.

'Blood on the neck,' she said, 'but only a trace on the pillow, and . . .' Very gently, she lifted the edge of the pillow on which Edwin's head rested. 'Blood—'

Mac came round to her side of the bed.

'—on the pillow underneath where his head is placed.' She pointed. 'I noticed that his head was at the wrong angle to be comfortable.'

'Petechiae?'

'Yes.' Miriam looked at Mac, horrified at the implication.

'What do they mean?' Rav asked.

Rina had caught on now. 'He was smothered,' she said. 'Miriam?'

Miriam nodded. 'It looks that way, Rina. Rav, did you see the door key when you came in?'

'I—smothered? What do you mean? You mean someone *killed* him?'

'I think it is a distinct possibility. The key?'

Rina pointed. 'There, on the chest of drawers.'

'Ah, yes. Right, we all need to leave and lock the door, then call the police and get some assistance here.'

'Right,' Rav said. 'No, you really mean it?'

'I really mean it,' Miriam confirmed. 'Rav, your friend didn't die of a heart attack. He was asphyxiated, and I'm guessing it was with this pillow. Whoever did it then placed the pillow under his head to make it look as though he'd died in his sleep. What they didn't realize is that either they'd scratched him or he'd struggled and scratched himself. The blood had flowed out on to the pillow he was lying on. When they put the other one beneath his head—'

'The blood was on the wrong pillow.' Rav stared. 'But no one would want to hurt Edwin. He was . . . harmless. Gentle, just a nice old man.'

Rina led him from the room. The others followed, and Mac locked the door. 'Best check what other keys there are,' he said. He looked grave.

Rav blinked, as though suddenly in too bright a light. 'Someone here did it? Someone here killed Edwin?'

'We can't rule that out,' Mac said gently. 'We should call the local police now.'

They returned to the dining room, and Mac asked to use a private phone. He took Miriam with him.

'Is he really dead?' Viv asked, eyes wide and a mix of horror and fascinated excitement on her face.

'He really is. Melissa, how many keys are there to each room?'

'Two,' Melissa told him. 'Why?'

'And a master key?'

'No, not to the bedrooms. We've got a master to the suite of keys for the downstairs doors, but the upstairs rooms are all just off-the-shelf stuff, we haven't got around to changing them yet. They were fitted when we took over.'

'Took over?' Rina asked.

'Um, yes, the consortium bought this place, spent a few months doing what was immediately necessary, and we've been doing it piecemeal since. The people before us tried to get it going as a country house hotel, they'd done it up, but I think most of their stuff was from the local DIY warehouse, we've been upgrading. Look, what happened to Edwin? What does it have to do with keys?'

Rav had sat down at the table, and someone poured him some coffee. He sat now with his hands around the cup. He looked sick, Rina thought. 'They think someone murdered Edwin,' Rav said.

'Murdered! Oh, for Pete's sake.' Toby was almost amused. Then: 'You mean it, don't you? Oh my God.'

'How?' Viv asked. 'Who? I mean, there's only been us here.'

'One of *us*?' Robin sounded less shocked than the others. He was watching Rina intently.

'We don't know that,' Rina said quietly. 'Melissa, where are the spare keys kept?'

'I'll show you.' Melissa almost fled from the room, clearly glad to be doing something. Rina and Tim followed her through the hall and back towards the kitchen. They passed Mac and Miriam in Melissa's tiny office, still talking on the phone. Mac was frowning, and Miriam looked anxious. Into the small but shining kitchen, and through to a back office opposite what Rina assessed to be an old boot room. A flight of stairs led down to a basement, and a cold draft blew upward.

'What's down there?

'The old wine cellar and various storage rooms. Why?' Melissa didn't wait for an answer. 'We keep the keys in here.' She pointed at a wooden cabinet fastened to the wall. There was a lock, but no key in it, and the door was held closed by a metal hook and loop that had been screwed to the door and the side of the box.

'We never had the key to that. And the door was off when I took over. I screwed it back on its hinges and then cobbled the hasp and staple together from stuff I found in the cupboards.' Melissa was babbling now.

'Here,' Tim said. A rough wooden table served as a desk in here, and an old mug stuffed with pens and pencils provided Tim with the implement he was looking for. He handed Rina a pencil with an eraser on the end. She used it to push the hook out of the loop, making as little contact as she could. The door swung open to reveal rows of hooks with keys hanging from them. Door keys and old-fashioned gate keys; a ring for the estate van and car. Each was labelled, the top two rows being bedrooms with numbers beside each one.

'Which was Edwin's?'

'This one.' Melissa pointed. The second key was still in place.

'Can you get into here from the rear of the building?'

'Yes, I suppose so.'

Melissa led them back out into the lobby and into what Rina had thought must be a cupboard next to the boot room. The rear door led out into a small courtyard with a gap in the wall through which Rina could see the carriage house across the lawn. Various outbuildings surrounded the courtyard, and Rina made a note to herself that she must come out and check them over later. When she actually had her shoes on and not the pink satin slippers. The snow lay thick and heavy, and various sets of footprints crossed the space.

'Have you been out here today?' she asked Melissa.

'Um, yes. Into that building there. We use that as the laundry, all the machines and so on are inside it.'

'So that set of footprints would be yours. There and back again. And those?' Heavier and larger, booted feet.

'I don't know. Oh God, you don't think . . . ?'

'It could easily have been one of the guests exploring,' Tim soothed.

They retreated into the lobby once more, and Rina glanced into the boot room, satisfying herself that no exit led from there. 'You say that's a basement. Can I go down?'

Melissa reached around her and switched on the light. 'The stairs are steep,' she said. 'And it's bloody freezing. Damp too.'

Rina and Tim descended. Melissa, arms wrapped around her body as though hugging herself, stood at the top of the stairs. The ceiling was arched and had been whitewashed, though this was now flaking and crumbling. Wine racks stood against the wall closest to the stairs, and it was soon evident that the staff, such as they were, rarely ventured beyond this point. Old wooden shelves filled a lot of the space; broken chairs and old crates took up much of the rest. 'There's so much of this place unfinished, undealt with,' Rina said quietly when Melissa was out of earshot. 'Why not just bring in a full complement of staff, get this up and running as quickly as possible?'

'Ah, yet another thing to nag at Rina's brain,' Tim said with a smile. 'But you're right, it is all a bit odd. Nothing down here though, except—' He pointed. The window was set high in the wall, as befitted a basement, but not so high that Rina could not see the snow settled against the broken panes.

'You think someone could have come in that way?' Rina upended a crate and stood carefully on its top. 'The latch is broken,' she said. 'You could just push it open from the inside, but no, the snow is thick, no one's disturbed it. My bet is they simply came in through the back door.'

'And do you have a particular "they" in mind? Something tells me you don't mean whoever killed Edwin.'

'No,' Rina confirmed. 'I still have that one down as an inside job. But twice now I've seen things that lead me to believe someone is poking around this place at night, and I don't want to guess yet if that's connected to Edwin's death or not.'

'You've not mentioned this before.'

'Nothing much *to* mention. Let's go back up, it's freezing down here.' She hopped off the crate and led the way back through the warren of basement rooms and up the stairs. Melissa didn't appear to have moved.

'Let's go and get warmed up,' Rina said, 'and see when the police are likely to get here.'

* * *

It had started to snow heavily again, Rina noted as they returned to the dining room. Lunch was untouched, and the company sat around the big table looking glum and rather lost. Mac followed close on their heels.

'When are the police getting here?' Rina asked.

'Well, that's a bit of a problem,' Mac said. 'There's been a multi-vehicle pile-up on the A1, abandoned vehicles and people trapped by the weather all over the county. As you can imagine, resources are stretched.'

'But this is a murder.'

'And, unfortunately, the two main access roads are blocked. The road through Hickling, where we stayed last night, is now completely closed. It looks like we left just in time. I phoned the landlord at the Oaks, where we stayed last night, and he reckons even his Land Rover can't make it up the hill, and there's been a landslide coming in from the other way.'

'That happened last winter,' Melissa said. 'Up by Crispin crags. It took three days to clear it that time.'

'So that will have to be sorted out before we can depend on help getting in, and then they've got the gated road to negotiate. The idea is, they'll get on to the local farmer and see what help he can provide, maybe get some officers in by tractor, but for now, folks, it looks as if we're on our own.'

'Oh, and to make it even more interesting, a lot of the phone and power lines are down,' Miriam added.

'We've got a generator for if the power does go down,' Melissa said. 'We learned that lesson last year. Phones might be more of an issue; let's just hope for the best there. But we can't carry on as normal with a dead body upstairs, it's just not right!'

'We don't really have a choice,' Mac told her. 'I've been talking to an Inspector Chandler, and he's going to call back as soon as he can. Meantime, we need to record the scene, take statements, work out where everyone was when Edwin died and so on.'

'So you're planning on taking over, are you?' Toby was oddly aggressive.

His hangover must be really bad, Rina thought. 'Do you have a better suggestion?' she asked.

'Poor Edwin,' Viv said softly. She glared at her professor. 'What can we do to help?'

'Well, first of all, Miriam and I need to record the scene. Melissa, do you have any kitchen whites? We don't want to risk contaminating things further than we already have, wearing our outdoor clothes.'

'Yes, yes, we have those.' She looked close to tears. 'What else?'

'Camera equipment. Toby?'

'No, you damned well can't.'

'Don't be an ass, Toby,' Tim said.

Toby glared at him for a moment, then sighed. 'Sorry,' he said. 'I'm just upset, and I don't like, well, being bossed around.'

That, Rina thought, was probably what everyone actually needed right now. To be told what to do.

'We should all stay in here for the moment,' she said. 'Just while Miriam establishes the extent of the crime scene.'

'What do you mean?' Viv was curious now.

'I thought the crime scene was just the bedroom,' Robin added.

'It's anywhere the killer might have left a trace,' Miriam explained.

'But that could be anywhere, couldn't it?' Viv said. 'Doesn't that mean we can't even go to the loo?'

Rina hid a smile.

'No, it just means we have to be methodical,' Miriam said. 'I suggest that Melissa takes us to the kitchen, we get changed, and then we start with that part of the house. That way everyone can get access to food and drink and the downstairs cloakroom. I doubt that will take long, but we still need to check. Later, they'll have to fingerprint the locks and so on and take fingerprints for comparison and elimination. Then we'll know, for example, if someone came into the house last night.'

'Carry your kit around with you, do you?' Toby again. 'Just in case you stumble over a body? Right little girl scout.'

'Toby, just cut it out,' Viv snapped at him. 'Ask Melissa for some painkillers and get over yourself.'

'I've got some pills in the kitchen,' Melissa said vaguely. 'Do you really have your stuff with you?' she asked. 'I mean . . . ?'

'No, but we can improvise, don't worry,' Miriam said. 'What we need to do is isolate anything that the local CSIs need to examine properly, so we'll do the obvious stuff like bagging and tagging keys and any trace evidence we find, photographing anything we can, that sort of thing.'

Rina glanced around the table. Miriam had them all focused on her, and the quiet, reasonable voice had them all in thrall.

'I suggest you all get something to eat, and Mac and I will deal with the main scene. Hopefully, we'll get some back-up soon,' Miriam said.

Quiet discontented murmurs and sounds of reluctant agreement followed. Mac and Miriam then left with Melissa to deck themselves out in chefs' whites and see what equipment they could improvise.

'Right,' Rina said. 'We should get ourselves some drinks at least and see if this lunch is still hot enough to eat.'

'Eat? I couldn't eat.' Rav shook his head.

Rina ignored him. She could see that the first shock was diminishing now and knew from experience that, despite protests and coyness about the propriety of gluttony, everyone would suddenly find that they were ravenous. She had just lifted the lid on the nearest dish when Mac reappeared carrying a small microwave, still in its box. He had not yet changed.

'Melissa sent me with this,' he said.

Rina beamed at him. 'Good thinking. Right, let's get it unpacked and plugged in.'

'My mum's got the same one as that,' Robin announced. 'Here, Viv and I will do it.'

'There's a plug over there, set it on the sideboard. Right.'

Rina stood back and let Viv and Robin take over. Rav seemed at a loss, but he took plates over when Viv asked him and helped to carry dishes to the sideboard to make serving easier. Terry joined in, getting in the way and offering helpful suggestions, glad of something that would break the tension.

'What's going on here, Rina?' Jay came over and stood beside her.

'I don't know,' she told him. 'Jay, did you see anything unusual when you were out this morning? Did you meet anyone?'

He thought about it. 'No,' he said. 'Nothing but crows and jackdaws out there this morning. I've never been in a place so quiet. I liked Edwin,' he added. 'I'd been reading his books for years—we'd attended the same events, even—but our paths never crossed properly until now.'

'What made you agree to participate in all this?'

He shrugged. 'Curiosity, I guess. I've participated in more bizarre events. None where someone got themselves murdered, though. Any word from Gail and David?'

'Not so far as I know. Did you know them before this weekend?'

'I arrived on Thursday, first time I met anyone here—except Terry, of course.'

'Oh?'

He laughed, 'You have a suspicious mind, Rina Martin. I was an adviser on one of his films. We hit it off and kept in touch. I heard about his new film and I was coming here so I was the one suggested it might be useful to him.'

'Sorry,' she said. 'I suppose I'm feeling suspicious of just about everyone right now.'

Jay nodded. 'Keep it up,' he said. 'Something tells me this isn't ended by a long shot.'

SIXTEEN

A sad little group left Aikensthorpe that morning. Elizabeth had not waited to be told to go; she had packed what she could and told Sally that she would replace Abigail, her lady's maid, for the journey. The girl had stared at her in horror and then murmured something that Elizabeth took to be agreement. In truth, that morning, Elizabeth had given little thought to the wishes of the servant girl, only to the fact that she could not travel alone. She had sent no word to her own family, knowing they would take Albert's side.

'Excuse me, ma'am, but where are we going?' Sally asked her.

'Rome.' Elizabeth had made up her mind only in that second.

'What? In Italy?'

'Yes. We have a villa there that my husband does not use. He will not care that I use it now.'

'On our own, miss? I mean ma'am?'

I wish I was a miss again, Elizabeth thought. 'We will engage other servants,' she said, realizing that she had never had to do such a thing. Her father and then her husband had taken care of such practicalities.

In the event, they did not go alone. Banks appeared just as they were loading the carriage. He had a carpet bag in one hand and a battered suitcase in the other. 'I will ride with the driver,' he said.

'Banks?'

'Begging your pardon, Mrs Southam, but Mr Southam won't want any in the house that witnessed . . . Well, that witnessed what went on. I think it best I remain in your employ rather than be dismissed from Mr Southam's, if you take my meaning.'

Elizabeth's eyes filled with tears. She had not thought any of this through. Not considered the way in which her actions would cause such waves.

'Thank you, Banks,' she said. 'I think we had better make speed before Mr Southam wakes, don't you?'

Two men watched them leave that morning. George Weston smiled at their departure, gratified that this troublesome young bride had been so easily duped and then cast aside. Albert Southam, staring out from an upstairs window, briefly considered going down and preventing their departure, and then thought better of it. She would, no doubt, go to her father's house, or maybe, if the thought of returning home in such disgrace had grown too much, to her sister in London. He did not yet know what to do about this or how he would ride the scandal about to break around them. Better for Elizabeth not to be here; her foolishness could only exacerbate the unpleasantness.

He tried not to think that he would miss her, comforted himself with the notion that she would return, seeking his forgiveness, his indulgence and the shelter of his reputation. No doubt he would indulge her wishes, but he would make her beg first.

The carriage drove away that morning carrying his wife and his unborn child, and Albert could not know that neither would ever return.

* * *

By two in the afternoon, blizzard conditions had set in and any thoughts of leaving faded. Mac had set up shop in Melissa's office and begun taking statements, though as he said to Rina it was a bit of a pointless exercise in some ways: he could hardly isolate everyone from one another, and he couldn't tell them not to discuss something that was bound to be the main topic of conversation.

Miriam had finished with the kitchen and had continued upstairs. To everyone's surprise, Joy had asked if she needed an extra pair of hands, and Miriam had agreed.

'Mac has to do other things,' Joy said. 'I'm not worried about dead bodies, and I know how hard it is to collate and collect at the same time.' So Joy, decked out in fresh whites and with her long hair bundled into a net, had accompanied Miriam up the stairs to Edwin's room.

Rina took Tim aside, and together they went back to the seance room. The fire in the big hall had been lit, but everyone had elected to settle in the small room next to the dining room where they'd had drinks on that first night. It was comfortable and warm, and Jay had drawn the curtains and shut out the blizzard. Despite the fire in the massive fireplace, the big hall was chilly.

'I hope Gail and Prof Franklin are holed up somewhere warm and not still out in this,' Tim said.

'I'm surprised they didn't come back. If both roads out of here are blocked, where have they got to?'

'Mac got through, and they left about the same time as he did. I suppose it depends which way they went. I don't really understand why they left so urgently,' Tim said.

'No, neither do I, but there's not much we can do about it.'

The snow was creeping in under the French windows in the orangery. Rina made a point of finding the door she now knew led from there into the kitchen area and the other wing, opening it to find a small lobby and short passage through which she could see the kitchen. The library was also chilly; the fire was not lit in there, and the cold that filled the glorified conservatory penetrated the book-lined room, despite its heavy door. It seemed like a silly place for a library, Rina thought. The damp would do the books no good at all. The unheated seance room was freezing; the shutters Rina had opened earlier that day were still locked back, allowing the chill of falling snow to bleed in through the badly fitting glass and leach what little warmth there might have been.

Tim shivered. 'Who opened the shutters?'

'I did,' Rina told him. 'I came in here first thing.'

'Find anything I missed?'

'Not so far. Tim, I felt a draft on the back of my neck several times during the seance last night.' Only last night. It felt so much longer ago. 'Did the door open at all?'

'No, we'd have seen it. It would have been caught on film.'

Together they examined the room again, tapping on the panelling, scrutinizing the floor. There was no electric light in the old study, and already, though it was not even mid-afternoon, it was getting hard to see, the swirling snow blocking out the daylight and turning everything to shades of twilight.

'I felt the table move,' Rina asserted. 'We all did.'

'And you can see it move on the video. We both know that can be made to happen in all kinds of ways.'

'But you found no evidence of any of them?'

'No, but that doesn't mean anything. We examined the room on Friday, but it was then left unattended for more than a day. It was locked, but frankly, that doesn't mean a damn thing, the lock is easy enough.'

He knelt beside the table. Then stood again. 'Help me with this, will you?'

The pedestal table was of a type that Rina understood was a tea table. The beautifully figured top was designed to swing upright, and the table could then be set back against a wall when not in use. It was solid and heavy, and she admired the flame veneer, stroking the smooth surface.

'Did Melissa polish this?' she asked.

'No idea. Why? What are you looking for? If the shutters were closed, there'd have been no fading, surely.'

'No, but there's no heating either. I'd have expected at least a bit of warping, some lifting of the veneer. I don't know. It's in lovely condition for something neglected for well over a hundred years.'

'True. OK, now tip the top back, right. Ah, now that's new.'

'What?'

'This, look.' What had looked like a perfectly flat rest at the top of the pedestal had been slightly modified. A small piece of wadding was slipped between the tabletop and the pedestal base; when they removed it and dropped the tabletop back down, they could tilt the table, just a little. 'Well, I'll be. So bloody simple.'

'I thought you examined the table?' Rina said. 'You were under it when we came into the room for the first time.'

'I was checking for microphones, hidden whatsits. Oh, I don't know. I understood the table had already been examined, and anyway—'

'You thought if there was going to be trickery, it would be clever trickery.'

'So bloody simple.'

'Hmm.' Rina recalled her conversation with Rav. Experimentally, she tested the ability to rap the tabletop. It wasn't easy, but a few practice tries convinced her that it could be done. 'And who would be in the best position to manipulate this?' she asked.

Tim stood back, visualizing the people sitting around the table. 'It would have been Edwin,' he said. 'In the dark, in that kind of atmosphere, well, no one's faculties are completely switched on. It must have been Edwin. None of us saw it.'

'But he had both hands on the table,' Rina argued, playing devil's advocate.

'True, but—' Tim grabbed the chair Edwin had used and sat down. 'Ah.' He tipped back slightly. 'The legs have been shaved off at the back, look, tilts.' He slid himself beneath the table and laid his hands on the top, as Edwin had the previous night. He tipped the chair and lifted his knee. The tabletop tilted and cracked down with a solid thump. 'Not easy,' Tim said. 'But eminently possible, and he was here right over Christmas so he'd have had plenty of time to practice.'

'Why would he do that?' Rina wondered. 'And anyway, Tim, we don't know for sure it was Edwin. Three of those chairs look identical. The room has been unlocked since last night, so it would have been easy for anyone to have swapped the chairs round.'

'True. But . . .'
Rina nodded. 'So who else realized?'

* * *

Mac had been on the phone to the local police again. 'More power lines down, accidents all over the place. I've told them we can hold the fort here, and they're going to try and get someone to us in a couple of hours.'

Miriam and Joy came down with a plastic box filled with freezer bags and camera equipment. 'I need to download the images on to a computer,' Miriam said. 'Then we can send them if the Internet connection is still OK.'

'Seems to be,' Melissa said. She seemed very subdued. 'I hate the thought of him just lying there. It doesn't seem right.'

'We've turned off the heating in his room,' Miriam said. 'That should slow decomp. I used the meat thermometer to take body temp readings so you might not want it back.'

'Oh God.' Melissa's colour drained, and she fled to the downstairs cloakroom.

'Sorry,' Miriam said. 'I wasn't thinking.'

'Time of death?' Mac asked.

'Best I can offer is between four and six this morning.'

'Between four and six,' Rina mused. What time had she heard the noises in the attic? 'There was someone else here around then,' she said quietly. 'I saw them the night before. I heard them last night and saw their footprints. Maybe Edwin saw them too?'

She shuddered at the thought that she might have gone to confront Edwin's murderer armed only with a heavy glass candlestick.

Quickly, she filled Mac in on what she had seen and done, trying to gloss over the fact that she had gone poking about unprepared and alone.

'Rina!' Miriam was appalled.

Joy giggled and then sobered. 'Sorry, I just have this image in my head of Rina in a pink dressing gown and slippers bonking an intruder on the head with a candlestick. It sounds like a Cluedo game, but really, Rina darling, why didn't you come and wake us up?'

'Because I'm not as sensible as I should be,' she told them. 'It opens up other possibilities though, doesn't it?' She sighed and glanced out at the heavy snow. 'Actually, I hope it was someone from outside, otherwise it all gets a bit grim, doesn't it? Amazing how helpless a bit of weather can make us, isn't it?' She pulled one of the big doors open and looked out. A blast of freezing, snow-laden air skittered in, and she let the door swing closed again. 'I hate to sound melodramatic, but I think we should all be careful, stick with the people we trust. We have one dead body; we don't want any more.'

SEVENTEEN

It was just before three in the afternoon. Joy, Tim and Miriam, along with Jay Stratham, were in the small room off the dining room, watching the videos shot the night before to see if Edwin had indeed been cheating.

Viv, Robin and Rav were sitting at the table, talking sporadically, trying to make sense of Edwin's death and also Edwin's insistence on setting up this event. Rav had been with him over the Christmas and New Year and was at a loss; Edwin had been excited but methodical, and it was he who had invented the character of Grace, the manufactured ghost.

'He never said where he got the idea from,' Rav said. 'Just told us she should be called Grace and also the various ideas he had about her life. We brainstormed the rest.'

Viv was thoughtful, something nagging at the back of her mind. 'There was a Grace in the news clippings, I'm sure of it. I just can't remember where I saw it.'

'Then he might have been influenced by that,' Rav agreed. 'I know he was very set on the name and the character. Maybe he found out something about the so-called ghost that Elizabeth and her group created?' He looked hopefully at Viv, who shook her head.

'I can't remember,' she said. Then: 'Does it really matter?'

'I suppose not.'

'We could go over the records again,' Robin said. The others nodded agreement, but no one seemed to have the energy to move.

* * *

In the large hall, Mac was trying to construct a timeline based on the statements he had taken. Jay paced while Terry watched. He held a script in his hand which he kept trying to read, but Rina could see he could not concentrate.

Toby had wandered off to his room.

Rina, bored with inaction, crossed the hall towards the kitchen wing to see if Melissa wanted any help. She was startled when the front doors swung open and Gail staggered through, supporting David Franklin.

'Oh, Lord, are you all right? Mac! Come here!' she called. 'Come on, sit down, you're both frozen through.'

'We crashed the car.' Gail was crying and obviously distressed.

Blankets were found, and warm drinks, and Miriam inspected the deep cut on David's head. Both Gail and David were chilled through.

'My God, you were lucky,' Rav said. 'You could both be dead just from the cold.'

'I know.' David was shivering uncontrollably now, hands clasped tightly round a large mug. 'We knew we couldn't stay where we were, but I really wasn't sure I could make it back across the fields. We could see Aikensthorpe, but it just seemed like forever away. I thought we'd freeze to death before we made it back.'

'Why didn't you call someone? We would have come out to find you.'

David Franklin shook his head. 'My phone is still back there somewhere in the car, we think—we didn't realize it was missing until we'd already set off. Gail tried hers and couldn't get a signal, then the battery died. The case was cracked in the accident, so we think it must have damaged the connector or something. I know she put it on charge last night just before bed.'

How does he know that? Rina thought.

'Simeon was there,' Gail said vaguely, leaning back into the armchair and closing her eyes.

'Try not to go to sleep yet,' Miriam told her. 'You're still really chilled and probably concussed.'

'Simeon?' Rina asked. 'Oh, you mean Professor Meehan. He left here before we arrived,' Rina explained to Mac. 'I replaced him.'

Gail lifted her head and looked around the room. 'Where's Edwin?'

Silence as the others exchanged glances. 'I'm sorry,' Rav said finally. 'Edwin died in the night.'

'What! Died? But how? His heart?'

Rav hesitated and then shook his head.

'Someone killed him, didn't they?' Gail demanded.

'Gail, don't be absurd, who would want to—' David Franklin broke off, the expected reassurances that it was natural causes obviously unforthcoming. 'I don't understand.'

'None of us do,' Rav told him. 'Mac and Miriam here are trying to make some sense of it, as the local police are on the other side of that landslide. It's all very unfortunate.'

Ah, the great British art of understatement, Rina thought. They should make competency in that part of the new Citizenship exam, along with drinking tea and talking about the weather.

'I'm sorry,' Gail said. 'Mac and Miriam? Who are you, anyway?'

While Miriam explained their presence and who and what they both were, Mac went back to Melissa's office and made another call to the local police. The news was no better. He told them about Professor Franklin's car and that both occupants had made it back to Aikensthorpe House. He was told that the route through should be cleared the next morning when the heavy equipment required would be on scene.

'Weren't you involved in the Cara Evans enquiry?' Inspector Chandler, his local contact, asked him.

'Yes,' Mac told him cautiously. 'I was.'

'So you're currently on suspension, then.'

'That's so, yes.'

'Right.'

Mac could hear the questions hanging in the air. Instead of encouraging them, he said, 'We've done all we can to secure the evidence and the scene, but I'll be very glad to be able to hand this over to you.'

Again, a slight hesitation. 'You're sure the old bloke didn't just pop his clogs?'

'I'm sure.'

'Right.' That word again, so full of unexploded meaning. Mac had become used to a certain notoriety being attached to his name this past year or so—inevitable, given his involvement in such a high-profile case as a child murder. Especially as he had been present when she died and was now a suspect in the death of her killer.

Mac closed his eyes and brought the conversation back to present matters. 'So, we can expect someone to arrive tomorrow morning then?'

'All things being equal, yes. Unless we get more bloody snow or another chunk of hillside decides to give in to gravity.'

Mac thanked him and rang off.

Returning to the main hall, he told everyone that help would be a little longer getting through.

'Don't they realize there's a killer on the loose?' Jay asked.

'I'm not sure they are quite convinced of that. Edwin was an old man, and they only have our word that it wasn't natural causes.'

'But you're a police officer and Miriam is a CSI.'

'And murder investigations cost a lot of money.' David was cynical. 'Better for everyone if this is just a heart attack. I suppose you *are* sure?'

Mac experienced a moment of uncertainty, then pushed it aside. Of course he was sure. He wasn't exactly a stranger to violent death, and neither was Miriam.

'I'm sure,' he said. 'Look, we don't know fully what went on here; I think we should all just be careful. The local police will arrive tomorrow and a proper inquiry can begin. In the meantime, I suggest everyone keep a lookout for anything strange and that tonight we lock our bedroom doors.'

'There are spare keys,' Viv pointed out. 'Maybe we should take the spare keys.'

'They need to be fingerprinted,' Miriam said. 'They need to stay in the key cupboard for now.'

'But—'

'If you lock your door and leave the key in the lock then no one else can unfasten the door from the outside,' Mac pointed out. 'We just all need to be sensible.'

No one actually argued with him, but the tension and fear were palpable. No one said it, but Rina could see the wary glances cast between the huddled little group and hear the unspoken question. One of them might have killed Edwin; would the killer strike again?

EIGHTEEN

The afternoon dragged on. Rina, Tim and Joy retreated to Rina's room and pored over the folder Viv had given them all on that first night and the printouts from the Internet that Mac had brought with him.

'So, as I understand it, the consortium that bought this place want to turn it into a conference centre and wedding venue,' Tim said at last. 'There are all these plans down on paper, and the local press report that it will bring jobs and opportunities into the area, that they will need tradesmen to do the restoration and kitchen staff and admin people to organize the conferences . . . and what do we actually see, eighteen months on?'

'Melissa and a bit of rewiring,' Rina said. 'Yes, the rooms are comfortable and the kitchen is well equipped and clean—'

'But the laundry room is one washing machine and a dryer,' Joy said. 'And the kitchen is fine for a smallish event, but I'd hate to have to cater an entire wedding.'

'Maybe they just plan to use outside agencies?' Rina suggested.

'And this event, this weekend, it's been a real oddity.'

'You mean even without the murder?' Joy said. 'No, but you're right. I looked in the visitors' book,' she added.

'You know, I like to see the comments and that. Well, there's hardly any.'

'Maybe we're reading too much into this,' Rina said at last. 'Tim, I'm sure I saw a list of shareholders somewhere?'

'Yes, it's . . . Ah, here it is.' He skimmed down the list of names. 'Well, what do you know?'

'Anyone familiar?'

'Yes, actually. Three names. The mysterious Professor Meehan—or at least I assume Mr S. Meehan is him. Then our friends David Franklin and Edwin Holmes. Edwin was part-owner of this place.'

Rina took the list from him and looked thoughtfully at it. Shareholders were listed: four of them, plus a company called Reality Enterprises for which they had no separate listing. She was willing to bet that many of the names would be on both lists.

She frowned. 'Look at the other name,' she said. 'Do you recognize it?'

'Oh, my God.' Joy's eyes were wide. 'Miss G. Wright. Could that be Grace Wright? But that's—'

'Impossible, or someone else with the same name,' Rina said. 'What on earth is going on?'

NINETEEN

Gail and David had dozed in front of the fire in the big room, Miriam not being happy about leaving them unobserved until she was sure they had fully recovered. By the time Rina and the others went back down, Gail had woken again and was looking better. It was clear, though, that she was worried about something and that David Franklin was not sympathetic.

'I felt Simeon's presence,' she asserted. 'I told everyone during the seance that I felt someone else, and I felt him again just before the car crashed. I'm sure of it. I think Simeon's dead.'

She was clearly agitated, and David Franklin was not helping by being so dismissive.

'I don't suppose anyone actually checked that he'd made it home?' Viv asked. 'He might have had an accident or something. I mean, with the weather being so bad.'

'The weather was fine when he left,' Robin pointed out.

'You don't actually *believe* her?' David Franklin was annoyed now.

'I'm keeping an open mind, just like you told us to,' Viv retorted.

'*Has* anyone heard from him?' Rina asked.

It seemed no one had.

'We didn't exactly part on the best of terms,' Rav confessed. 'He didn't like the idea of Edwin's ghost. He thought the project was doomed to failure.'

'Why was that?' Joy wanted to know.

'Oh, as Rina pointed out, it was nigh on impossible to reconstruct what happened in 1872. Edwin was adamant he wanted to continue, and Simeon equally adamant it was a bad idea.'

'Look—' Mac sounded tired and irritated—'what's the harm in calling his home and making sure he's all right? I'd like to ask him a few questions, anyway.'

'What about?' Robin asked.

'I'd like to know why Edwin was so adamant about continuing with this experiment and Professor Meehan so much against it.'

'You think this experiment had something to do with Edwin's death?' David Franklin scoffed. 'Get real, Inspector, or whatever you are; it was a thief, an opportunist. It was—'

'We're in the middle of nowhere,' Robin said thoughtfully. 'You'd have to be an odd kind of opportunist thief to trek across the fields in the snow, just on the off-chance, and then not steal anything.'

He had a point, Rina thought, mentally kicking herself for not trying to discover sooner where the strange man she had seen had come from.

'If the thief had arrived by car, wouldn't we have heard it or seen tyre tracks or something? And it's not exactly a quick getaway, is it? Not down a gated road,' Rina said.

Rina's gaze met Mac's, and she could see that he, too, was processing this train of thought through and reaching the same conclusion.

'What other houses are near here?' Mac asked.

'Only the farm,' Melissa said. 'But the farmhouse is a good two or three miles away. Most of the land round here belongs to the estate. There's just, like, a narrow spit of farmland running along that back boundary. He uses it for grazing; I think there's some kind of covenant on the use of the land. There's a lot of that kind of thing round here.'

'Other buildings? Barns or anything?'

She shrugged. 'Estate cottages that used to be let to the estate workers. They are going to be renovated eventually.'

She, too, sounded bone weary, Rina thought.

Mac nodded. 'Could someone give me Simeon's number then?' he said.

Rav produced his mobile phone and began to scan through the entries.

Rina drew back one of the heavy curtains and gazed out on to the white landscape. The sky should have been night black by now, but instead was a deep, heavy grey, bellied with snow clouds and oppressively low. Light flakes had begun to fall again, and something told her it would not be long before they grew much, much heavier and more numerous. Tomorrow the police would arrive, she told herself, if they could get through. Either way, they would have to venture out when it was light, see if they could find the barn or half renovated cottage where the man might have holed up.

Had this stranger killed Edwin? That didn't work, somehow, though Rina was not sure she could explain why.

Mac returned looking oddly put out. 'Simeon didn't make it back home,' he said. 'I spoke to his son. None of them have seen or heard from him in over a month, long before he came here. In fact, they didn't even know he *was* here. They reported him missing more than three weeks ago.'

Silence as everyone absorbed this.

'I know he was getting divorced,' Rav said slowly. 'We didn't talk about it, but he mentioned that his marriage had broken down.'

'I knew it.' Gail seemed caught between horror and triumph.

'You knew nothing,' David Franklin said. 'A vague feeling is *not* knowing.'

It looked as though their dispute was going to flare again, and Rina, for one, didn't think she could be bothered with it. 'I understand that you and Simeon are both shareholders in this place,' she said. 'Edwin too. What will happen to his shares if he really is dead?'

She saw Mac frowning at her, wondering what she had dug up that he hadn't.

A beat of silence, and then David Franklin shrugged. 'What of it?'

'You never told me that,' Gail said.

'I didn't know either.' This from Melissa.

Interesting, Rina thought, that both women felt they should have been informed. 'Apparently, there was one other individual shareholder,' she added, 'and a parent company of some kind? Reality Enterprises?'

'Who is the other shareholder?' Mac asked her.

'Well, that's the interesting thing. Miss G. Wright. Grace, perhaps?'

'What?' Gail looked from Rina to David. 'I don't understand. Edwin created Grace, he—'

'Oh, he just borrowed the name,' David Franklin said. 'He said there'd be a better connection if the name sounded real, or something, I don't know. Anyway, your point is?'

Rina shrugged. 'I just found it interesting, that's all.'

'I think we all do,' Melissa said.

'I told Edwin I thought Simeon was dead. What if—'

'Oh, for goodness' sake, Gail. We all heard you tell him.'

'Actually, some of us had gone up to bed before that.' Until now, Jay had remained silent; merely observing.

'Yes, well. It has no bearing, anyway,' David said irritably.

'Look, it's late, I suggest we all get some food inside us,' Melissa interrupted. She looked, Rina thought, particularly upset by this latest revelation, and Rina wondered why.

'Do you need a hand?'

'Thank you, no. I'm fine. Someone had best give Toby a call. Food will be just a few minutes.'

Toby. Rina glanced round the room, wondering why she hadn't noticed his absence earlier.

'I'll go,' Tim said.

Mac followed him, that unspoken anxiety now permeating the room. They returned a few minutes later with odd news. 'Toby's gone,' Mac said.

TWENTY

They had searched the house and then gone out with torches to look for Toby, investigated the outbuildings and looking for footprints in the snow, but there was no sign of him. His clothes were still in the room, but not his coat or gloves, and Viv noted that one of the small video cameras seemed to be missing.

'What would he go out for?' Viv stamped cold feet on the floor of the boot room. 'It's bloody freezing. Toby hates the snow.'

'And what would he want to film?' Robin was clearly really puzzled.

'Whatever it was will have to wait until morning,' Terry said practically. 'We can't see to search any further out, and it's starting to snow really heavily again.'

'But what if he's hurt or . . .'

They looked at one another, completing the sentence but not wanting to say anything aloud.

'Would he have had his mobile?' Terry asked.

'In his pocket, probably, but you know what the signal's like round here.' Viv gnawed at her lip. 'What should we do?'

'Tell the local police and look again in the morning. Nothing else we can do,' Terry said.

Rina agreed, but a feeling of deep dread and even deeper sorrow had taken a hold of her. This would not turn out well, not for anyone.

TWENTY-ONE

Morning brought clearer weather, and the heavy machinery arrived, following in the tracks of the snow plough. Slowly, the rocks and mud were cleared.

'How long now?' Inspector Chandler shouted up to the digger driver.

'About an hour, if we don't hit any snags. I can see that car, by the way. On its side, it is. They were lucky.'

Chandler nodded and went back to flapping his arms and stamping his feet. It was fiendishly cold, the temperature actually falling now the sky had cleared. Just what they needed, he thought: ice atop snow where the roads had not yet been cleared, and where it had, on top of the compacted skim of snow left behind on the tarmac. He had no illusions about the gritting lorries getting up this way; their energies would be focused on the main routes and town centres, and the rural areas would get what, if anything, was left.

At least the two in the car had got themselves out; there had been three weather related deaths so far, and he had no doubt there would be more.

He got on the phone and tried to call Aikensthorpe to let them know help was finally on the way. 'No frigging signal.'

The police constable with him, a local boy, just grinned. 'You could try climbing a tree, sir.'

'I've got a better idea, Constable. I could send you up the tree.'

'My mum wouldn't like that, sir, and you know what my mum is like when she doesn't like something.'

Chandler laughed. 'Oh, I'd be the last person to upset Mrs Brown,' he said. He'd known the lad—not that he was a lad now, he reminded himself—and his mum for more years than he cared to think about. 'You been up there since the new lot took over?'

'What, up to Aikensthorpe? No. Me sister applied for a job. They advertised for casual staff to help out with events, and she did an interview and they said they'd let her know when something come up, but—' He shook his head. 'She did a wedding, I think, just serving food, like. They had a massive marquee on the lawn, but she's not been asked back. She don't know anyone what has. *And* they were slow paying.'

Chandler nodded. That chimed with what he'd heard. He tried the phone again, just in case, but the road had been cut between a sheer rock face on one side and a bank rising behind the hedge on the other, and every time he dialled the signal dropped from only just there to not at all.

'Once we get past the bend the phones'll work,' the constable predicted.

Chandler sighed and went to see how the digger was doing.

* * *

The driver had been about right; it was just under the hour by the time he broke through the last section of mud, tipping the final load of clay and rock on to the verge. Here the rock face dropped down almost to road level and slowly gave way to scrubby woodland and deep gullies where the run-off from the winter rain was channelled off the road. Chandler followed the digger through the gap and went to check on the car before the digger driver prepared to nudge it over on to the verge, where it would lie until the recovery lorry could be brought up.

Definitely no one inside. He glanced into the rear of the hatchback, making certain that no one had been thrown out of the passenger compartment and into the rear. He'd known it happen when a vehicle rolled.

Satisfied that it was empty, he pulled open the driver's door with some difficulty, checking for personal belongings that might need urgent retrieval and, more to the point, might actually be in reach. A mobile phone had got itself wedged beneath the passenger seat and, reaching in, Chandler managed to grab it. Out of habit, he slid it into an evidence bag before putting it into his pocket.

Seeing nothing more of interest, he gave the signal for the digger to shove it over to the side of the road. The driver beckoned to him and then called to him to climb up into the cab.

'Something wrong?'

'Take a gander down there. Looks like someone else crashed out on the bend.'

Chandler looked. They would never have spotted it from the road, he realized. It needed the height of the cab for anyone to see into the narrow fissure that dropped down from the road.

'He's a long way down though,' the digger driver said.

Chandler agreed. Getting down from the cab, he called the constable and together they stomped through the thick snow to where the car now lay half buried. Chandler brushed snow from the windows and peered in. No one inside, that was a blessing, though there was a suitcase on the back seat.

'Someone was planning on going somewhere,' the constable commented. 'Though you'd think they'd have put it in the boot.'

Chandler nodded. 'Doors are unlocked,' he said. 'It looks like someone parked up here and decided to walk. Maybe they thought about taking the case and then changed their minds. I'll have a quick look for some ID; you uncover the number plate and we'll call it in.'

Chandler tugged at the driver's door while Constable Brown went round to the rear of the car and began to excavate the number plate. The doors were frozen closed, and it took several minutes of persuasion to get them open. Chandler stuck his head inside and began to root in the glove compartment. Then he stopped. Something wasn't right. He knew that smell. Faint though it was, he knew that smell.

Withdrawing his head, he came round to the back of the vehicle and tried the boot. Again, the lock was frozen shut.

'You got a lighter?' he asked his constable.

'Um, no. I don't smoke.'

'You *do* smoke. I've seen you sneak the odd one. Don't worry, I won't tell your mum.'

Constable Brown produced the lighter, and they heated the lock. Cautiously, Chandler pressed the button and propped it open.

'Christ!' Brown jumped back.

'I don't think so,' Chandler said softly. The cold had dramatically slowed the rate of decomposition, but it couldn't completely obliterate that faint whiff of death Chandler had detected. Once sniffed never forgotten, he thought grimly, looking at the dead man's face and the massive gash between his eyes that had obliterated most of what had been his nose. One blow, so far as Chandler could tell. Hard and heavy and without hesitation, if he was any judge. One blow to kill the man. Whoever delivered it had either been dead lucky or had known exactly what he was doing. Beside the body was a towel and a plastic bag, and from the amount of blood on it, Chandler assumed it had, at some time, been wrapped around the head. Why bother taking it off again?

Unless someone had wanted to check the man really was dead.

Gently, Chandler lowered the lid of the boot and led Brown back up the slope. He hopped back up on to the cab. 'Reckon I can get a signal from up here?'

'Try it. Find anything?' asked the digger driver.

'Unfortunately, yes.'

'Damn. Reckon they hit the rocks?'

'No,' Chandler told him. 'I don't think he hit anything. In fact, I reckon you'd be more accurate if you said that something hit him.'

* * *

It didn't take long to identify the body; Professor Simeon Meehan still had his wallet and driving licence in his pockets, and the police computer soon turned up the information that he had been reported missing.

But it also didn't take long before Chandler knew the confusing fact that Professor Meehan had actually been at Aikensthorpe for much of that time.

'We've got ourselves a real can of worms,' Chandler muttered as he got off the phone to Mac. 'Looks as though our roving inspector might actually be on to something.' Truthfully, he hadn't fully believed that the death reported at Aikensthorpe could be other than natural. In Chandler's experience, the deaths of old men in their beds tended to have very normal explanations.

TWENTY-TWO

Mac was thoughtful as he returned to where everyone had gathered in the main hall. Today, any sense of camaraderie seemed to have vanished and the group had become factional. Not hostile to one another, just oddly tribal and protective of themselves. Rina and Joy sat with Tim on one side of the fireplace. Terry and Jay close by, but not quite belonging. Rav seemed to have joined forces with Robin and Viv and presently they were playing cards with Miriam, an activity Mac knew she didn't really enjoy.

Gail and Professor Franklin maintained an uneasy silence over by the window, near to one of the solid old cast-iron radiators. They could have moved to the fire, he thought, but since Rina's challenge the day before, Franklin seemed to be avoiding her. His relationship with Gail puzzled Mac, though, like Rina, he guessed they must be having some kind of an affair. He still couldn't figure out what might have drawn them together; they really didn't seem to like one another.

Melissa seemed to be avoiding everyone, staying in the kitchen as much as she could, and he was sure she had been crying. Her reaction to the discovery that Franklin was part-owner of this place also puzzled Mac. Was it simply that she felt she should know who she was actually working for? That she felt she was being spied upon? Or was her reaction more personally based than that?'

And where the hell had Toby got to? A renewed search that morning had turned up nothing.

All eyes turned to look at him as Mac entered the room.

'Inspector Chandler and his people expect to be here soon,' he said. 'But I'm afraid there's more bad news.'

'Toby?' Tim asked, concerned about his old friend, even if he felt let down.

'No, sorry, nothing on Toby. It's—'

'Simeon. They've found him, haven't they?' Gail demanded, a hysterical edge to her tone.

'I'm afraid so. They found his car when they cleared the mudslide.'

'Had he crashed?' Viv asked. 'Oh, Mac, that's dreadful. He must have been there for days.'

'It wasn't snowing when he left,' Robin reminded her. 'The mud slide hadn't happened.'

Viv's mouth formed a perfect 'o' as this sank in.

'What happened to him?' Rina asked.

'Someone caved in his skull,' Mac told them, watching closely for reactions.

'What?' Viv almost squeaked the word.

'From what I've been told, it seems that he was killed, probably by a single blow to the face. He was then probably put in his car and driven away, the car was concealed and no doubt the killer intended to move it later.'

Consternation, fear, was that guilt? Hard to tell.

'But he *left*.' No one seemed to have noticed before that Melissa had followed Mac into the room. 'I saw him leave. He went out the back way, through the coach house. I saw him go.'

'You saw him clearly?'

Melissa nodded.

'You saw his face?'

'Well . . .' She frowned. 'No. He had his coat collar pulled up, and he was walking away from me. I'd gone into the yard at the back of the kitchen to get the washing out of the dryer. I saw him walk across the lawn carrying his suitcase and with that old leather bag of his slung over his shoulder. I mean, it was getting late, nearly dark, but . . .'

'It most likely wasn't Simeon,' Mac told her.

'You mean it was whoever killed Simeon? Oh God.'

Robin got up and led her to a chair. 'Shall I get you a drink or something?'

'No, I'll be fine. Thank you though. I just can't believe all this is happening. None of it makes sense.'

Amen to that, Rina agreed silently. But there was sense hidden in amongst the chaos, of that she was certain. Or reason, then, if not sense. Edwin and Simeon were both shareholders in this place . . . and so was David Franklin. Did that make him a potential victim or a potential killer?

So, she thought, who had been here when Simeon was killed? Gail, Franklin, Melissa, Toby, Edwin and Rav. Which of them could have impersonated Simeon? Not knowing what he looked like, Rina found that hard to guess.

'How tall was he?' she asked. 'How heavily built?'

'Tall,' Gail said. 'Tallish, anyway.' She shrugged. 'Not heavily built or fat or anything, just a bit podgy round his middle and going a bit thin on top.'

Vague, Rina thought. She waited to see if anyone had more to add, but no one did. Given that kind of description, just about anyone could have passed themselves off as Simeon Meehan had they dressed in his coat and carried his bags. It could even be the stranger she had seen, heading across the lawn and towards the boundary hedge.

TWENTY-THREE

The police and CSI arrived just after two that afternoon, and Rina was aware of the sigh of relief that seemed to echo through the house. Mac spent an hour with Inspector Chandler and Miriam spoke at length to the CSI manager before both gratefully escaped to Rina's room.

'You won't be involved in the investigation?' Rina was surprised. 'I thought they'd be glad of the assistance.'

'You're forgetting, Rina. First, I am well out of my area of jurisdiction, and second, I'm still technically suspended until after the enquiry. I'm still a suspect in the killing of Thomas Peel, remember.'

'No one believes that; we all know who was actually responsible.'

'True, and if anyone was serious about me being a suspect then I probably wouldn't be here, but, well, I don't want to mess things up for Chandler. If he asks me to help out on the quiet, then I'll do it, but that's all.'

'I thought we might take a look at the attic,' Miriam said, 'and then I thought you might like to come to our room and we could go through the box of papers Melissa found when the seance room was opened up.' She smiled wickedly. 'Not that I want to be involved or anything, but, well, since we have the box, it seems silly not to look through it.'

'Oh my goodness, I'd forgotten about that with all that's been going on. Does Melissa know you have it?'

'She might do.' Miriam shrugged. 'I asked, she said it was in the office somewhere, I went and found it. Actually, Rina, I think she was a bit cagey about it. It's funny, but since you outed David Franklin and the rest as shareholders she's been very upset about something, and I don't think it's just the two deaths.'

'No, I don't think it is either. Mac, have you told this Inspector Chandler that Toby is missing?'

'I did, but I don't think he's giving it priority. Why?'

'Because I do wonder if he actually went anywhere. I mean, this is a massive house and—'

'And there are plenty of places to hide should you want to disappear for a while without going to the trouble of getting cold and wet in a snowstorm. It's falling again, by the way,' Mac said.

Rina sighed. 'I never thought I'd be sick of the sight of snow,' she said. 'But I wish it would just stop. Mac, is Chandler planning on keeping us all here?'

'I doubt it. Jay and Terry are both starting to make "do you know who I am this could ruin my reputation" noises. Not that it would, I'm sure. I think in Terry's case it would just add to the mystique, but I can understand them playing that particular card.'

'Is Chandler going to be influenced?'

Mac laughed. 'Not a chance, I'd say. I don't think he's the kind of man to be impressed by a bit of stardom. I suspect he might get Viv and Robin out of here first. After all, they only arrived a short time ago, and it's highly unlikely they are involved in any of this; there's no motive so far as I can see.'

'That's because we can't see a bloody thing at the moment,' Rina said tartly. 'No, but you're probably right, and Tim, Joy and Miriam, as well as ourselves, by the same reasoning.'

Mac nodded. 'But, as I said, I don't have any influence.'

* * *

Rina led them up the attic stairs and into the large rooms she had entered, candlestick in hand, only a couple of nights before.

'What an amazing space,' Miriam said. 'It's bigger than the boathouse.'

Rina stood on the threshold and studied the attic room. Had anyone been here since she had come to investigate the strange noises? One set of scuffmarks in the dust, she remembered from before. Then her own, lighter and smaller. Then another.

'Someone else has been here recently,' she said, pointing out the different tracks and, now she was looking more closely, the way the boxes had been moved and disturbed. Miriam had brought a compact camera with her, and she took contextual images before they went further into the room. Slowly, more methodically this time, they examined the boxes and tea chests stored there, trying to discern what the late-night visitor might have been after, but unless he was interested in tacky porcelain or books stinking of mouse urine, Rina really couldn't see what was so interesting. Unless they—whoever 'they' were—had already found whatever it was they were looking for.

Feeling rather deflated, they made their way downstairs to find a rather confused looking police officer wandering the corridors. His countenance brightened when he saw Rina.

'Mrs Martin?'

He's got it right, Rina thought, gratified. Mac's young police constable still referred to her as miss, even though she'd corrected him countless times.

'Inspector Chandler would like a word, please. Just a quick statement.'

'Any sign of Toby?' Miriam asked him.

'No, miss, sorry. We're a bit understaffed. If you'll come with me, Mrs Martin.'

Rina shrugged and obediently followed the constable down the stairs.

* * *

Inspector Chandler listened and another officer took notes as Rina explained who she was and how she came to be there and described the events that had taken place since she had arrived. He was particularly interested in the man she had spotted, and Rina knew he was seeing this as a solution to his problems. Some thief had come in, attacked people, taken whatever he had come for and gone again. And, unlikely as it might seem, he had done that twice.

She could see his point in that this was a neat and nice resolution to a ravelled and messy situation, but she truly hoped he could improve her swiftly diminishing opinion of him.

Mac would never have looked for such an easy and inelegant way out.

'Miss Perry seems very insistent that she sensed or felt Professor Meehan's presence at this so-called seance,' Chandler said, taking Rina a little by surprise. 'May I ask what you think of that?'

Rina raised an eyebrow. 'Are you asking if I believe that Gail receives messages from the dead or are you asking if I think she might be implicated in Simeon Meehan's death? I had left the others arguing and gone to bed before she made that particular announcement, anyway.'

She saw Chandler's mouth twitch as he tried not to smile. 'You're very direct, aren't you? Inspector McGregor said you would be.'

'I don't like beating round bushes. I don't see the point.'

'Right. So what do you think is going on here, Mrs Martin? What's your take on this?'

'Are you asking everyone this, or just a chosen few?'

'Well, I made the mistake of asking Miss Perry, and she offered to do a reading or some such for me; hold an intervention, whatever the . . . one of those is.'

Rina laughed. 'Inspector, we all make sense of the world in our own way. If that's what she feels will help, then of course that's what she will offer to do.'

'And you? Not into crystal balls and tea leaves?'

'No, Inspector. Only in the tea they make. I do have a thought or two though, but I don't know that you'll approve.'

'Oh and why is that?'

Rina considered the man sitting across the dining table from her. He was older than Mac, probably not far off retirement. His hair was as grey as hers, though she had the years to justify that; he did not. His eyes were brown and oddly serious even when he joked and jibed. He was, she decided, a boxer. A slugger. He'd like it direct.

'This place was bought by a so-called consortium about, what, eighteen months ago? Since then, while appearing to make plans to turn this lovely old house into a wedding venue and lord knows what else, they have done very little. Any bookings they have taken, it seems to me, have been almost accidental or at best *in*cidental to the main purpose of buying this house, and I ask you, Inspector, what group of business people buys a place like this and then, effectively, lets it stand idle, when a little care, attention and advertising could turn it into profit?' She paused and looked keenly at him, seeing that her thoughts made sense to him thus far.

She carried on. 'I think this place is a front for something, though I don't know what. I also find it interesting that the two dead men and David Franklin are shareholders in this scheme, and that the one permanent employee they have—'

'Melissa Burrows.'

'Yes, Melissa, had no idea that they were in fact her employers until yesterday. She was very put out.'

'I suppose she might well be. Anything else?'

'Yes, but it gets a bit what you might call tenuous. The other named shareholder is a Miss Grace Wright.'

'Who is not here.'

'That depends on your interpretation. Grace Wright is the name of the ghost the seance was trying to contact.'

'A ghost?' Chandler was amused. 'Mrs Martin—'

'No, I'm not about to start reading the tea leaves. Grace Wright was a supposedly invented character. The point of the seance was to reconstruct a series of events that happened here in 1872. Edwin was attempting to re-enact events, and I believe he knew more about those original events than he let on, but that's aside from the point, possibly. I'm not yet sure. I told you it got tenuous.'

He was regarding her with the air of one who is not sure how to react because he feared a wrong reaction might cause hysterics or worse. Rina wondered just how traumatic a time he'd had with Gail.

'Look,' she said. 'I don't know what's going on either, but something is, and I can't help but feel that whatever modern scam is being enacted here has its roots way back then. The motives for the killings are somehow tied up with that night.'

He leaned back in his chair and steepled long crooked fingers. 'Mrs Martin,' he said. 'I think you're way off on most of this, but we can agree on one thing. This house was never intended to be the business it's advertised as being.'

Rina nodded, finally satisfied that this man might actually be worthy of his job title. 'Anything else, Inspector?' she asked.

Chandler smiled. 'Not at the moment, Mrs Martin, but, as they say in the movies, don't leave town.'

Rina looked out of the window at the blizzard conditions beyond. 'Somehow, Inspector, I don't think any of us will be doing that tonight, do you?'

TWENTY-FOUR

Chandler had asked Rina to send Mac down to see him, and Mac found him wandering restlessly in the entrance hall, glaring out at the blizzard.

'Bad winter,' Chandler said by way of greeting. 'Makes you wonder about this global warming lark when it gets like this.'

'It's going to make it hard to move the bodies,' Mac agreed.

'Oh, I heard from the team down on the road; they just made it out before it all started again. I'm afraid poor old Edwin Holmes is going to be with us for a bit longer though. That Melissa woman is organizing accommodation for us if we get stuck here overnight—which, I'm afraid, is looking far more likely.'

'So,' Mac said. 'What can I do for you? Unofficially.'

'Unofficially, you can come into my office—Melissa's office, actually—and tell me what you think of this lot.'

Mac followed him across the tiled floor. 'I don't really know them,' he said. 'Rina, of course, and Tim and Joy, but the rest were strangers until yesterday.'

'Which gives you a full day's advantage over me. That Mrs Martin, she's a tough old bird, isn't she?'

'I'm not sure she'd like the description.'

'You don't think I'd be daft enough to say that to her face, do you?' Chandler laughed. 'Actually, I think she's shrewd. Now, what about the others? You say you know Tim Brandon and Joy Duggan? Sit yourself down,' he said as they arrived at the office, 'and I'll make a brew. You're not a coffee man, are you?'

Mac said that he was not. He hoped Chandler would accept him vouching for his friends and that the enquiries would not become too personal. Joy's father had been a well-known hard man, a career criminal. Mac had actually been inclined to like him, but, well, you would have to understand the circumstances to understand that, and he really didn't feel like explaining. As Rina had pointed out, something wasn't right here, and he didn't want this man leaping to false conclusions just because of Joy's dead father.

'I've known them all for about a year,' he glossed. 'Since I moved to Frantham.'

'Odd move, that.' Chandler cocked his head and observed Mac carefully.

'I'm sure you've read all about me,' Mac said. 'So can we just get a few things out of the way? Yes, I'd been on the sick for a long time. Yes, I'm fine now. And yes, Frantham is meant to be one of those places they put people out to grass, but I happen to like the place and it's been far from slow since I got there.'

Unexpectedly, Chandler laughed, and Mac decided that he would probably let things rest. For now.

'As I understand it, only Tim Brandon from your lot has any connection to the other guests, anyway,' Chandler said.

'To Toby Thwaite, yes. They were at university together.'

'And Mr Brandon, Miss Duggan and Mrs Martin all arrived here on Friday afternoon.'

'Yes.'

'So, presumably, are out of the running for killing Professor Meehan. Right, so who does that leave us with? He was last seen on New Year's Day at about three in the afternoon. That's if you discount the sighting of him leaving about an hour after that.'

'Melissa saw someone she assumed was Meehan crossing the lawn and going to get his car. Safe to assume, I suppose, that it wasn't him.'

'And this man your Mrs Martin has spotted?'

'Rina didn't think it was one of the guests.'

'And that this outsider might have killed Meehan?'

Mac thought about it. 'Possible,' he said. 'But the coincidence of Simeon Meehan and then Edwin Holmes both being killed is a little bit of a—well, we should be looking inside the house first. That's what I feel, anyway.'

'Given the weather, I think you're right. For the moment at least. Soon as this lot clears we get people out to the estate cottages, see if there's any evidence of this mysterious stranger.'

'You know the estate well?'

'I've lived this way all my life. Constable Brown knows it better, though. His mum and dad used to work here. He grew up not a mile across the fields. When this place changed hands about five years ago, everyone got their notices to quit. The cottages were tied to the job, you see. You don't get that happening in many places now, but some of the big farms and old estates still haven't made it into the past century, never mind this one.'

'Five years ago? I thought the present owners bought it more recently. Oh,' he said, recalling something Rina had told him, 'it was a country house hotel or something, wasn't it?'

'Run by morons,' was Chandler's opinion.

'But didn't they need staff? What was it before, then?'

'Believe it or not it was a horticultural training college. The gardens were bloody fantastic.'

'So, what happened?'

'They leased the place. The company that owned the lease refused to renew. The place stood empty for a year, and then the hotel lot moved in, started ripping the place apart, lost money, moved out, this lot arrived with full fanfare, promising to employ local people and turn this into some kind of five-star wedding venue.' Chandler laughed derisively.

'From what I've seen, it could work.'

'Could, but where's the investment? Where's the staff? Where's the local jobs? Anyway, before the gardeners it was a private school. Constable Brown's parents worked for them too. Before that, long before, it was leased by a family who used it mainly for summers, Christmases and entertaining their friends. Brown's grandparents worked for them.'

'It must have been a wrench to leave,' Mac commented.

Chandler nodded. 'But the odd thing is, no one has actually owned this place since old Albert Southam's time. It's been a lease, managed by some trust or other. Then, suddenly, they up and sell. More than a century and a half after old Albert died, and suddenly the place is for sale.'

'Could there have been some legal reason? Some codicil of the will?'

'Who knows? Anyway, this lot take over, all big plans, and open up Albert's room, and suddenly we've got bodies all over the place.'

Mac was laughing. 'I'd never have taken you for a superstitious man.'

'And I'm not. I just don't like that kind of coincidence. It's got to mean something, that's what I think.'

'Hang on,' Mac said. '*Albert's* room? Why do you call the seance room that?'

'Everyone who knows Aikensthorpe calls it Albert's room. There were silly rumours that he died there. Locked himself in and shot himself, according to some of the stories. He was poisoned by a servant, according to another. Died of grief after his wife left him or he heard his daughter had died, according to others. Actually, he died in his bed. Nothing more dramatic than pneumonia, I understand.'

'Just a minute,' Mac interrupted. 'Daughter?'

'Rumour is Elizabeth was pregnant when she took off for Italy.' Chandler shrugged. 'Who knows? The fact is this house is not a settled place. It's a sad old pile—and now this.'

'You sound as though you think some places attract tragedy,' Mac observed.

Chandler just shrugged again. 'So,' he said. 'Who do we have in a position to kill Simeon Meehan on January first?'

'Well, as I understand it, Gail Perry and David Franklin. Melissa, of course. Edwin Holmes, I suppose, though from what you've told me the blow took considerable force.'

'And Edwin was killed shortly after,' Chandler said.

'But different MO. His killer asphyxiated him.'

'Obvious method, maybe, seeing as the old boy was asleep. He'd have been an easy target. Plus, if it hadn't been for your sharp eyed girl, it might well have been passed off as natural causes. He was under the doctor, had a heart condition.'

'True. There was also Rav Pinner here over New Year. That's it, I think,' Mac said.

'That's where you're wrong. It seems Toby Thwaite and the kid, Robin Hill, were here too. They'd called in to do some of the set-up and get a first look at the room.'

'I didn't know that.' Mac was thoughtful. 'I don't think Tim or Rina knew that either. So, who admits to seeing Simeon last? Melissa's sighting apart, of course.'

'Well, Melissa also says she went up to speak to him before he left. She was worried, she says, because he'd had rather a lot to drink at lunch and she wasn't sure he should be driving. He apparently told her he was fine and that it was none of her business. Rav Pinner says he passed Simeon's room on his way down; Melissa was just leaving, and he spoke to Simeon briefly. Then he went for a walk.'

'And the others?'

'Well, they're keen on tramping about the countryside, this lot. David Franklin also reckons he went out. Gail Perry was in her room—meditating, apparently.' Chandler rolled his eyes. 'Boy, but she's a funny one.'

Mac smiled, but said nothing.

'Melissa then retreated to the kitchen; Edwin sat in the library and read.'

'The library? So he might have seen Simeon leaving. Or rather, whoever was posing as Simeon.'

Chandler steepled his fingers and tapped the tips together slowly. He had very bony, crooked fingers, Mac thought. 'He might indeed, and if he did, he might have seen the face or noticed something Melissa couldn't see from the back.'

'And Toby and Robin?'

'Might have been in the back room, Albert's room, talking about camera angles, or they might have been in the kitchen with Melissa, or they might have been exploring the house.'

Mac raised an eyebrow.

'Quite,' Chandler said. 'Toby not being here, we have only Robin's recollection of events, and he is, shall we say, somewhat vague. The only thing they can all agree on is they had tea at four and that Rav was late getting to it.'

'And Simeon, or someone dressed as Simeon, was seen leaving at three. The car was driven away. How far is it back across the field?'

'Too far and too uphill. The timing is too tight. Me or the lad, Constable Brown, we could probably do it. But we know the lie of the land and where you can cut across. A stranger—'

'We're *assuming* everyone here is a stranger.'

'True. We're also assuming Melissa got the time right. Half an hour earlier, gloomy weather, half dark outside—'

'And that would give someone time?'

'Well, they might be a bit late back for high tea, but I'd say so. Yes.'

TWENTY-FIVE

When Mac wandered back upstairs a while later it was to find that his bedroom had been invaded. Joy and Miriam knelt on the bed, spreading documents and newspaper cuttings, while Rina and Tim had taken some of them over to the dressing table and seemed to be trying to collate them.

He reported back what Chandler and he had discussed.

'Toby and Robin were here? I didn't realize that. Do you think it's relevant?' Tim said.

Tim looked hopeful that Mac would say no, but Mac didn't think he could. 'Possibly. It's worth having a word with Viv and Robin together, see if they can add anything not in the statement. I've noticed that Viv is good at helping Robin get his thoughts in order.'

'Toby and Viv had a real set-to the night of the seance,' Joy said. 'She really doesn't like him.'

'I'll bear that in mind. What are you doing, anyway?'

'Trying to put all of this in some kind of order. Did you know Elizabeth had a baby?' Miriam said.

'As of about fifteen minutes ago. Yes. Chandler says she died?'

'Nothing about that here. She was born seven months after Elizabeth left. There's a letter here to Albert, telling him he has a daughter, but it isn't from Elizabeth. But here's the thing, Mac, she called the baby Grace.'

'Edwin is supposed to have based the ghost on a real person,' Joy said. 'What if he deliberately based her on Elizabeth and Albert's child?'

That seemed logical. 'What else do you have there?' he asked, eyeing the newspaper clippings and foxed papers they had unearthed. 'Was all of this found in the seance room?'

'In the deed box Melissa is supposed to have found just inside the door, yes.'

'You don't think she did?'

'I don't know. We're trying to piece the story together. Melissa was right, though. This stayed in the news for months.'

'So, what happened then?'

'So far as we can make out—' Tim was shuffling papers on the dressing table—'it started with that death of the gamekeeper. It was supposed to be accidental, but there were rumours that his wife had been in a relationship with a man called Rico Spinelli. He was a vicar or something, but he held seances, and Mrs Creedy, that's the gamekeeper's wife, is supposed to have been involved. Creedy is reported to have spoken Spinelli's name before he died and there's the inference that if the shooting wasn't accidental then Spinelli might have done it. Anyway, Albert Southam heard the rumours and brought in a private detective to investigate, but he wasn't able to get to the bottom of it. Albert Southam then seems to have taken care of the widow and her children, and she lived in a cottage on the estate.'

'Then there's this George Weston person. He's the estate manager,' Joy said. 'He more or less took over after Elizabeth left and Albert seems to have gone to pieces. When Albert died, George Weston goes missing with a large amount of cash and some diamonds. Or at least, they go missing at the same time he does.'

'Then this place is leased out,' Rina added. 'Neither Elizabeth nor the daughter ever seem to have come back here.'

'It was still being leased until about five years ago,' Mac said. 'Chandler says it had never been sold until the people who tried to start the hotel bought it. He says he thinks there was some kind of trust administering the place. It's a terrifically long time for something like that to continue, don't you think?'

'Nothing about Aikensthorpe is what you'd expect,' Rina said quietly. 'My question, I suppose, is what happened to Elizabeth and Grace?'

'And why did she leave, and why did Edwin model his ghost on her?' Joy wanted to know.

'All very interesting,' Mac said. 'But the questions we need to be asking right now are who killed Simeon Meehan and Edwin Holmes and where on earth has your friend Toby got to? More to the point, is the killer still here? Most likely, I'd have said. In which case, does he have anyone else he wants to be rid of?'

* * *

The CSI team had been roaming the house, fingerprinting and taking photographs. Miriam showed them the attic rooms, and Melissa found an old map of the Aikensthorpe Estate and the cottages the farm workers and other employees had used over the years.

Finally, with the darkness closing in somewhere behind the white-out, they had to concede nothing more could be done that night. Jay and Rina helped Melissa set out a buffet in the dining room and find bedding and spare mattresses for the unfinished bedrooms so that people could camp out in relative comfort. No one said much; the police presence, small as it was, seemed to intimidate everyone—that, and the constant reminder of Edwin's body still lying upstairs, though enclosed now in a white sheet and body bag, ready to be moved. Although the police presence should have spelt security for the other guests, Rina felt that it just intensified the sense of threat. There was a murderer among them, and no one but the killer themselves knew who.

Rina found she was examining everyone with unwarranted closeness. Was the bracelet on Rav's wristwatch sharp enough to have caused the scratches on Edwin's neck? Was Gail's psychic persona just an act after all? Could Melissa be tempted to put something unpleasant in the food? (Unlikely, as she tasted everything she prepared, but still.)

Mentally, Rina gave herself a good shaking and an even better telling off.

She was lucky; there were people here she knew unquestionably that she could trust. Could any of the others now feel the same way?

* * *

No one had yet spoken to Robin and Viv about New Year's Day, and when Viv waved rather pathetically as Rina entered the dining room, she decided that now would be a good moment to try.

'Do you want anything more?' she called as she helped herself from the buffet.

Viv shook her head. Robin was pushing food around on his plate, but didn't seem to be eating, so Rina assumed a no from him too. She joined them at one end of the long table. Miriam was chatting to the CSIs at the other; their conversations seemed to be about a television series rather than work, Rina was relieved to note. She didn't think Viv was up to forensic conversations over the supper table.

'How are you holding up?' she asked.

'I was doing OK until I called my mum,' Viv said. 'She's all anxious and fussed, and that set me off.'

'She's bound to be,' Rina said. 'Have you called your family, Robin?'

'I . . .'

'Robin doesn't really have family,' Viv said.

'I'm sorry to hear that.'

'Oh, it's OK,' Robin said. 'My mum died when I was young. Dad remarried, and I didn't get on with his new wife.

I went to uni and sort of moved out completely. We don't really talk now.'

'That's sad,' Rina said.

He shrugged. 'It happens. My half-sister is planning on going to uni next year. She phoned me and asked advice. That was nice. I like Fliss.'

He didn't seem to want to pursue this topic, so Rina introduced her own. 'You were here with Toby at New Year, I understand.'

Robin nodded. 'Just for the afternoon. I'd been at Viv's for New Year's Eve. Toby said we should drive up to see the place. Viv wasn't keen, so I came up with him on my own.'

'It's a long drive from London, isn't it? Just for a few hours?'

'Not really. Well, it is, but we were going back to uni then anyway. Toby had been down in London visiting friends or something; he said he'd give me a lift, and it saved on train fares. Viv came up the next day.' He grinned suddenly and unexpectedly. The smile transformed his face. 'She was too hung-over to drive up with us, anyway,' he added.

'Was not! Well, maybe, yeah, but it was a good night, wasn't it?'

'I spent the holiday with Viv's family,' Robin said. 'Christmas and New Year. It was nice being with people.'

Rina nodded sympathetically. 'Robin, what was the mood like that afternoon? We know Simeon had quarrelled with everyone, but it would be good to hear an outside view.'

Robin thought about it, nudging the food on his plate with the tines of his fork. 'We didn't really get to talk to anyone except Melissa and Edwin,' he said. 'Or, at least, I didn't. Melissa was nice, she showed us the seance room and made sure we had a sandwich before we headed off. Edwin was lovely. He came with me into the room, and we talked about camera angles and so on, and then we went back into the library. He said he'd found some books he wanted to use in his new research. Then he laughed and said he was probably being a bit ambitious, planning another book at his age, but that he couldn't seem to break the habit. I liked him. I can't understand how anyone would want to kill someone old like that.'

It happened all the time, Rina thought. 'What was Toby doing while you were in the seance room?'

Robin shrugged. 'I don't know. I left him in the kitchen with Melissa. He came and checked what I'd decided, but I did the main survey.'

Rina nodded, recalling the impression she'd had at the start of their stay that Toby and Melissa knew one another well already. 'Did Toby give you any indication he wanted to leave here before he vanished?'

Viv and Robin looked at one another. 'No, not really,' Viv said.

'You don't like him very much, do you?'

Viv wrinkled her nose. 'It was like he thought he was God,' she said.

'Thought?'

'Yeah.' She didn't seem to have noticed her own change to past tense. 'When I asked if he'd be my supervisor for the MA, he was like, well, of *course* you're going to ask me, I'm the best. Then when I got more involved with him, you know, he got kind of like—' She looked at Robin.

'Possessive,' he said.

'He's been better since we came here,' she added, changing back to present without a blink. 'Or at least he was, then he started acting like we were all, well . . . Like he was too good for all of us. I can't make him out.'

Robin nodded. 'Viv had a row with him, said she didn't want him to be her supervisor.'

'It's pointless, of course. I'm much too far through to switch to anyone else, but he made me so mad, just the way he talks to everyone.'

'I hope he's OK,' Robin said quietly. 'I mean, where's he gone?'

They both looked at Rina as though she might be able to provide the answer. Where indeed, Rina thought. And was he still all right? She doubted that very much.

TWENTY-SIX

Rina had locked her doors that night and been glad that Mac and Miriam were literally next door. Mac and Chandler had insisted that no one be alone, and he'd included the CSI and his own people in that directive. Melissa had reluctantly agreed to share her room with two of the female CSIs, and Constable Brown had bedded down with the crime-scene manager. The degree of paranoia had seemed to increase exponentially through the evening, and by the time Rina finally made it to her room, she had practically been twitching.

'Pull yourself together, woman,' she had told herself sternly and allowed a moment of amusement that no one had suggested *she* required company that night.

Morning brought clarity. Bright skies clear of threatening snow clouds, frozen ground; the layer of frost clearly visible overlaying the covering of snow. Clarity of mind, too, Rina thought, waking with the—probably unfounded—sense that today would bring solutions. Unfounded or not, it made her feel better.

Over breakfast, Chandler divided them into search teams: a police officer or CSI as lead and the rest allocated to one of four groups. The hope was that the roads would be clear again by midday and Edwin's body could finally be moved.

By half past eight, decked out in warm clothes and borrowed wellingtons, Rina was with her assigned group, led by DI Chandler himself, and joined by Rav they set off across the fields towards Aikensthorpe woods on a search for any sign of Toby.

'Virgin snow,' Rav said. 'Just bird tracks and fox footprints. At least the sky has cleared.'

'For now, anyway,' Rina said.

'Do you think we'll find him?'

'I think if Toby had simply up and gone, he would have had the grace to call someone and tell them that's what he'd done. Tim, if no one else. Tim would not have judged him. Toby knows that.'

'You think he's dead.'

'I think that's crossed everybody's mind. None of us want to put it into words, that's all.'

Rav nodded, then said wryly, 'I'm sort of surprised, then, that Gail hasn't claimed to have sensed it.'

'There's still time. No, that's unkind—and disrespectful too.'

'I'm sorry.'

'For what? It amused me too. We can be bad people together.'

Rav laughed aloud at her comment, and Chandler, a few paces ahead, looked quizzically at Rina.

'Where are we headed?' she asked.

'To the tower. We can start there. There's a bit of an underground thing there too, like a crypt; that's if we can still get into it. The roof was coming down last time I looked.'

'Tower?' Probably the ruins Tim had spotted.

'An old church, don't know what period. I think it was from the big house that was here before Aikensthorpe was built. The house burned down in the civil war, so I'm told. Then there was a small hunting lodge type of thing that got turned into the Dower house later. It's been boarded up for the past few years, but it used to belong to the headmaster when this was a school and was offices when this place was a college. The church was left to fall down, and the tower is about all that's left of it.'

Rina tried to recall what the map had looked like. 'Where have the other groups gone?'

'One search team to the three workers' cottages over on the other side; one to the cottage and barn down towards the main road; and the third team is looking at all the outbuildings.'

'We searched those already,' Rina objected.

'You may have done, but it doesn't hurt to look again with a different eye.'

Rina couldn't argue with that. They had reached the woods now, skirting the edge. The going was difficult, deep snow and cold air making it slow and wearing. When the tower came into view, Rina was surprised by its height and solidity. Definitely not a folly, she thought. This was much older.

Chandler paused, and the others gathered round him, suddenly anxious about what they might find.

Chandler called out: 'Toby. Toby Thwaite, are you here? Can you hear me?' He glanced round sheepishly at the others as it dawned on all of them that there would be no answer. If Toby had come to this grim place and had been able to return to the house then he would have done so, not remained here in such bitter, unforgiving weather. Had he been alive, but unable to make it back to Aikensthorpe, then the chances were he could not have survived the two intervening days. He would have frozen out here.

'Right, go slowly,' Chandler instructed.

Suddenly reluctant, Rina followed Rav towards the tower.

'You think he might be here?' Rav asked.

'I don't know.' Chandler had moved towards a broken wall; she saw him sweep snow aside from what looked like the top of a narrow flight of steps.

'No one's been here,' Rina said. 'Look.'

The wooden door had been padlocked. The padlock was so heavily rusted that it must have been years since anyone had entered the tower. She tugged at it just in case, and the hasp pulled free from the wooden door-frame; the padlock refused to budge.

Rav pushed at the door. It creaked and groaned, and the hasp gave way completely, cracking part of the wooden frame. The door itself was frozen to the stone floor. Knowing it was a pointless exercise, but nonetheless caught up in the moment, the act of actually doing something, Rina helped as Rav leaned against the rotten timber. It gave with a sharp crack, and they both fell forward. Rav caught Rina's arm as she almost fell.

'Everyone OK?' Chandler called to them. 'Can you see anything down there?'

'We're fine,' Rav said. 'But the way in is completely blocked. Rocks and snow and an old bird's nest.'

Chandler tramped over to them. Rina peered into the tower herself, examining the small, circular room with a flagstone floor and drifts of autumn leaves pushed back against the walls. That isn't right, Rina thought. She withdrew her head and looked again at the padlock and the hasp and staple it secured, recalling how the hasp had torn away from the frame when Rav had shoved at the door. She could see now that the screws which should have held it fast had been exchanged for smooth, short nails, enough to fool the casual observer into thinking the door was secure. Enough, indeed, to fool the not so casual observer, but in fact very easy to lever out and thence to open the door.

'Look,' she said. 'And look inside. The door was open long enough for leaves to collect inside. The roof must be reasonably intact, the floor is dry. But you'd expect the leaves to have been blown just inside the door, maybe against this closest wall, not—'

'Swept to the back. Scuff marks on the floor. Something was kept here. Recently.'

Chandler examined the lock, coming to the same conclusion as Rina. He was about to comment further when his phone began to ring. It was one of the other search teams reporting in. They had found Toby. It was not good news.

TWENTY-SEVEN

Mac went with Chandler to the cottage where Toby's body had been found. The windows had been boarded up, but inside some of the furniture remained. Kitchen table and a couple of chairs, an old sofa in the living room. Someone had brought in a camping stove, and a half-dozen tins of food had been lined up beside it, together with a small kettle and a battered saucepan. There was evidence of a fire recently lit in the living room fireplace.

'Wouldn't anyone have seen the smoke?' Mac asked.

'I doubt it,' Chandler said. 'The barn blocks the view from the road, and the cottage is in a dip; you can't see it at all from the house. You didn't even know it was here, did you?'

Mac had to agree that they had not. 'Who would want to stay here?'

'Rina's stranger?' Chandler suggested.

Toby's body lay on the hall floor. He was very cold and very dead. Blood congealed on his temple and matted his hair. It had pooled beneath his head, testament to the fact that he had lived long enough to bleed for a time after the blow had landed.

The floor was tiled and chill, and the air frosted as Mac breathed out. 'Time of death? Best guess?'

'Best guess on body temp is at least twenty-four hours. We can hope our friends the flies can give us a more accurate account, though I reckon it's too cold even for them to be out. Potassium decay in the eyes might help, but, again, time and chill are not on our side.'

'Toby went missing the day after the seance. No one saw him after lunch, but we only noticed he had gone later that afternoon,' Mac said. 'He ate lunch.'

'Analysis of stomach contents might help then.' Chandler sighed. 'We both knew this is what we'd find.'

'Sir?' Constable Brown beckoned them into the living room. 'You should see this.' He pointed to where the crime-scene manager was photographing a little pile of plastic. 'We think it's from a video camera. The LCD screen.'

'No sign of the rest of it, I suppose? No memory card carelessly dropped by a fleeing assailant? No? Pity. It means he was filming something, though.'

'Toby's room was at the back of the house, looking out this way. Maybe he saw someone and followed them here.'

'Your Mrs Martin's mystery man, maybe. Right, let's get back to the house. Let the mortuary ambulance know it's got another passenger.'

* * *

Back at Aikensthorpe, Rina was dealing with a hysterical Melissa.

'No! Not Toby, not Toby, not Toby.'

Screams gave way to sobs, and Rina wrapped her arms around the younger woman, shushing and soothing and finally convincing her to sit down and drink the tea Joy had brought for her. Miriam had gone off to see if she could be useful, and Tim and Joy were now with Rina and Melissa in the little room she used as her office. Tim stood helplessly by the door while Joy perched on the desk, not quite knowing what to do for the best. Tim was horribly shocked; Melissa something far deeper.

'You knew him well, didn't you?' Rina said gently.

'We're cousins. Toby said best not let on.'

'Why?'

Melissa shrugged.

'Melissa, someone killed Toby, probably the same person who murdered Edwin and Professor Meehan. Whatever you're hiding has got to be brought out into the open before someone else gets hurt. It isn't going to end here.'

Tears began to flow again, and Rina did not try to stop them. Sometimes people just needed to be allowed to cry.

Joy stood with Tim now, not saying anything, just holding his hand and looking at Melissa with deep compassion. Joy knew what loss felt like.

'Why did you come to work here?' Rina asked.

Melissa shrugged. 'I just thought, I mean, we've all grown up knowing about this place. I used to drive up here, just to look at it. When the job came up, it seemed perfect. When I got here it was all as if . . . It just felt right.'

'Why, Melissa? What is this place to you?'

She sighed and slumped back into her chair. 'It sounds so stupid when you say it out loud, but I used to fantasize about it. You know the way kids do. That one day they'll marry a prince and live in a big castle?'

A small bell rang in Rina's mind. What was it Rav had said about Melissa when they had all been planning to leave? The poor princess, alone in her castle.

'But why this place?' Joy asked.

'Because a long time ago it belonged to our family. It was home.'

'You're related to the Southams?' Tim asked.

Melissa nodded. 'Elizabeth and Albert had a daughter. She never lived here. Her name was—'

'Grace,' Rina said.

'Yes. How did . . . ? She was born in Italy, but eventually she came back to England and married Theodore Wright. Grace Wright was my great, great grandmother.'

TWENTY-EIGHT

'We were as close as brother and sister when we were kids,' Melissa said. 'The whole family knew about this house and what had happened. It had become mythic, and we lapped it up. It was all so romantic. Toby and I, we'd talk about getting the house back and living here. No one ever thought we would, that was just impossible, but we dreamed about it.

'Once, my dad brought us both here. It was a horticultural college then, and the gardens were open in the summer so we came to look at our house. It was so beautiful. We found out later that Albert Southam had set up some kind of trust fund, just in case his daughter came home. No one else was allowed to buy Aikensthorpe, even after he died. It could be leased or rented, but Grace was the real owner—and Grace was our ancestor.' She laughed weakly.

'So, when you came to work here?'

'I loved it. I just had to look after the place, supervise the renovations and take bookings at first. Then we started to get a few weddings, and I really thought we could make a go of it. I started to look for local caterers and staff, but the solicitor that handled everything said the owners only wanted this one catering firm to be used. I mean, they were good, but I knew if I shopped around I could get a better deal and maybe support local companies.'

'So you got suspicious?' Chandler asked.

'Not at first. Then, I don't know, it seemed a bit odd. The caterers would arrive with more vans than they needed, more people than I saw actually working in the marquees. Toby was over here for one weekend when we'd got a wedding on, and he filmed some of the so-called security staff. I mean, who needs security staff here? He called me up a week later and said he knew who they were, but I shouldn't say anything. He said I should resign, but it was all getting a bit more complicated.'

'In what way?' Mac asked.

'You were stealing from the estate, weren't you?' Rina asked.

'How did—?' Melissa nodded. 'Yes.'

'Stealing what?' Mac asked.

Chandler fixed Rina with a curious look before turning his attention back to Melissa.

'Books, mostly. The library had been left intact. It was a condition of the lease, just like it said we had to leave Albert's old study closed up. Apparently, when the place was leased, an inventory had been taken, and every couple of years the trustees would send someone up to check. When the place was eventually sold, that stopped, of course, but the Prices, who tried to run the hotel, they'd not bothered with the library. To them it was just quaint, atmospheric. Anyway, they left, the consortium took over. I came to work here, and Toby and I thought, hell, this should all have been ours anyway, so I started selling the odd book and other bits that the Southams, my ancestors, had left behind.'

'What did you do with the money?'

She hesitated. 'Toby had a gambling problem,' she said. 'He was in debt to some really nasty people.'

'Who knew the people who were doing whatever is going on here.' Joy sounded oddly wearied by the inevitability.

Chandler's attention shifted to her now.

'What?' she said. 'Networking doesn't just go on with legitimate business, you know.'

'I know that,' he said caustically. 'I'm surprised that you do.'

Joy fixed him with a steady gaze. 'My dad was Jimmy Duggan,' she said. 'I'm guessing you've been a policeman long enough to know all about him.'

Chandler said nothing, but Rina could hear the cogs whirring.

'So,' Joy went on. 'I'm guessing you found yourselves being blackmailed into being cooperative?'

Melissa nodded. 'Toby was scared. But we were told that if I kept on running this place the way I'd been doing then they'd turn a blind eye.'

'And the strange man I saw leaving two nights in a row?'

Melissa looked away. 'He didn't kill anyone. His name is Clive Harding, and he's a dealer in antique books. I'd let him come in to see the library, and we'd found some stuff in the attics I thought might interest him so he came in to have a look around. I know it was stupid. It was a risk he'd be seen, but Toby was up to his neck. I had to do something.'

'The casino had increased his credit limit,' Joy guessed.

'How did you know?'

'It's obvious,' Joy said. 'They drag you in deeper, and you have to do more just to keep from drowning.'

She sounded sad, and Tim put an arm around her shoulders and hugged her tight. Joy had loved her father; he'd been a good dad, whatever else he was, and Rina knew it must be hard for her to have to look at Melissa's situation and know how her father would have acted in similar circumstances.

'Jimmy Duggan was almost legitimate by the time he died,' Rina said. 'He was a businessman.'

Chandler snorted his disbelief, but Joy smiled briefly, gratefully.

'So, what do you think they were moving?' Mac asked.

'My guess would be drugs,' Melissa said. 'One group of catering vans would deliver, and then when the lorry came back—to collect the marquee and the tables and such—the boxes the caterers had unloaded would be picked up at the same time.' She shrugged. 'I don't know any more than that. I didn't want to know.'

'It's a good front,' Chandler said. 'A legitimate business, vehicles moving to and fro that no one is going to think twice about. And a safe place for storage should they need to hold stock back.'

'And then you find out that Edwin and David Franklin and Simeon are all shareholders, and that they were using Grace's name as well.'

She nodded. 'I liked Edwin. I trusted him. I never thought—'

'No wonder you were so shocked. Melissa, it's possible they don't know what's going on. Or that Edwin didn't, anyway.'

Melissa looked hopefully at Rina and then at Joy.

'The other shareholder is a company called Reality Enterprises,' Rina said. 'Then four individuals who may or may not have been involved with this. Melissa, how long had you known Edwin for?'

She thought about it. 'A year, maybe. He came here to see about setting up the experiment last winter. We'd started to advertise Aikensthorpe as a venue, and he'd got to hear about it. He was interested because of the Southam seance.'

'And so you saw him, how often?'

'A half-dozen times, I suppose. Sometimes he'd stay over. I told him why I wanted to be here, about the family connection, about the stories we were told when we were kids about there being an updated will hidden in the library, all that stupid stuff.' She smiled sadly. 'I never believed it, but it was a nice idea, you know?'

'I know,' Rina said gently. 'But did you confide in him about anything else?'

Melissa hesitated. 'Yes,' she said at last. 'I was scared. Toby said he owed so much money and he was being threatened. Edwin was looking for a particular book in the library.'

'But you'd sold it.'

'Yes. I don't know, somehow it all came out. He seemed so shocked.'

'Do you think he told anyone else?' Mac asked her.

She shook her head, and then nodded. 'I think he might have told Simeon. Everything was fine, and then suddenly Simeon was rowing with everyone and threatening to leave and telling Edwin that the whole experiment had been ruined.'

'So, perhaps Simeon knew, and they had arranged for the disagreement so that he had an excuse for leaving,' Rina wondered. 'I suppose we can't ever be certain.'

'But as a working theory . . .' Chandler agreed. 'If he and Edwin had decided this needed reporting.'

'I told him in confidence.' Melissa was hurting.

'And he confided in his old friend,' Joy said thoughtfully. 'And someone must have realized, or overheard, but whichever, it cost both of them their lives. Toby too.'

Melissa began to cry again.

TWENTY-NINE

The mortuary ambulance had arrived, along with another scientific support van to continue processing the scene. The original CSI team had left gratefully, and only Chandler and Constable Brown remained, though new bodies had been promised to relieve them and a mobile incident room was supposed to be en-route.

'Good luck with that one,' Mac said, thinking about the route it would have to take to get to Aikensthorpe.

'I love an optimist,' Chandler agreed. He shrugged resignedly. 'No one's worried about us getting home, just about the number of overtime hours we'll be claiming for.'

Mac laughed. 'No one actually *gets* them,' he said. 'It'll be Time Off In Lieu, which you'll never actually manage to take.'

'Ah, but you're a cynical man.'

Rina had brought Melissa through to the main hall. She had ceased to cry, but her face was pale and her eyes red rimmed.

'So, when can we leave?' Terry Beal wanted to know.

'Soon,' Chandler soothed. 'We need to take statements and—'

'Oh, please. We've done all that. There's nothing you can do to keep us here.' David Franklin sounded bored.

'Charge us or let us go, isn't that what they say on the television?' He seemed ready for the applause, but it never came.

'Professor Franklin. Three people are dead,' Chandler said. 'Now, my colleagues and a mobile incident room will be arriving shortly. I ask you all to be patient for just a little longer.'

'We should be going while there's a break in the weather,' Jay Stratham objected. 'Some of us just stumbled into this situation. You can't really be serious about suspecting us.'

'Just a little patience,' Chandler said again, and Jay gestured annoyance but sat down beside Rina.

'Some of us have to be elsewhere.' David Franklin again. 'We are expected back at work.'

'I don't imagine you're the only ones unable to make it in,' Chandler said. 'This weather is countrywide—and there's more to come, apparently.'

A collective groan from the company.

'I used to like snow,' Jay said. 'OK, so what more do you want to know, and when are the reinforcements going to arrive? I don't know about anyone else, but I'd feel a lot happier if we had a few more neutral bodies around.'

Rina saw the general exchange of glances and knew that none of them actually wanted to say it out loud, so she took the task upon herself. 'You mean, it's becoming increasingly obvious that one of us might be a murderer.'

David Franklin started to protest, but Jay nodded. 'Look, I'm sorry, but what else are we supposed to think, and surely it's better to get that thought out into the open? I don't mind admitting, I'm pretty spooked by the whole idea.'

'Scared rigid,' Terry Beal confessed readily, though he looked anything but. 'But frankly I'm also not happy about driving out of here in that.' He pointed to the window. The snow had returned, suddenly and vehemently, a solid, muffling curtain of white through which it was impossible to see anything.

'Well, I suppose that settles that,' Jay conceded. 'So, what do we do, all sit here and watch one another? Split into groups and assign a police officer to each one?'

No one responded. Rina surveyed the collection of glum expressions and made up her mind that she'd had enough of sitting there. She got up and headed for the library. A moment or so later, Jay followed her.

'Mind if I join you?'

She glanced back at him. 'May I ask why?'

'Because I'm bored to tears and you look like a woman on a mission.'

'Can I come too, or is three a crowd?' Terry Beal stuck his head around the orangery door.

'Feel free, but I'm warning you both, there's lifting to be done.'

'Better than sitting around staring at one another or listening to platitudes,' Jay said.

'Or listening to David and Gail bickering,' Terry added. 'Or Melissa crying. I'm sorry, that sounds cruel.'

'No, it sounds human,' Rina told him. 'We can overdose on the grief of others very rapidly. It doesn't make us bad people, just people who are made for doing and not for comforting.'

Terry laughed out loud at that. 'Ah, Rina,' he said. 'I've seen you in comforting mode, and very good you are too, so don't try and play the hard-man card, that's my job. Right,' he said, rubbing his hands together, 'what are we looking for?'

'I don't know,' Rina admitted. 'Probably for what is no longer here.'

* * *

Chandler had gone off to make phone calls. Constable Brown was prowling between the rear lobby and the main hall as though he felt he ought to be patrolling somewhere. Mac and Miriam had taken up residence in one corner of the main room with Tim and Joy and were sitting playing cards and talking quietly about their situation, Mac's change of career, and the logistics of Miriam moving in. Oddly, it was the practicalities of life after this was all over that seemed to occupy them most.

Gail seemed to be reading a magazine, but it was ten minutes since she had turned a page, and David Franklin was working on some papers. It looked, Mac thought, like marking, and whoever the unfortunate students were, Franklin's pen indicated dissatisfaction with their efforts.

Melissa had fallen asleep tucked up in a large wing-backed chair. People often slept when they could no longer cope with grief or stress, Mac observed. He was glad she had found a means of escape, however brief.

Rav, Viv and Robin had set-up a laptop on a coffee table and were watching a film. A small stack of DVDs sat beside it, and Mac wondered if they planned on sitting out the storm—both real and metaphorical—watching films. He could think of worse ways of coping.

No one had sought to go to their own rooms or looked for sanctuary elsewhere. It was as though, by common consent, everyone wanted to keep everyone else in view. Suspicious and yet also social in their behaviours with the reading and the card playing and DVD watching, it made for a disconcertingly surreal atmosphere.

'What's Rina up to?' Joy wondered.

'You could go and ask her.'

'If she'd wanted any of us there, she'd have said.' Joy didn't sound resentful of that fact. She laid down a card and announced that she'd won yet another hand. Mac had suggested gin rummy rather than poker, hoping it might give the rest of them some shot at victory, but so far that didn't seem to be working.

'I think she wanted to talk to Jay alone, and I don't think she minds one way or another about Terry Beal.'

'She doesn't see him as a suspect then?' Mac was amused.

'Oh, I didn't say that. I don't think she's ruled anyone out. Have you?'

'Present company excepted, no,' Mac agreed.

'Why rule out present company? We were all here for at least two of the murders.'

'True, but—'

'And we're all capable of it, aren't we?' Joy continued.

Miriam laughed. 'Are we?'

'Yes, if you think about it. If we thought someone threatened a loved one, if we thought someone might be out and out evil, then I don't believe any of us would hesitate for long. Put me in a room with the men that killed Patrick and I wouldn't promise anything.'

People often said that sort of thing, Mac observed, but he felt that Joy actually meant it, and his own actions had demonstrated his own capacity for violence and irrationality. It was not a comforting thought.

'True.' Tim nodded. 'So who tops your suspect list then?'

Joy dealt the cards again, and Mac watched carefully. If she was cheating then she was bloody good. She shrugged. 'I don't know about the murders,' she said, 'but I know at least two people here are lying about something. Don't ask me how, I just do, and I think Rina thinks so too.'

'You want to say who and what about?' Tim asked her.

'Melissa is one,' Mac guessed. 'I think David Franklin might be the other?'

Joy laughed. 'Well, he's lying to his wife, but that doesn't count, and have you actually listened to anything he's said? It's all noise and nothing. No, he's still on my suspect list, but he's not actually said enough of anything for it to count.'

'Surely Melissa wouldn't hurt Toby,' Miriam objected. 'Or this Edwin. She seemed to be fond of him.'

'I said not telling the whole truth, not killing,' Joy pointed out. 'While there's probably some overlap, motive-wise, it's not necessarily the same thing, is it?'

'No. So if you think Melissa is hiding something, then who else is on your list?' Mac asked.

Joy picked up her hand and rearranged it, then rearranged it again. 'Viv,' she said. 'I don't know why or what, and I like her and I don't think she'd kill anyone, but she's not telling us something and I think I might know what.'

* * *

Back in the library, Terry and Jay were earning their keep, taking heavy volumes down from the shelves and laying them out on the central table. It was cooler, but not cold, and Rina soon realized that heating was being channelled in through elaborate vents below the shelves.

She had told them, without revealing Melissa's part in all this, that there were suspicions some of the books had been sold. She was now trying to get some sense of what was here and what might have gone; Melissa was unable to provide them with a sensible list of titles, and the inventory Rina knew had been taken was certainly not available in the library itself.

It was obvious to Rina that the young woman had little knowledge on which to base her thefts, so who had told her what to look for? Did this book dealer she claimed had been acting on her behalf know the library and tell her what he wanted?

'You know,' Jay said. 'Being able to see this library was one of the reasons I accepted the invite.'

'Oh? And why is that?'

'Old Albert collect magic books, did he?' Terry asked.

Jay laughed. 'Actually, this has nothing to do with Albert Southam. He started collecting, true, but it was after Albert was dead and gone that things really began to get interesting.'

'You're talking about the mad scientist who rented the place after Albert's death.' Terry showed that he, too, had read Viv's notes.

'Well, mad or not, he knew his books.'

'So,' Rina said thoughtfully, surveying the volumes spread out on the table that they had identified as of special interest. Jay, it seemed, also knew his books. 'If you wanted to sell any of this collection, what would you go for?'

'Don't auction houses carry out checks? You know, make sure they're not handling stolen property?' Terry asked.

'Well, that's true,' Rina said, 'but there are always ways.'

Jay nodded. 'Sure. A book comes on to the market from a deceased collector—how is anyone going to prove it's not legitimate? Book dealers buy up collections and then go through them to see if there's anything really unusual. I know; I have three who regularly call me with items of interest, and a lot of the time it's an odd volume that's turned up amongst a whole load of mediocrity.'

'But that's not the case here,' Terry objected. 'Rina, from what you say, this collection has been inventoried often over the years.'

'Until the house was sold, yes,' Rina reminded him. 'Aikensthorpe was sold complete with contents, including this library and Albert's closed room. While the previous owners don't seem to have taken much notice of either, you couldn't prove with certainty that they'd not sold or otherwise disposed of books that had come into their possession legitimately. Anything could have been taken from the library, and provided it was filtered through legitimate channels before it came up for public sale, it would be really hard to prove that it wasn't a right and proper sale. Even if it could be traced back to Aikensthorpe, there's nothing wrong with someone who owned the house having sold the books.'

'So how come no one sold these?' Terry pointed to the volumes on the table. 'And we're still no closer to knowing what is actually missing, if anything. Rina, where did this information come from? Are you sure anything has actually been taken?'

'I'm sure,' Rina told him. 'Suffice it to say that Melissa told me. Let's leave it at that, can we?'

Jay and Terry exchanged glances, and Rina knew she didn't need to spell it out for them.

'But—' Terry began to object.

Jay waved him into silence. 'OK, we'll let that lie for the moment. Let's just assume that maybe these were considered too rare, too noticeable to shift yet. That would make a kind of sense.'

'OK.' Terry looked far from satisfied. 'So what isn't here?'

'Do either of you happen to know what Edwin was researching?'

Blank looks. 'Here?' Jay asked. 'I didn't know that he was.'

'He said he had another book planned.'

'He did,' Jay confirmed. 'But nothing here would have helped him. In fact, that's why he really wanted us to get together, what we talked about. I was going to help him with the technical stuff.'

'You're sure there would be nothing here? I mean, even if he wasn't researching for the next book, maybe he—'

Jay was shaking his head. 'Oh, I don't doubt he'd have loved this place, but he was planning on writing about a man called John Murray Spear: he was a minister and medium in the 1830s. He did early experiments with magnetism and then claimed to have built a machine that could help him speak directly to God. There's been a fair amount of research done in the States, but I've recently unearthed some schematics which no one else seems to have connected to Spear's machine. I ran the idea past Edwin, and he believed I was on to something. Edwin was going to edit the book, add a monograph of his own and the research on the new schematics, and invite others in the same field to contribute their own essays.' He laughed. 'Frankly, if we sold a few hundred copies we'd have both been happy. We'd already found a printer and someone to help us with the technical stuff, but it was never destined to be a best-seller. It's the sort of thing only geeks like us get excited about.'

'I'd have liked it,' Terry objected plaintively. Rina thought she may have done so too.

So, she thought, if Edwin hadn't needed to use the library for his own research, was he just coming for the pleasure of being among so many splendid old books? Melissa said he'd stayed about a half-dozen times this past year, carrying out his studies, that he had noticed a book missing because he needed it.

Was that true? Was Jay mistaken? Or was Melissa being economical with the truth—and if so, what did she hope to gain?

THIRTY

Melissa was still asleep when Rina and the others returned to the main room. It was four in the afternoon; the curtains were already closed against the dark, and there was still no sign of the promised incident room and accompanying officers. Twitching the drapes aside to look out, Rina could understand why.

'I'm going to make some tea and cobble some sandwiches together,' Rina announced.

'I'll come and help,' Joy said.

'I'll give you a hand too.' Viv slipped off the sofa from between Rav and Robin.

'Oh, but the film's nearly over. Shall we pause it?' Robin barely took his eyes off the screen, and Rina wondered what they had been watching.

'No, it's fine. I'll catch it later. If I don't move I'm going to set in that position.' She dropped a kiss on Robin's head and joined Rina and Joy by the door.

'Anything interesting in the library?' Joy asked. 'Do you think we should wake Melissa or let her sleep?'

'We can wake her when we've got the tea ready. As to the library, yes, it's a rather wonderful collection. You should take a look.'

She closed the kitchen door and filled the hot-water urn, set it to boil. 'I think we might as well use that rather than bother with all the kettles. Right, one of you find bread while I raid the fridge, and we'll see what cake there is left, and then, Viv, you can tell me what's on your mind.'

Joy raised an eyebrow, and Viv laughed uneasily. 'You don't let much slip past, do you?'

'I try not to.'

'Right,' Viv said. 'You see, Rina, I've got a bit of a problem.'

* * *

Chandler had called Mac into Melissa's office.

'Phone lines are down,' Mac said. 'We've still got erratic mobile coverage.'

The lights flickered, but did not completely fail. 'Not good,' Chandler said. 'I understand this place has a generator? We should sort it out. I'll send Brown and borrow your Tim.'

'I wouldn't,' Mac said. 'Tim is wonderful when it comes to modelling obscure and ancient trickery, but if it needs a spanner then you're best finding someone else. Terry's looking bored, send him.'

Chandler laughed. 'Can I trust him with my constable? He might be a suspect.'

'So if Brown gets hit over the head, we'll know who did it. What have you found out?' Chandler seemed to have spent half the afternoon on his mobile telephone.

'That I've been treated like a mushroom yet again.'

'Kept in the dark and fed shit?'

'Right.' Chandler sounded bitter.

Mac looked at him expectantly.

'This place is already under investigation. No one thought to tell us locals, of course, and what I know now you could write on the back of a fag packet.'

'Serious crimes unit?'

Chandler nodded. 'My boss tells me we've got someone on the inside. He doesn't know who, of course.'

Mac nodded; even if Chandler's boss did know, he wouldn't say. 'I suppose we should hope it wasn't Edwin, Simeon or Toby.'

'That would complicate matters.'

'Any news on the cavalry arriving?'

'Stuck in a snowdrift ten miles down the road. There's a public footpath that cuts across below the cottage and the barn where we found Toby. If anyone can get through that far, they'll walk the rest of the way over the fields.' Chandler didn't look hopeful.

'Up to us then.'

'So it would seem. Right, let's get Brown on to the generator and find the candles, just in case. We should make sure everyone charges their mobiles while we've still got electric and get out extra blankets.'

'Blankets?'

'If the power goes out, the generator will take care of essentials, but the rest of the house is going to be very cold and very dark.'

* * *

Using Melissa's old tea trolley, Rina and the others took food through to the main hall. They had met PC Brown and Terry in the hallway going off to sort the generator, and Melissa—awake now, if a little vague—had been dispatched with helpers to find quilts and blankets.

'Do you think the power really will go out?' Gail looked scared.

'We should be prepared, and we should all stay together,' Chandler said. 'Round here most of the lines are above ground, just like the phone, so it's not unusual.'

PC Brown and Terry returned, snow-covered and chilled, with news that the generator was fuelled and ready to go and they had found paraffin and a cache of lamps in the same outbuilding. They had brought them into the boot room.

'So, what now?' Mac asked.

Chandler shrugged. 'We eat our sandwiches and we drink our tea and we let Melissa tell everyone what's been going on, see who reacts. Any better ideas and I'm ready to listen.'

'No, given the current situation, I'm not sure I do, unless it's to do nothing until we get back-up. Three dead already, it's not an encouraging figure. One thing I didn't ask—did you get anything on the book dealer Melissa claimed was the stranger Rina saw?'

'I'm still waiting to hear back. In fact, there's a few loose ends I've only half tied up, one of which looks very interesting.'

'Care to share?'

Chandler smiled. 'Later, when I've got all the pieces. We'd better go in. Rina is waiting.'

* * *

Melissa had managed not to cry as she had told everyone about her background and Toby; how she had come to work here; and how she had stolen to protect Toby and pay his debts.

On one side of the room Mac sat beside Miriam, watching the reactions. Chandler leaned against the fireplace, mug of tea in hand. How come, Mac wondered, he had a mug, when the rest of them were making do with silly little white catering cups?

Rina sat with Tim and Joy. She knew the story already and made no comment as Melissa reprised her tale. She seemed to be watching Viv and Robin rather than Melissa, Mac noted, and he wondered why. Joy was frowning fiercely, as though something puzzled her, though Mac knew that she, too, had heard this before.

'So, that's it then,' Gail said, her voice rising angrily. 'It's this gang, whoever they are. They killed Simeon and Edwin and now Toby.' She turned to Chandler. 'I demand you let us leave, get us protection.'

'I would love to,' Chandler said evenly. 'But as your previous attempts to leave must have demonstrated, wanting and doing are two different animals.'

'Melissa,' Rina asked, 'the box of papers you said you found in the seance room—is that true?'

A moment's hesitation. 'The box was there, some papers in it. The rest were from the family. I brought them here.'

'Why?'

She shrugged. 'I don't know.'

'Can you sort out for me what was in the box and what wasn't?'

'Why? What does it matter?'

'If you could just do what Mrs Martin asks,' Chandler told her.

Melissa shrugged and looked away.

'I've got another question,' Chandler said. 'About the ownership of this place.'

Mac saw Melissa flinch, the reaction barely perceptible but definitely there.

'It's owned by some consortium or other,' David Franklin said. 'We all know that. Oh, and Edwin and Simeon had shares, didn't they?'

'Edwin, Simeon, you and Grace Wright did, Mr Franklin.'

'*Professor* Franklin.'

'How do you come to own shares in this place? Why Aikensthorpe House?'

David Franklin opened his mouth . . . and then shut it again.

'Professor Franklin?'

'Simeon told me. He said that this consortium, Reality whatsit, had bought Aikensthorpe and were selling a small number of shares. I don't know how he heard, but we both found the idea appealing. I think he must also have told Edwin.'

'Your reasons?'

David Franklin glared. He controlled his emotions less effectively recently, Rina noted. 'It's buying a little bit of history,' he said. 'Like you buying a piece of police memorabilia.'

'I think an old truncheon might come in at a lower price,' Chandler said. He turned his attention to Melissa. 'Though maybe you gave them mates rates, did you?'

'What?' Melissa got to her feet. 'I don't know what you mean.'

'Ah, well, you see, all my phoning around turned up some interesting bits and scraps. Like the fact that when Albert Southam died, he tied this place up in trust so it couldn't be sold, not until either his daughter or his daughter's descendants came back to claim this place, or until those who held the trust judged that wasn't likely to happen or financial problems forced a sale. Well, five years or so ago that came about. The law firm that had administered the trust finally closed, and those responsible for winding up its affairs decided the house should be sold on—all but ten per cent of the value, which should be held in the form of shares in whatever business took over.' He shrugged. 'I don't begin to understand the ins and outs of it, but the fact remains that a proportion of the value and ownership of this place remained in trust, just in case some relative of Southam's showed up. It seems he forgave his wife and loved his daughter.'

'So why did Elizabeth never come back?'

'Because she died,' Melissa said. 'Giving birth to Grace. It happened a lot back then. I don't know why it was concealed, but Albert knew, and the servants who went with Elizabeth to Rome continued to look after Grace until Albert died.'

'Then what happened?'

'More scandal.' Melissa shrugged. 'Though it was hushed up by friends of Albert. It all got very messy. George Weston challenged the will, saying Albert Southam had promised to marry his mother but had then cast her out. He had letters and papers to support that. He threatened if he ever caught up with Grace he'd kill her, so the servants went into hiding with her. Grace only found out who she was when she got married and became Grace Wright. It all faded into family history—you know, the kind of legend lots of families have about lost rich relatives. No one really believes them.'

'But you found out there was truth to the rumours.'

'Eventually, yes. It was Toby who found out, really. He saw that Aikensthorpe had come on the market. There was an article in some magazine or other, and it mentioned the strange mystery of the Aikensthorpe heirs, and suddenly what we'd imagined and wished for when we were kids, it all seemed possible.'

'But you couldn't claim the house?' Mac asked.

She shook her head. 'No, it had all gone too far, the trust wound up and all that.'

'So what happened to the money from the sale?'

'It's still going through the courts, isn't it, Grace?' Chandler said. 'But it seems there are other descendants challenging now.'

'*Grace*?'

'Melissa is my second name,' she said flatly. 'I've never cared much for Grace. It's so bloody insipid. This house should have been mine. I've already proved that.'

'Granted,' Chandler said. 'My legal contacts tell me you'd proved enough to get hold of the ten per cent. You are a direct descendant of Elizabeth and Albert Southam, but I'm told your chances of taking the rest are pretty minimal because of certain codicils in the will favouring George Weston and his kin.'

'Forged!' Melissa said fiercely. 'They were forged. Weston was an evil man, a criminal.'

'Aside from that, both the previous sale and the current one were totally legitimate, even if those that bought this place are using it as a front for illegal activities.'

'So can't their assets be seized?' Rina asked. 'This house included?'

'That won't help Melissa, will it? Not if there's any hint she was implicated in any of it.'

'I've done nothing wrong.' Melissa spaced the words emphatically.

Chandler did not comment on that. 'So you sold on part of your share. Was that to get Toby out of debt too? You must really have resented that. Selling your birthright to get a wastrel like Toby out of the shit again.'

'It wasn't like that.'

'So you were Grace Wright?' David Franklin was outraged. 'We bought our shares from you?'

Melissa shrugged. 'I told Edwin, he liked the idea, he told Simeon and Simeon persuaded you. No one but Edwin knew I had a connection to this place. Edwin was just amused.'

'Sounds like Edwin,' Jay muttered.

'But I still don't understand what brought Edwin here in the first place,' Tim said. He seemed to be going off at some kind of tangent, Rina thought, when the question should have been: did Melissa kill Toby?

'I told you—well, I told Rina. Edwin heard we were setting this place up for conferences; he wanted to know if he could see the library and Albert's room. We became friends, sort of. I liked him, and I liked the idea of him having a share in this place. I didn't realize he'd then sold most of his shares on.'

Hence the shock when she heard the names on the list, Rina thought. That's if she was telling the truth now.

'And did you kill Toby?' Chandler asked. 'Did his demands become just too much? After all, he was frittering away your birthright, wasn't he?'

Melissa did not respond. She stared past him at the curtained windows.

'Especially when you found out that Toby wasn't a Southam after all. That his family descended from George Weston's side.'

'I didn't care about that,' Melissa said. 'You just don't understand, do you? I loved Toby. I always had. Why should I care what part of the family he came from?'

'But did you kill him,' Chandler pursued.

Melissa's look was pure malice. 'No,' she said. 'I did not kill Toby, or Edwin, or Simeon. Why would I? You want to find a murderer, Inspector Chandler, then you'd better start looking elsewhere.'

THIRTY-ONE

The evening dragged on. Slowly, people drifted off to their own rooms, leaving Mac and Chandler and Rina by the fire. Miriam and Jay had wandered back to the library and were poring over esoteric texts on early microscopy which, Miriam told Rina, she had only ever heard about, never thought she'd be able to actually handle.

Jay, it seemed, was a polymath. Early science, magic and what came to be known as stage magic were all closely related, he told Rina excitedly. Rina had looked in on them to see if they wanted anything from the kitchen, and they had been deep in conversation about some obscure sixteenth-century treatise on what Rina took to be alchemy. She ducked out again when the talk switched to red dragons and cinnabar.

PC Brown was back to pacing, and Terry, for some reason Rina had yet to fathom, had perched on a high stool in the kitchen and was investigating Melissa's store of recipe books.

'Are you all right?' she asked him.

'Yes, I just phoned my wife. She's snowed in too. I told her I'd find a recipe for potato bread.' He shrugged. 'It's something to do.'

'What have you told her?'

'That we're cut off and that Edwin died. I was worried just in case something made it on to the news, but I didn't want to worry her too much. If she knew the truth she'd be going frantic.'

Rina nodded; she'd indulged in similar half truths when she had made her own phone call home. 'Why potato bread?'

'My mum used to make it. Daft how that sort of thing suddenly becomes important, isn't it?'

'Not so silly,' Rina told him. A rattle from behind the kitchen attracted her attention.

'Rav's bringing the lanterns through. The lights keep flickering. I've found some candles too.' Terry pointed to where several boxes had been laid on one of the counters. 'And I've filled the Thermos flasks and the tea urn.'

Rav appeared with his hands full of lanterns. He smiled at Rina. 'I thought I'd put these in the hall. They've all been filled.'

'Matches?'

'With the candles.'

'Looks like we're all set then. Where's Melissa?'

'Gone to her room,' Rav said. 'I told her to lock the door.'

Rina nodded. She gave Rav a hand to bring the other lanterns through and then wandered back to Mac and the fire.

Passing Melissa's office, she saw Chandler speaking on his mobile; he looked annoyed about something. Moments later he followed her through and flopped down on the small sofa.

'More problems?' Mac asked.

'No, not exactly. They picked up Melissa's dodgy book dealer. Surprise, surprise, he had form. He admits being here on the Friday night, which is when Rina saw him leave, presumably. He said Melissa left a package for him in the boot room in one of the cupboards, as was usual. He trekked back across the fields and picked up his car not far from the cottage where we found friend Toby. He denies going in. Forensics will tell us more on that, but he is adamant he's not been back since, so the footprints you spotted must have been someone else. Always supposing, of course, that he's telling the truth.'

'What reason would he have to kill Toby?' Rina mused. 'None that I can see. Toby knew what Melissa was doing, so he's not likely to have caused trouble.'

'Any record of violence?'

'None.'

'So who did I see on that second night?'

'Well, whose *footprints* did you see?' Chandler corrected her. 'It's entirely possible that someone just went for a walk.'

'True, but don't forget, Toby followed someone and tried to film them. They killed him.'

'That's the assumption,' Chandler agreed. 'I now know that Toby was passing on information to whoever we have undercover,' he added. He frowned, the lack of information clearly nagging.

'Do we know if that officer is here? Or just part of the broader set-up?' Mac asked.

'No, but I'm guessing maybe a driver or one of the caterers. They have reason to come here, opportunity to see what is going on.'

Mac nodded. 'That would make sense.' He glanced at Rina, expecting an opinion, receiving none, but Mac recognized that look and wondered about it.

THIRTY-TWO

Later, when she heard Mac and Miriam return to their room, Rina unlocked her door and knocked on theirs, glad now that this wing of the house was so cut off from the rest.

'So,' Mac said, when Rina had taken up possession of the window seat, 'what is it you haven't told me?'

'Viv came to me earlier this evening with some interesting information,' Rina said. 'I'm honoured that she made such a judgement call and decided I might be trustworthy; I happen to know that she is a very frightened and confused young woman.'

Mac waited, but Miriam was ahead of him. 'She's the undercover police officer, isn't she?'

Rina nodded. 'Apparently, she really is doing the MA, and she just happened to know Toby because of that. She was offered the chance to do her master's full time rather than stretch it out over two years if she took the job; originally, she'd cut her hours and turned down a promotion so she could study. I think there's a bit of family pressure being brought to bear.'

'There'll be even more now,' Miriam noted.

'She's just a kid,' Mac objected.

'She is twenty-four, and you and I are just feeling our age. She was Toby's link; he passed his information on through her. Melissa didn't know. Toby was allowing her to sell items from the house on his behalf and at the same time was working as a police informer. Viv says he seemed to think that might give him some leverage, afterwards, when the house was sold again.'

'Or someone allowed him to believe that,' Miriam suggested. 'Just to get him on side.'

Mac absorbed this. 'Then why didn't Viv come to me or Chandler?'

'Because she doesn't know you, and she has reason to suspect Chandler. He's been under investigation, Mac. They think he might be mixed up in all this.'

'*Chandler*? Why? No, I can't accept that. What evidence?'

'She doesn't know. Only something about financial irregularities in his bank account.'

'Which could be anything.' Mac frowned. 'I don't see it, but—'

'But we have to keep it in mind. She's out of her depth, Mac.'

'And Melissa knows nothing? About Viv? About Toby feeding her information?'

'No,' Rina said. 'Melissa just kept paying Toby's debts; she didn't know anything of what else he was doing.'

'So, if Melissa confided in Edwin; and he told Simeon; and our assumption about them going to expose what was going on here—' Miriam began.

'If our assumption is correct, then someone either overheard them talking or Melissa talking to them, but the sad thing is, whoever killed them did it to protect cover that was already blown. Toby had already exposed what was happening here, and they died for nothing.'

'It looks that way,' Mac said.

For a minute or two they sat in silence, then Mac said, 'OK, so we need to cover all bases here. Has Chandler lied about what back-up we can expect? How much suspicion is actually attached to him?'

'How do we find that out?' Miriam asked.

'We call someone who can do some quiet checking for us,' Mac said. He plucked his mobile phone from the bedside table and skimmed through the contacts. 'Alec,' he said. 'No, we're both well. Sorry to be calling so late, but we need a favour. A discreet favour.'

Rina smiled. Of course. Pinsent was only forty miles or so away; it was quite likely Alec Freidman would be able to discover something, and at least they then had a trusted outsider ensuring they would not be forgotten.

She twitched back the curtain and looked out on to a white world. Soft fields of snow were overhung by fat bellied clouds from which the occasional flake escaped. Would it hold off long enough for the cavalry to arrive? she wondered, though there was no way of knowing what drifts blocked the roads.

'There's no television here,' she said suddenly. 'No radio, for that matter. At least, not that I've seen.'

'I expect Melissa has both in her room,' Miriam said. She shrugged. 'I'd not given it any thought.'

Mac finished his call. 'He's looking into it for us,' he said.

'Good,' Rina approved.

At that moment, the lights went out and plunged them into the dark.

THIRTY-THREE

The sound of the handbell ringing in the lobby drew everyone downstairs. PC Brown met them at the foot of the stairs. 'Boss says everyone should gather in the big room,' he said. 'We've got the lanterns. Power's out,' he added unnecessarily.

'We should go and switch on the generator.' Terry's voice sounded from deep shadow by the kitchen door.

'Right you are.' Brown sounded quite cheerful about the whole thing. 'Boss is calling round to see how local the power outage is,' he added. 'Likely, the lines are down. It happened last winter and the one before.'

He went off with Terry to see what lights could be restored, and Mac, Rina and Miriam joined the others in the main room.

Viv and Robin were already there. Rina smiled at the girl, nodding encouragingly to indicate that it would all be all right. She hoped.

'Can we make toast?' Robin said. 'By the fire?'

Viv laughed. 'What?'

'Isn't that what you do in a power cut?'

Silently, Rina blessed him for breaking the tension. 'Toast sounds good,' she said, 'and I think I saw some crumpets in the kitchen. I'll go and find us something to use as a toasting fork.' Chandler met her as she crossed the dark reception hall, lantern in hand. 'Power is out for a ten-mile radius,' he said. 'Lines are down.'

'Just as well we have the generator.'

He nodded. 'Ah, good.'

The lights flickered and began to shine, albeit dimly. 'Robin will be disappointed,' she said. 'He wants to make toast in a power cut.'

'He obviously didn't live through the three-day week,' Chandler observed.

Terry and PC Brown emerged from the kitchen looking triumphant. 'We should just use what lights we need,' Terry said. 'So someone should go and check what's on upstairs.'

As he and PC Brown loped off up the stairs to do that, Rina foraged in the kitchen, finding bread and a barbecue fork that would do for toasting. A sound behind her caused her to turn, startled. It was only Mac.

'Sorry,' she said. 'I'm more jumpy than I thought. What is it?'

Mac glanced behind him and then came close, speaking quietly. 'Alec called,' he said. 'Chandler didn't lie about problems with reinforcements, though he does seem to have downplayed what went on here.'

'How can you downplay three murders?' Rina wondered out loud.

'And he *is* under investigation. There are big rumours that he's been on the take, that he knew exactly what was happening here.'

'But you still aren't sure?'

Mac shook his head. 'We both know what a few well-placed rumours can mean to a career. I'll wait and see how this turns out before making judgement. In the meantime—'

'In the *meal*time, grab some bread, we are making toast.'

THIRTY-FOUR

It was not until everyone had settled by the fire and Robin had taken on toast-making duties that they noticed Rav was missing. No one seemed to know when he had left.

A search of the house; Rav was not there. Footprints led from the boot room door out across the yard and into the grounds.

Mac, Chandler, PC Brown and Tim took torches and prepared to follow.

'He was here when we all came down,' Terry said. 'I spoke to him. He lit a lantern in the kitchen and took it through into the hall. Then Paul—PC Brown—and I, we went to sort out the genny.'

'You didn't see anyone, hear anyone go past the outbuilding?' Mac asked.

Terry laughed. 'The din that thing makes, he wouldn't have heard if you'd all walked past. I didn't notice footprints either, but I wasn't looking, if I'm truthful.'

Brown hadn't seen anything either. Rina had the impression that both men were in a hurry to get back into the warm, and she couldn't blame them for that.

'He could have left at any time this evening,' she pointed out. 'Why now?' Then she considered that it was close on midnight. In the usual run of things, the household would probably have been asleep, or at least in their rooms.

She watched the four men leave, hoping that Mac's faith in Chandler was justified.

Viv came over to her. 'Did you tell Mac?' she asked anxiously.

'Yes, I did. Don't worry, my dear, this will soon be over.'

'I should have gone with them,' Viv said.

'No, no you shouldn't. What you need to do now is to get on the phone to your handler and let them know just how urgent the situation is.'

'I've left messages,' she said.

'Then try again now. Mac has contacted a friend of ours, and he is doing what he can too, so don't worry. This will all turn out well enough.'

'Will it?' Viv was wide eyed and clearly scared, and Rina felt for her. Gently, she hugged the younger woman.

'Yes,' she said. 'Mac and I have been in tighter corners than this. Believe me, dear, it will all be fine.' She just hoped she would not be caught now telling an outright lie.

* * *

It was only a few minutes later that they noticed Melissa had also left. Rina was furious. How could she have missed that the woman was no longer there?

'Dammit,' Rina said. 'I don't like this at all. This is not good.'

'What's going on?' Joy asked. 'None of this makes sense. Where would she have gone?'

'There are clearly things we don't know yet,' Rina said. 'Things Melissa omitted to tell. Right. I'll get my coat.'

'You can't be serious?' Joy said. Then, when Rina nodded: 'Then I'll come with you.'

Rina shook her head. 'I need reliable people here to keep an eye on everyone else. Terry, Viv, get yourself wrapped up, we're going out.'

'Why Viv?' Robin demanded. 'You go, I go.'

'We can't all go,' Rina told him sharply. 'Robin, please, explanations later.'

He seemed about to argue, but Viv handed him her phone. 'See that number there? Keep trying it until someone answers, and then tell them what's happening, OK?'

'Viv?'

She kissed him lightly. 'Love you,' she said. 'Just hang in there. I'll explain everything when I get back.'

There were other minor protests, but Rina could see no one else really wanted to venture out or to risk getting more involved in something they did not understand.

'Joy, Miriam, keep everyone in one place and lock the doors, OK?'

'OK.'

Minutes later they were heading out into the snow.

'You do know I'm not a real action hero, don't you?' Terry said. 'I mean, there's no stuntman tonight, is there?'

'I know, but you're the closest I've got handy right now.' The footprints in the snow were clear. Rav's, and then those who had set out to follow him, and weaving unsteadily through all of these were smaller steps that Rina knew must be Melissa's.

'What's the woman playing at?' Terry asked.

'I'm not sure,' Rina said. 'But I suspect she's after revenge.'

* * *

In the cottage where Toby's body had been found, crime-scene tape hung limply by the door. Rav glanced at the place where Toby's body had lain, at the bloodstained carpet and a stray evidence marker, forgotten in the race to pack up before the weather closed in again.

'You've got them?' The man stepped out of the shadows by the stairs.

'Of course. Let's get going.'

'Show me first.'

'I'll show your boss. They'll have noticed I'm gone by now. We should leave.'

'And my instructions are to make sure you've got the goods. Show me now.'

Rav sighed. He dug into the pocket of his overcoat and withdrew a table napkin. Unfolding it he revealed—

'Are they the real thing?'

'Of course they are. You think I could fake something like this?'

Elizabeth's diamonds glinted in the low light of the cottage. 'He'd locked them away,' Rav said, after she left. 'No one's worn these in more than a hundred and thirty years.'

His companion was unimpressed. 'Very romantic.'

'Everyone assumed that George Weston had taken them, but they were there all that time, just locked inside that room.'

The other man was uninterested. 'Like I said. Romantic. Car's down on the road. It's a long walk.'

* * *

Chandler and Mac watched the cottage closely. Tim had moved down towards the road, with instructions to keep well back from anyone emerging from the cottage. PC Brown had crept towards the window. Dimly, they could see his outline as he watched what went on inside. He jerked back and ducked down, and a moment later two figures emerged. Rav and a stranger, roughly the same height and build.

'Let them go, and we'll follow,' Chandler whispered. 'We don't know if he's brought company.'

Mac nodded, his attention on Brown, willing the young man to keep very still. The night was now clear and cold—ideal conditions for the slightest sound to travel—and Brown's position at the side of the cottage was very vulnerable should either Rav or his companion look directly back from the path they were now taking.

Mac could see no sign of Tim, who he guessed was probably now close to the road.

He and Chandler began to move, preparing to follow. The sound of the shot came out of nowhere. Mac hit the ground. 'What the—!'

Chandler lifted his head slowly. 'Fucking hell.'

'Whoever it was, they missed,' Mac said.

Rav and the other man had retreated towards the cottage, and Mac could see now that the stranger held a gun.

Chandler saw it too and swore again. 'But he wasn't shooting, so who the hell was?'

'I don't know.' Mac was still watching Brown, willing him to hold his nerve and keep still. He felt Chandler move.

'This is the police,' Chandler shouted. 'You are surrounded. Put your weapon down.'

'What the hell are you doing?' Mac hissed. 'Let them go! We can't do anything on our own.' But it was too late for second thoughts. A shot fired in their direction, hitting the bank a few feet away, told them what the stranger thought of losing his gun. And at the same moment, Brown moved back and Rav spotted him.

The gunman grabbed Brown and hauled him out of his hiding place. 'Who the bloody hell are you?'

Chandler and Mac could see the gunman staring out into the night, searching for whoever was out there, and now he had a hostage . . .

* * *

'What the hell is she doing?' Terry stopped in his tracks, stunned as Melissa raised the shotgun and fired. 'And where did she get the gun?'

'This is the countryside,' Rina observed tartly. 'Every farmer and his dog needs access to a shotgun. My question is: where did Melissa get hers? I thought Aikensthorpe had been properly searched.'

'And who is she shooting at?' Viv asked.

Rina started forward again. 'Oh, that would be Rav,' she said.

Melissa spun around as they came closer. She was clearly distressed, waving the shotgun dangerously in their direction. 'I missed,' she said. 'I *missed* him.'

'You think Rav killed Toby?' Rina asked.

'Melissa, put the gun down, why don't you?' Terry said. 'Come on, you don't want to shoot either of us, surely?' He spread his hands wide and smiled at her.

'They killed Toby.' Melissa was crying now. 'They killed Toby, and Rav is with *them*.' Tears poured down her cheeks, and Rina gently took the shotgun from her hands. She gestured to Viv to take Melissa away from the scene and then moved slowly forward, keeping in deep shadow. She could see the cottage now, Rav and a stranger and—

'Oh, good Lord,' Rina breathed. 'This is a real pickle. *Another* gun.'

Terry moved up behind her. 'That's Paul Brown,' he whispered. 'They've got Paul.'

'I can see that. Terry, does your action-hero self know how to shoot?'

'Shoot, yes, hit the target—'

'Right. Well, I guess it's up to me then.'

'Rina?' Terry was horrified. 'OK, look, what do you want me to do?'

'Can you see down there, just behind the cottage? Two figures.'

'Mac and Chandler.'

'Can you get to them without being seen? Tell them what's happening?'

'Yes. What are you going to do?'

'Tell them to keep back, out of the line of fire. Melissa only fired one shot—that means I've got one left.'

With one last disbelieving look, Terry did as she asked.

* * *

'He's just a local copper,' Rav was saying. 'There's no back-up. Chandler, Mac,' he shouted. 'Bloody idiots.'

Paul Brown knelt upon the ground. The gunman had his weapon pointed at Brown's head. He glanced wildly around, trying to figure out if Rav was telling the truth. The fact was that a shot had been fired.

'He's just a local copper,' Rav insisted. 'It's a bluff! Can't you work that out, you idiot?'

For an instant the gun wavered between Brown and Rav. 'Who the fuck are you calling an idiot?' His eyes still on Brown, he took a mobile phone from his pocket. The number he wanted must have been on speed dial. He listened, then swore again.

* * *

'No way he'll get a signal,' Chandler muttered.

Lying prone on the snowy ground, Mac was disinclined to comment. He was annoyed, anxious, and completely at a loss.

'Mac.' Terry dropped down beside him.

'What the hell are you doing here?' Mac hissed.

'Rina sent me. She's up there with Melissa's shotgun. She's sent Melissa and Viv back to the house, and she says you've got to stay put, out of the line of fire.'

'Out of the *what*?' Chandler demanded in a low voice.

'Just try and get his attention so she can take the shot.'

* * *

Rina could hear Chandler's voice. He was talking to Rav and the gunman, urging them to let Brown go, telling them that he was just a kid, that it was Chandler's fault he was even here. To let him go and Chandler would take his place. The gunman had retreated further towards the cottage, taking Brown with him.

Rina hesitated. It had been years since she had handled a firearm of any kind, though she'd always been a pretty good shot.

Not that 'pretty good' was enough now. It had to be *bloody* good. She'd only get the one chance.

She took a deep breath and held it, said a brief prayer to whatever gods had jurisdiction over such acts and a brief supplication to her beloved husband, and then she pulled the trigger.

The gunman fell, shot peppering both legs and the gun falling from his hand. Rav made a grab for it, but PC Brown kicked it away, and then Terry, action-hero moment come at last, was on top of Rav and wrestling him to the ground.

Rina released the held breath and closed her eyes. 'Oh Fred,' she whispered and fancied that she felt his hand briefly clasping hers.

EPILOGUE

Rina sat in the kitchen sipping tea. Bone weary, all she wanted to do now was go home, but she knew there'd be questions first and statements and all sorts of palaver before she was free to leave. Her victim had been transported to the local hospital, and Rina anticipated that it would take a while to remove the shot from his legs. Nothing life threatening, she thought, but it had certainly distracted him.

'The diamonds were in the rose bowl,' Joy said wonderingly. 'Can you believe that?'

Rina nodded. 'Apparently, Melissa found them when they opened the room. She didn't let on to Toby; selling the books to cover his debts was one thing, but selling what she saw as her birthright for his benefit was quite another.'

'But she told Rav?'

'She knew Rav was involved with the criminals that owned this place and thought he could get her a good price for the jewels. Melissa was naive; for that matter, so was Toby.'

'They were way out of their league,' Joy said softly. Rina knew she was thinking about her father. 'And Chandler?'

'I don't know,' Rina said. 'He was photographed here, talking to the caterers, but it might simply be that. As he says, he was curious. Not our problem, Joy.'

* * *

Robin sat on the stairs beside Viv, watching the to-ing and fro-ing from the police incident room and the CSIs donning over-suits and moving off towards the cottage in the woods. It was nine in the morning, and his world was upside down. 'So, did you ever—'

'Like you, care about you, or were you just part of the job? That what you've been trying to ask for the past hour?'

'I suppose it is.'

'Robin, you are such an idiot sometimes.' She took his hand and held it tight.

THE END

ALSO BY JANE ADAMS

RINA MARTIN MYSTERY SERIES

Book 1: MURDER ON SEA
Book 2: MURDER ON THE CLIFF
Book 3: MURDER ON THE BOAT
Book 4: MURDER ON THE BEACH
Book 5: MURDER AT THE COUNTRY HOUSE

MERROW & CLARKE

Book 1: SAFE

DETECTIVE MIKE CROFT SERIES

Book 1: THE GREENWAY
Book 2: THE SECRETS
Book 3: THEIR FINAL MOMENTS
Book 4: THE LIAR

DETECTIVE RAY FLOWERS SERIES

Book 1: THE APOTHECARY'S DAUGHTER
Book 2: THE UNWILLING SON
Book 3: THE DROWNING MEN
Book 4: THE SISTER'S TWIN

DETECTIVE ROZLYN PRIEST SERIES

Book 1: BURY ME DEEP

STANDALONE

THE OTHER WOMAN
THE WOMAN IN THE PAINTING
THEN SHE WAS DEAD

Thank you for reading this book.

If you enjoyed it please leave feedback on Amazon or Goodreads, and if there is anything we missed or you have a question about, then please get in touch. We appreciate you choosing our book.

Founded in 2014 in Shoreditch, London, we at Joffe Books pride ourselves on our history of innovative publishing. We were thrilled to be shortlisted for Independent Publisher of the Year at the British Book Awards.

www.joffebooks.com

We're very grateful to eagle-eyed readers who take the time to contact us. Please send any errors you find to corrections@joffebooks.com. We'll get them fixed ASAP.

Printed in Great Britain
by Amazon

80777558R00133